If You Find Emory Walden

James Wallace Birch

BEACON PUBLISHING GROUP

For information, or to order additional copies, please contact:

Beacon Publishing Group
P.O. Box 41573 Charleston, S.C. 29423
800.817.8480 | beaconpublishinggroup.com

Cover Art by Peter Cizmadia. "Twenty-Four Hour Service," Linoleum Block print on paper, 2019.
All rights reserved.

Publisher's catalog available by request.

ISBN-13: 978-1-949472-11-0

ISBN-10: 1-949472-11-0

First Edition. New York, NY 10001

DEDICATION

For those who never stopped listening.

"When your ideas are everywhere, where are you?"
- Emory Walden

THE STARTING LINE

Chapter 1

I was sitting on the kitchen counter without any shoes on, staring at the junk drawer. I wasn't even seeing it in front of me; really, I was staring through it. But the concept of it was there in my mind. I could see a series of scenarios playing out, each a little scene that I was watching as though I was sitting in the dark staring at an old slide projector.

Should I get down and open it?

I saw that scene. I saw all the little actions leading up to it, one flashing slide at a time. *Click.*

But I didn't move.

If I did open that drawer, I wasn't sure where I'd stop. Or, if I'd stop. Opening that drawer was like opening the past and all the junk that I'd shoved inside and tried to hide would come pouring out. I had put it in there. I had closed the drawer. And I had tried to turn away. And yet, here I was staring.

So I took a swig from the bottle I was holding. *Click.*

As the gin fell down my throat like a torch falling into a well, something my wife used to say to me appeared on the next mental slide: "Cultivate a mind that clings to nothing".

Just then, the little scene in front of me was shattered by the sound of a knock at my apartment door.

I was back in the kitchen of that apartment. That shitty apartment, my surroundings no longer protected by my thoughts.

I capped my drink, slid open the knife drawer beneath me, and laid the bottle inside.

I eased the drawer closed and sat quietly. Go away, I thought. I tried to be still but my heart was pounding and I was sure the person outside could hear it banging against my ribs, desperate to get out. My body was this derelict prison and my heart was an inmate fighting for freedom.

Maybe a minute passed. Maybe it was ten seconds.

I heard another knock. I tried to slow my breathing and quell my pounding heart. It didn't help. Whoever it was knocked again.

Go away.

"Professor B," the voice called through the door. "I've got your mail."

It was a voice I used to know. A voice I hadn't heard in some time.

I didn't know what to say. I suppose I wanted to see her, since I hopped down and went over to the door.

"Just leave it outside," I called back.

"I'd prefer to make sure you get it," the voice replied.

"Better if you leave it outside," I said again.

If there was a way that I could have seen her without her seeing me, I would have chosen that option. And, if you were to press me about it, I guess I'd have said that about everyone at that point in my life.

But I didn't get that choice. She twisted the door knob and pushed it in towards me, saying, "I think I ought to make sure this gets to you." I guess the door wasn't locked because suddenly we were face to face. She was standing a step into my apartment, standing where I should have had a little doormat, maybe with some Pollyanna quote about life, or maybe a Cheshire cat.

But I didn't have a doormat.

"What the hell is wrong with you?" I blurted. "Do you just walk into people's homes?"

I shoved her out the front door and into the hallway. The second I did it, I couldn't believe what I'd done, how I'd acted. If you knew me years ago, then, well... let's just say I used to be so meek I'd just as soon go thirsty than ask someone to pass the water at a dinner party.

But, since you're going to get to know me now, when I'm done telling you my story, I don't even think you'll remember that I shoved Melanie like that. It'll seem so blasé.

"I'm sorry," I said. And then, "I. Um -"

"Can we go inside?" Her eyes looked past me and into my apartment. She wore a white t-shirt, red cotton gym shorts, and furry red slippers.

"No. What is it?"

"I guess the post guy put your mail in my box."

"That happens sometimes," was all I could think to say, noticing her hips. There's something about a woman's hips that tell you what she's unwilling to say. But Melanie's hips never gave away much, though they were always worth looking at. One of those tan sleeves with the bubble wrap on the inside and a yellow envelope were propped on the inward curve at the shelf of her hip, held in place by her arm.

"Hope the letter wasn't urgent," she said. "Lost my mail key. Took forever for the landlord to replace it."

"So, can I have it?" I asked.

Melanie held the mail up before her, but her clutch said she wasn't offering it.

I snatched it anyway.

Her phone vibrated and she seemed to wince. She checked her phone, looked away, and then glanced at her phone again as if hoping to see something different.

"You opened my mail," I groaned, finding the sleeve was slit.

"Yeah-yeah, just the one. I didn't realize -"

She looked up at me and we finally saw one another.

"What happened to your eye?" I asked.

"Oh," she touched her face. "It's nothing. My cat. She -"

"Your cat?"

Melanie's eyes fell to the floor and a snortish chuckle escaped.

"You okay?" I asked.

"I'm fine. Listen, I better go." The words slipped out from between her lips.

Those lips.

They had this way of separating in the front so that the upper lip turned up and puffed out just slightly, almost like it was pouting, lifting the curtain on her two front teeth so that they just barely showed, even when she thought her mouth was shut. It's hard to put a finger on it, but there was something alluring about that slight opening in her mouth. She was permanently teasing you with this way in, this forever-possible chance to get inside her. Or maybe it was just a sign that she was vulnerable; a sign that she didn't have a way to lock her defenses.

"Thanks." I said. "If you need anything." I don't know what I meant by that.

"Yeah-yeah," she replied dismissively.

I was heading back inside, closing the door, about to head back to my kitchen counter and hop back up on it to be alone with my bottle and my junk drawer, when Melanie said, "Wait."

"What?"

"What's it mean?"

"What's what mean?"

"The note in the book." She was pointing at the sleeve. There was only one book she could have been talking about.

Chapter 2

I could tell you I had a nice apartment, but that would be a lie. Truth is, my apartment was not something I'd ever want any former student to see. But I sensed that I needed to invite Melanie in.

"There's like, nothing in here," she said.

That wasn't true. I had a small kitchen table shoved in the corner with a stack of CDs and a stereo on top of it. Admittedly there weren't any chairs, which is why I liked to sit on the kitchen counter. But, what you may call redeeming, was the fact that I had lots of books stacked along the wall, which I felt gave the place an air of sophistication.

"Towards the end there, my wife and I were trying out minimalism," I said, which was true in a way. We were minimizing contact with one another.

"Do you want something to drink? Soda?" I asked. All I had was booze and water.

"No thanks." She walked over to the CDs and began flipping through them. I took the opportunity to throw the small envelope in the trash, as well as a stack of eviction threats that were fanned out on the kitchen counter.

"What kind of music is this?" she asked, picking up a Pietasters CD and eyeing the back.

"It's a ska band from the 90s."

She nodded.

"What kind of music do you like?" I asked.

"Mostly hip hop," she shrugged, as if I was asking a stupid question.

"That's about what I had you pegged for," I said, trying to shrug her off.

"How about you?" she asked.

"The good stuff," I said. "Stuff you probably never heard of."

"You mean stuff no one's heard of," she yawned, turning the CD over. "So the note in the book, what do you think it means?" She put the CD back atop the pile.

"It doesn't mean anything."

"You haven't even looked at it," she complained.

"I don't need to."

"But what if it's a note from him?"

"It's not."

"How do you know?"

"Because," I sighed. "What if he's dead?"

"But what if? You know-"

"Look," I cut her off. "I get mail like this sometimes. Emory's got fans. Do you know any happy teenagers?"

"Happy teenagers?"

"Never mind," I said. "Look, I don't mean to be rude, but I'm kinda busy."

"Oh," she said, stepping back. "I, um, I just think you owe it to him."

I laughed. "Owe it to him? I never asked for any of this."

"But you took it." She paused. "Sorry. That wasn't what I meant. Of course, anyone would."

"I had to make a living," I grunted.

Melanie walked over to the kitchen sink, picked up the bubble wrap sleeve, and pulled out the book *Discontents: The Disappearance of a Young Radical.*

I've seen the cover of that book a thousand times, and my reaction to it has changed over the years. Relationships confound life in ways we can never anticipate and can only hope to outlast. And I guess I realized something as I saw the words on the red book cover under the blue fluorescent kitchen light in my crummy apartment of white walls, cheap carpet, and sticky linoleum. I realized that all I was to the world was the guy who published Emory Walden's memoir some seven years before.

So I took the book from her and opened the cover. There was the foreword I had written to the reader back in 2011 when I was jobless and alone and had no clue that publishing a little book to help a former friend tell the truth about his disappearance would change my life forever.

So much happened in those intervening years. And yet, here I was again, jobless, alone, and about to get kicked out of my apartment. The only difference was that this time I no longer had a television to curse or a fancy townhome to lose to some bank. Instead, I was renting a college apartment in a termite-infested building behind a row of bars on University Avenue. I may as well have called these bars home.

At the end of the book's foreword I found the note Melanie was referring to. It was typed along the edge of the page as though someone had slid the book sideways into the top of a typewriter. It read:

JUST DOWN THE HILL, JAMES HAD A THRILL. IN THE MIDDLE OF MAY, JAMES WAS A HERO TODAY. JUST UP THE LANE, JAMES LOST HIS...
-    YOUR BIGGEST FAN

"This poem is terrible," I said, looking up at Melanie. "It reads like some dropout wrote it. And what's with this signature? Is that some kind of jab at me?"

Just then, the apartment door blew open as though a grenade erupted in the hallway. In place of an explosion there stood a well-groomed man in skin-tight jeans. Closely cropped blonde hair and a receding hairline accentuated a strong forehead that sat atop a strong head connected to a strong body. Then, there was his jaw. It jutted distractingly forward, offering up an unfortunate assortment of bad teeth like a bowl of misshapen restaurant mints. His blue collared shirt hung off his shoulder, the top splayed open as though it had been clawed and torn apart. On his exposed chest, three scratches were sliced in red parallel lines across his dog tag necklace tattoo.

"I found you," he declared, pushing his chin out and pulling his lower teeth up over his upper lip. He laughed, fidgeting. "I'm Christopher Fucking Columbus, too."

"Do I know you?" I asked.

"He's talking about me," Melanie clamored, sliding behind the kitchen table.

"Darling, I'm Columbus. See? The Nina, the Peanut. You know that, you fucking know that! The Peanut." He laughed. "Searching for new lands on the Peanut. Enough of your crazy bullshit. Don't make me. Don't you dare," he threatened, rolling his shoulders as if stretching before a game. He rolled his neck, too. His left hand clenched. It loosened. His fingers stretched out. His hand flattened. Then he clenched again.

"Darling?" I laughed. The liquor spoke for me.

It took me a moment, but I recognized him as Melanie's boyfriend, Nick.

"Well, this is awkward," I continued. "But I'm afraid you -"

"Stay out of it," he grumbled, pointing a finger at me. "You, you, you goddamn poser with your goddamn poison." He marched towards Melanie.

"I mean, I was," I said, "until you flew in here like a drunken pilot from a Cary Grant film and -"

That's about when he charged me, shoving me back and into the air. There are moments in life that occur both quickly and slowly, that seem both

years and an instant in the making. My head smacked
the linoleum and I remember hearing the thud, then
the stickiness of the kitchen floor on my back. My last
thought was one of embarrassment. I really wished I
had mopped that nasty linoleum sometime in all the
months I'd lived there.

I awoke. I couldn't have been out for long
because the apartment door stood wide open and I
could hear Melanie's screams down the hallway.

The James Wallace Birch approach can
generally be described as one of cowering in corners
and trying not to be seen. As a people, us Birch's have
excelled for millennia in the same conflict
management style. Pretend it didn't happen and hope
things blow over. If we can make ourselves disappear,
the way Emory did, we'd all be better off. I truly
believe it. I envied that about him. He'd walked away
from the fire in the trash bin and was free. It was
something I couldn't do by myself. I'd need someone
to shove me off the edge, and then I'd yell back thank
you to them as I fell.

So everything I tell you from here on out
would not have happened if Nick had shoved me just
a bit harder. Because then I could have thanked him.

But he didn't.

So I got up, ran to the door and peered into
the hallway. Nick held Melanie by her hair, dragging
her around the corner and out of sight. I ran back to

the kitchen, opened the knife drawer, grabbed what I could, and raced back out into the hall after them.

Chapter 3

I could tell you that I was a great professor. But it's not my place to say. That's really up to the students. What I can say is that I loved teaching. As an adjunct, the pay was poverty level. It should come as no surprise to any American reading this that getting a degree beyond a Bachelor's isn't worth a dollar in this country. But being in the classroom brought me to life. Plus, I'll admit, I sort of cashed in on the whole knowing-a-famous-fugitive thing. After I published Emory's book, I got a lot of speaking gigs up and down the east coast. Maybe you saw one.

I doubt Emory would have approved. But it was the Great Recession, so forgive me, and don't tell me you wouldn't have done the same if you were trying to climb your way out of bankruptcy.

I gave one of my book talks one evening about two years ago to the regional English honors society. The society was comprised of maybe twenty of the top writing students from our university and two other universities nearby in the Shenandoah Valley. A few renowned faculty members sat in the back, glancing up over their glasses, their suspicious eyes below the envy that perched on either edge of greying temples.

There, in that sweeping auditorium of wooden folding chairs and walls cluttered with paintings of dead men with knowing stares, is where I first saw Melanie. She was young and verdant, and her blue sun dress with orange and yellow flowers clung to her hips and torso in the heat. It was late August and she strolled in among a group of laughing students. Even then she had about her a different vibrancy and, although a part of the group, she seemed to walk alone.

She took a seat in the front row. She crossed her legs and took out a notepad. She looked up at me, took out her phone, snapped a photo and began typing. I had a feeling that she had been watching me for some time. Her eyes, a deep green like a lost corner of a shaded forest floor, pulled at you the way a leaf pulls at light. Her short maroon hair swept over to her right side, and her black glasses with white triangle patterns squared a small nose above pale pink lips. She was tall, but her translucent skin and petite features gave off the sense of smallness. Seeming to possess a vulnerable curiosity, her shoulders rolled slightly forward. The sweat on her exposed neck and shoulders caught my eye. Had I been one of her classmates, I would have spent the evening plotting ways to get some of that sweat on me.

"Professor Birch, how was your summer?" a student asked. "Did you and your wife ever get a chance to go kayaking?"

I popped back to reality. "We did, thanks for recommending it, Kyle. You get out on the river much this summer?"

After my speech, we did a brief Q&A.

A student from another university I didn't recognize started off. "Professor Birch, I, um," the kid cleared his throat. He stopped and caught his breath. "I read the, um, the book and it's an amazing story. It's got, ya know, political conspiracy, criminal behavior, the works. Really, the works. I mean, real damning for Emory. So, so. Sorry I'm nervous. So, here's my question. So, Emory disappeared and then wrote out his story and secretly sent it to you to publish. Sorry this is the question part: Why did he choose you?"

"First, thank you for your question. I appreciate it. See, Emory didn't just disappear. He was a wanted man. The authorities and others wanted to dispose of him. He fled for his freedom. For his life."

"Yes," the student said. "But, um, what I'm asking is, why do you think he chose to ask you to publish his story?"

"That's a great question and one I've thought a lot about," I said. "I think he knew I was a very loyal friend when we were teens. I was his sidekick, his follower, helping him out and never ratting him out on all the stunts he pulled. For example, he was a prolific graffiti artist, as I'm sure you know from reading the book. But he was getting into graffiti way back in high school and I, well, I might have helped him a bit when he was getting started. So I think he felt he had a history with me. He could trust me. And he could rely on me to publish it."

The student followed up, "But didn't he, um, didn't he take your girlfriend? Why help someone who did that? I'd, um, excuse me for saying so

Professor Birch, but - well, to be honest   I'd let the guy rot."

"It certainly wasn't easy. I guess in the end I felt like his apology was sincere. The smoking stuff he wrote about in the memoir was about me. So, in a way, I felt he wrote the book in part to say sorry to me. I, I don't know. I was touched by it all. You have to understand, Emory did a lot for me growing up. We were very close."

A few of the students in the audience took notes, including Melanie. Then, Melanie stood and a microphone was brought to her. She took the microphone, wrapping her fingers with blue nails around it. She wore a metal wrap around her left thumb that circled below the knuckle two times and I couldn't quite tell if it was a snake or the figure eight symbol for infinity. At her wrist hung a black woven band that was cinched together with a metal clasp and a piece of leather with something imprinted on it that I couldn't make out.

"Professor Birch," someone called. I must have lost a minute.

"Yes?"

"A student, a Miss Melanie, has asked you a question."

"Oh right," I said. "I'm sorry. Can you please repeat the question?"

A few giggles rose from the back.

"Professor, you're married right?"

I cleared my throat. "Yes." The giggles bubbled back up.

"And what does your wife think about all of this?"

Droplets of sweat seeped through my pores around my hairline and on my neck at the edges of my shirt collar. "Um, I'm not sure I understand the question."

"What I mean is," she tapped the metal wrap on the stem of the microphone. "Being tied up in all of this - well, drama I guess - surrounding Emory and his memoir and how he vanished. It's like you're his spokesperson - our connection to him and the things he knows. What does she think about that? About Emory?"

"She thinks it's fascinating." I turned to the crowd. "Other questions?"

Another student I didn't recognize asked a question. "Like, um, what did it feel like when you found all the money Emory left for you? That's like a boatload of money. Millions, right? I've got to think it was insane."

I felt a shift in the room. Everyone seemed to lean forward, their chairs creaking in harmony.

"Thank you for your question. I didn't go to find the money," I replied. "I didn't think -"

"Bull crap, man," a voice called from the audience, but I didn't see where from. Another voice called, "Where you hiding it, bromine?" A few people laughed. The professors in the back chatted among themselves.

The student who had asked the question weighed back in, "So what you wrote in the foreword, that you didn't go get the money that Emory hid for you to find, was true? Why? You said you were broke."

"It didn't feel right at the time," I shrugged. "I felt unethical about -"

"That dude took your girl, man. That's your money, man," yelled the first of the two voices that had called out from the audience.

"Look, I didn't want anything from Emory."

"Bull crap," called one of the voices. "You're here exploiting the guy. You're trying to tell us you're some innocent victim? You poser."

"That's enough, Nick," said one of the professors, standing up and walking towards the podium. "I'd like to thank Professor Birch for speaking with us today and taking time from his busy schedule to share these powerful insights from this remarkable story."

"The book was slow anyways," called the guy whose name was apparently Nick. "And Emory was a pretentious, clueless, unlikable loser. Just read the Goodreads reviews."

And like that, the speaking gig was over.

It's magical what a podium can do for a person. But perhaps what's truly incredible is how a podium changes how others see you. Because after my talk, I came out of the bathroom and overheard a group of female students talking in the adjacent women's bathroom.

"He was on point up there," one said.

"Have you seen his Insta? I love his aesthetic. He's got like the perfect marriage. His wife is hella pretty and she posts the cutest stuff," said the other.

"Bible, okay? Don't judge."

"He's married."

"Whatever. Guys around here are trash."

"It's different. He's kinda famous. If he wasn't, would you?"

The two women laughed and meandered off. So I left the bathroom and headed for the exit. But Dr. Sherry Schnell and a few other professors I didn't recognize asked me to join them at Ricky's Pub for a drink. Ricky's was the bar that graduate students and faculty hung out at. It had a wall of old books on birch wood shelves and the music professors played jazz there a few nights a week. I had seen them in there through the window.

"We're off for a drink and would love for you to join us," Dr. Schnell declared.

"How fortunate you were to have this, err, manuscript of sorts fall into your, err, lap," noted an eager woman with long silver-brown hair that, were it not so long, would have stood straight up in it's frizzled, stringy state. "We'd love to, err, pick your brain."

"Yes, I love what you said about fate," nodded a V-neck teal sweater.

"It's not quite literature," said a pumpkin-faced man with lemon-orange hair that age had squeezed some of the color from. "But it's an entertaining story no doubt."

The funny thing is, I could talk to students all day. But I have never felt comfortable around other adults. "Thank you so very much for the kind invitation," I said. "But I told my wife I'd be home by eight." They seemed to buy it. But who knows really. There are always two layers to every conversation. The things we do to be polite, and the truth. And the amazing thing is that both sides play along even in the face of a bad lie or an obvious false statement. It's easier to just smile back and keep the story going. Maybe it's that we take the lie and turn it into our own version of the truth. And the big truth falls away like leaves from a dying tree and we're left rooted in a story pieced together from a thousand branching perspectives and little prevaricating twigs and we feel that as long as the trunk is still standing, so must we. So we might as well tell another little lie. After all, you can't revive a dead tree.

Chapter 4

So I ran after Melanie and Nick. Melanie was screaming as Nick dragged her now by her hair, her legs flailing and her arms up around her head as she tried to break free. Her ass was dragging along the floor, her red shorts sliding off her butt a bit, exposing her violet underwear. Those hips weren't hard to read now.

At the end of Nick's thick arm was a massive fist like an anchor with fingers, and those fingers pulsed red with veins. They rooted below the canopy of maroon hair atop Melanie's head. He looked down the hall as he headed towards the elevator door and didn't notice me coming up behind him.

At the door he stopped, mashed the button several times and turned back in my direction as though he were a lion with a zebra in his clutches prepared to fend off any starving hyenas.

I ducked into a vestibule by an apartment door. I don't think he saw. As I heard the elevator door chime, I peered around the corner to see him dragging her in. It was two body lengths away.

I clenched my fist in fear, sensing then the object in each hand. In my rush of adrenaline, I had completely forgotten what I was holding. I glanced down towards my hands, sucked in a cloud of air, mumbled something about fate to myself, and sprinted towards the elevator. Nick looked up, eyes meeting mine. He smashed the button to close the door with his free hand, and, like the lion he had become, gnarled his teeth.

It is strange, the choices we make.

Chapter 5

After the speech I drove thirty minutes to a small town in the sticks west of campus. There, I worked the drive thru at a chicken sandwich restaurant. I'd gotten the job because it was far enough away from campus that I figured no students would ever come there. And it was open late, so I could work until two in the morning, head home, and be up to campus for 9 a.m. classes.

I worked the drive thru late that night. A silver Audi A4 pulled up to place an order. I heard two couples laughing on the other end of the call box.

"The guy is a joke. His whole story is made up," said a male voice.

"No it's not," laughed a female. "You just hate on anything you don't get."

"It's true," agreed a different male voice.

"You sure do," said the other female.

"Shut your trap. I'm trying to order," the first man demanded. A whack came over the intercom. Maybe a bird flew into the car window? The car fell silent.

I clicked the call button and said my lines. "Welcome to the Chicken Country Counter, would you like to try a Clucking Combo tonight?"

"No, fry boy," he bellowed. "Give us four Big Tasty Chicken Sandwiches and four fries."

I told the guy on the other end that for only 95 cents more per order, they could all get the combo which came with a drink.

He told me to shut up and asked me, "Hey asshole, who do you think knows what we want, us or you?"

I dealt with my share of drunken customers working the late night shift and quickly apologized. To this he said, "Damn Skippy." Whatever the hell that meant. Then he added, "Go make our food, Douche-o Baggins. We're coming 'round."

In the background someone said, "You're a fucking lunatic when you're blasted."

I glanced at the closed circuit video screen and saw, in shades of grey and black, Melanie in her flowered sundress sitting in the front seat. Then I saw the driver. It was the heckler from my talk earlier that night.

Shit, I thought. I can't let them see me.

I grabbed Rita, who worked the register, and told her I had to use the bathroom.

"It's an emergency. I ate some bad wings for lunch." Now normally I wouldn't say something like that to a teenage girl. But desperate times call for desperate lies.

I ripped off the headset, tossed it at her, and did what I do best. Hide.

My supervisor was Mandy, a 17-year-old high school dropout with a YouTube following and plans to head to California in search of, well, more YouTube followers. Mandy's rule for us was simple.

No phone use while on the clock. Meanwhile, Mandy livestreamed, Tweeted, Snapped and otherwise broadcasted every banal waking moment of her small town nightmare of a life. With her cutesy narrations and twangy smile, she could make working the fry hopper look like a truly fulfilling experience. But she threw an atomic tantrum if Rita or I so much as sent a measly text once in a while.

So while in the bathroom, I pulled out my phone. That little red LED flashed, begging for attention. I wish I hadn't given in to its lure and checked it. But I did.

A text from my wife read "BLOOD in the toilet. Lots of it. I can't do this again." A second text consisted of a single crying emoji.

I don't know why, but I didn't text her back. I wish I had. It was a mistake I didn't realize I was making, like a small earth tremor that humans don't notice but which starts a crack in the foundation of your home. In time, the earth will shift again. And again. Soon, nothing is stable. Yet we don't notice. We are sprawled out on the couch with our noses jammed up against our smartphones, our souls slowly vanishing to the soundtrack of our most brilliant distraction mechanism yet, the looping lunacy of outrage, idiots and YouTube influencers. Or, in this case, it was much simpler. I simply didn't know how to express compassion and sadness through a text message while standing beside a box of urinal cakes.

And of course, neither my wife nor I ever posted about what happened online, or told anyone else. That's not the kind of thing a family, perfect or not, posts on Instagram.

Chapter 6

The elevator door began to close. Nick pushed up against the far wall in the corner as though trying to back right through it. His knees were bent, his head cocked. Melanie hung by the wad of hair in his fist, her butt on the metal floor, red shorts at her knees, her thrashing legs entangled in the shorts.

I ran towards the closing door.

Melanie saw me. She gasped. It was a brief respite from her screams, an eerie moment of silence.

Nick swung his free arm around Melanie's chest, up under her armpit. He thrust her in front of him as a human shield. But he didn't quite have the strength to get her high enough with just one arm. He didn't think to let go of her hair with the other arm and use it to help. So she dangled with her head at the height of his chest.

I burst into the elevator with a steak knife high in my left hand as the door clipped my heel.

I chucked the knife towards his head, aiming high. He ducked down and to his left. He never saw me swinging the bottle with my right.

The barrel smashed into his right temple, exploding. Barbs of glass splattered the elevator walls and crashed down, gin pouring all over Melanie.

Nick's knees buckled. His head sagged. He crumbled to the floor on top of Melanie. Melanie started screaming again. But these screams weren't the carnal yelps from before. They were screams of shock.

"What do we do?"

Melanie crouched over Nick's limp body in the elevator. I stood by the elevator door with my finger on the door close button. The plant like smell of gin mixed with the scent of wet metal, like the odor of wet coins in swim trunk pockets, filled the enclosure.

"I don't know," I answered. "It's not like I've ever been in a situation like this before."

"You're sure he's breathing, right?"

"Yeah, I checked three times. You can check if you like."

"I trust you," she said, brushing glass from her hair.

"We just need to, you know, put him somewhere," I said. "Then come back and clean this up."

"It's not a murder scene. Why do we need to clean up?"

"I don't know. I guess out of a sense of stewardship. You know, community pride."

"This place is a shithole," she laughed, slipping towards hysteria. "We need to call the police if someone hasn't already."

"It's Friday. Everyone's at the bars. If someone had called the cops, they'd be here by now."

"Ok, I'll call," she said. "Where's my phone?" Melanie poked around the elevator floor like a bird looking for bugs. "Shit, I can't find it."

"Look," I said, grabbing her wrist. "Let's stop and think. Do we really want the cops involved? I don't want to be charged for assault with a deadly weapon. Rotting in prison isn't in my plans."

"You were just protecting me, and, and yourself really. He attacked you too."

"What if the cops don't see it that way?" I pleaded.

"He's gone mad. He's smoking some, some, some shit. It's that stupid war. It's made him insane. Oh my God! How the hell did this ever happen? Fucking Afghanistan. I love him, I love him, but, but he needs help. I'm - oh, I can't believe I'm saying this, but he needs to be locked up or I'm never going to feel safe again," Melanie cried. She tumbled to the floor, tucking her hands between her knees.

I crouched down beside her.

"I agree," I said, trying to console her. "I just think we got to get ourselves out of the picture first. Then, maybe we can call in an anonymous tip," I suggested. "You said he was doing some kind of drug? Why don't we just plant some on him?"

Chapter 7

"It's so beautiful out here," my girlfriend moaned, as if letting go of some deep tension in her gut. We stood beneath a moon halfway between dark and light, its visible side a corn yellow. The sky was deep and the stars shone through like a million crystals that had been scattered whimsically by an heiress. The river swept below us, a few hundred feet down from the cliffs. In the dark, we felt the cool air rising from the river as it washed against the rocks below.

I reached around my girlfriend's waist and pulled her back to my chest. "Move here," I said. "Move here and live with me."

"Move here?" she asked over her shoulder.

"Yes," I smiled, nibbling at her ear. "Get out of the suburbs. It's a little better a little further west, don't you think?"

"It's beautiful," she nodded. "And I could get away from Jessie."

"Jessie Whetstone," I said. "She's still struggling?"

"Did I tell you she stole $200 from me? You know me, Jamey. It's not the money. But to lie about it? I can't live with someone I can't trust."

"Then move here."

"What'll I do for work?"

"Maybe you can teach at the university too."

"I would need a Master's degree."

"It's just two years. Take one of the programs here. Or, I don't know, they have other jobs."

"That's true," she said. "I'd love to do it. I'd love to leave the traffic and the noise behind."

"Then do it," I said. "Marry me."

She turned her head and met my eyes. "Did you just-?"

"I think I did."

"Jamey, are you kidding? You don't say it to a girl unless-"

"I mean it," I said. I dropped to a knee. I pulled her hands into mine and held them out before her. "Marry me." I had no ring. But I held her hands anyways. "Will you?"

She looked down into my eyes, the moonlight cast across her neck and down her pigtails.
"You will never regret it. I promise," I said.

She leaned down and threw her arms around my neck. "Yes," she said. "Yes, I will."

"Yes you'll regret it, or yes you'll marry me?"

"Yes, I'll marry you." She kissed me. We fell together onto the cliff rocks.

"We better move back from the ledge," she panted between kisses.

We scooted back, careful to not let go of one another.

We made love on the forest floor before the moon and stars and the breeze that rustled the leaves. After, our bodies warm with sweat, we lay on our sides facing one another, our heads resting on balled up clothes.

"What day is it?" she asked.

"What?"

"What's the date?"

"It's April 14th."

"April 14th," she whispered. "I got engaged in April."

"We got engaged in April," I corrected, throwing a loose arm over her naked body.

"We got engaged," she said. "This night will always be special, Jamey. Every year until we die we will celebrate this night naked under the stars."

"I can't argue with that," I laughed.

She laughed and jabbed her little fingers playfully into my ribs.

"Star night. April 14th. It's on my calendar."

"Mine too," she said.

Chapter 8

Melanie's apartment wasn't a great spot to leave Nick. But we needed somewhere to store him while devising a plan. So we took the elevator to her floor and, after finding the coast was clear, we managed to drag him inside her place. Good thing she lived alone.

The inside of her apartment was buoyant and comfortable. It was as if we didn't live in the same building. A cushy beige sofa sat in the corner under a tall reading lamp. A coffee table nestled nearby, adorned with candles and travel books. Sprawled next to it was a red duffle bag, unzipped with clothes pouring out. A fast food bag and the debris of a meal littered a small kitchen table. A handle of cheap tequila and a few empty beer cans dirtied the kitchen counter.

"He stays here. Only on weekends, of course. Just sometimes," Melanie offered.

Her cat wandered out of the back bedroom and brushed up against me. "Okay, so, um, we should be quick. Where are the drugs?"

"We can't do this, we can't do this," Melanie shook her head.

"Can't do what?"

"This!' She pointed at Nick. "This is crazy."

"I know. But stop and think," I said. "What'll he do when he wakes up?"

"He'll be fine."

"I mean, to you? To me?"

"He'll be fine. He won't remember."

"Are you sure?"

Melanie looked away.

"Melanie, are you sure?"

"He…I… Yes."

"He dragged you by your hair."

"It wasn't serious."

"It wasn't serious? Are you kidding? I thought he was going to kill us both."

"It's not his fault."

"It doesn't matter," I pleaded. "Look, you want me to leave, I'll go. Take your chances. But stay the hell away from me."

"I love him. I'm sorry."

I turned towards the door. Then I turned back around. "Take my cell number and when you need help, call me. Trust me, it's going to happen again."

Melanie typed my number into her phone.

"Good luck," I said, turning to leave.

"Thanks," Melanie said. I opened the door and stepped into the hall.

"Wait," Melanie called.

"What?"

"He keeps the drugs in his overnight bag with his toothbrush. It's mostly weed and sometimes blow. It's in the bathroom."

"Are you sure you want to do this?"

Melanie looked at Nick who lay sprawled in the entryway between us. "No," she said. "But, what if it's the only way?"

"Okay then. We gotta be quick. Can you go get the drugs?" I asked.

"I'm so embarrassed, Professor B," she blurted. "I'm so afraid." She walked towards the couch and looked at it as if deciding whether to sit or stand. She grabbed a decorative pillow and wrapped her arms around it. "He loves me."

"I understand," was all I could think to say.

"I swear, he's never acted like this," she said, putting the pillow down on the couch and fluffing it. She headed towards the bathroom in the back, and said over her shoulder, "It's like he's on something totally different."

It occurred to me that I should tell her, "None of this is your fault."

She turned back towards me, tears in her eyes, and mouthed, "Thank you."

With a moonless sky and a sleeping town, we got Nick's sandbag of a body down the elevator and hoisted into the back of my Honda Element.

The plan was to drop him off behind the closed down strip club at the edge of town by the old highway. We shoved two small baggies of white powder into his pocket. One of the baggies Melanie said looked like the cocaine he did but the other looked different and she didn't recognize it.

We figured an abandoned building was the kind of place a drug addict would be getting high and that an anonymous tip to the police would solve the problem. Plus, it was far enough outside of town that if he woke up, he would have nowhere to go until the cops arrived.

We drove in silence. I pulled the SUV around back, shut off the lights, and killed the engine.

"We'll toss him here and then call him in. We just got to find a payphone."

"I don't think those exist anymore," Melanie pointed out.

"Shitty shit," I muttered. "Good point."

"I don't know how much drugs someone needs to have in their possession to get locked up."

"Yeah, me neither," I shrugged. "Grab the bag of pot - that looked like a lot - and the rest of the powder."

Melanie reached for Nick's duffle bag in the back seat and we got out of the car. I opened the hatch. I grabbed Nick's feet in his nice desert boots and pulled. Melanie's head swiveled nervously. "What if he gets out on bail?"

"I don't know. Maybe a few days in prison is enough to figure out your next move."

"You mean jail."

"What?"

"It's jail. Not prison."

"What?"

"If he's locked up a couple days, it's just jail."

"Well, whatever. It's not like I've had time to think this through."

"What if he gets out and comes after you?"

"Shitty, shit. I didn't think of that," I said.

"I don't know. It feels drastic."

"Hey, you're the one who said you wouldn't feel safe unless he was locked up. Remember?"

Melanie nodded.

"Do you have a better idea?"

"No."

"Then grab him and help me out before I change my mind."

She reached out one hand to grab him, clutching the duffle bag in the other.

"Put the bag down," I said.

"Sorry. I'm nervous."

"I am too. But we got to be quick. I can't believe he's been out this long."

"You're sure he's not dead?"

I pointed. "See his chest there?"

"Yeah-yeah, kinda."

"Well, so he's kinda not dead."

We lugged him, his boots dragging on the gravel, to a dumpster and propped him up so he'd be seen when the police pulled around back.

"Maybe we should tie him here so he can't leave," Melanie suggested.

"Good idea. No, wait. It's gotta look like an accident. Otherwise the cops will be looking for a suspect."

"Like he fell? His head is busted up."

"Maybe against the dumpster. He hit his head on it?"

"Oh, right. I guess." Melanie eyed the dumpster. "You don't think he'll tell the cops what really happened?"

I eyed the dumpster too. "They're gonna think he's a drug addict, right? Drugs on him. Drugs in his system. Any story he tells, he's making up. Right? Right?"

"Yeah. I guess. Yeah that makes sense. Okay. The dumpster."

"Okay. Okay. Where are the drugs?"

"In the duffle bag."

"Where's that?"

"You told me to put it down when we were at the car."

"Oh yeah. Shit. Um, go get it. We gotta plant them on him."

"Then what do we do?"

"We leave."

"I mean with the duffle bag."

"I don't know. We'll toss it somewhere."

"Are you sure we should be doing this?" Melanie asked.

I paused. "No," I said. "No we should not be doing this."

"Maybe we should stop."

"It's not like we're leaving him for dead," I said. "It's just prison or jail or whatever. You want to be safe from him, right?"

"Maybe he's sorry."

"Maybe. But I get the sense we're past the apology stage."

Melanie touched her face. She turned and scurried across the gravel to the Honda. It seemed much further than it had while we were dragging Nick. And as I watched her disappear into the dark I felt as though she would never return. The frogs of night croaked the seconds away, each croak pounding off the building wall.

Just hurry, I thought.

I heard a grunt. I turned back toward Nick. Something grabbed my shirt. Instinctively, I swatted it away as though it were a fly. But it wasn't. It didn't let go.

I grabbed at it. It was his wrist. His fist had locked onto a wad of my shirt.

"Let go," I whispered. I'm not sure why I whispered. I guess I was hoping he was half conscious and confused and maybe it was like being in that half asleep state of suggestibility.

But he didn't let go.

I grabbed his wrist and yanked. "Let go," I said. "Let go, let go." I yanked again. In the blackness of the night I could feel him pulling forward, muttering something. I felt his legs underneath me coming to life. "Let go of me," I shouted, yanking and yanking.

Melanie yelled from behind me, "What's going on?"

"Just hurry!"

I could see his face now. He had pulled me close to him. And in the black night, amid the frogs croaking and the damp early spring air, were two eyes. They seemed to come online, as if shifting from a state of blankness to a piercing awareness, the eyelids flickering, pupils clicking on.

I spun his wrist downward away from his shoulder, his head rolling with it. Still, he clutched my shirt.

His other hand cracked across my left cheek. Then, he hit me again. My mouth burst open, an involuntary grunt shot out with a wad of spit and something else.

I pulled back hard and lunged into him, his head slamming into the dumpster. He went limp.

I peeled myself from him. I hopped to my feet. I turned to see Melanie racing toward me with the duffle bag swinging beside her.

"Go, go, go. Let's get the fuck out of here."
She turned and ran.

Something grabbed at my ankle. I kicked at it, stumbling. My hands skidded across the gravel pebbles as I fell, rolling in pain, my knee tearing across the ground. I inhaled a cloud of gravel dust as I gasped. Lurching to my feet, coughing on gravel dust, I fled towards the Honda. Behind me, somewhere in the dark, Nick let out a primal, snarling yowl.

Chapter 9

Outside, the rain crashed against the side of our home as the clouds brought forth an early nightfall. Ella Fitzgerald filled the air, Louis Armstrong trumpeted behind her, his gruff whimsy a counterbalance to the melancholy she hid below the smooth harmony of her voice.

Wasn't it a lovely day in the rain? Ella and Louis romanced the idea, cajoling one another.

A candle in one hand and a bottle of Shiraz in the other, I slipped into the bathroom where my wife was showering, her golden body glistening behind the glass in the light cast down from above her. I stood, taking her in as she pulled her hair back, the water darkening its normally lemonade-like hue. Her face, eyes closed, turned up into the stream of water pouring upon it. The water cascaded onto her shoulders, curved down her back, arched over her rear, trickled past her vulnerable and inviting hips, slid down the smooth skin of her legs, and dripped off her calves and ankles to swirl once, maybe twice around the drain and, having lived its brief purpose, vanished. I lifted the bottle to my lips, poured wine into my mouth, swished its sweet and bitter over my teeth, and invited it down.

As moisture filled my lungs, I turned towards the mirror to find it fogged. The words "Happy Star Night, Jamey" were scrawled across the glass by my wife's finger.

I tiptoed to the shower, placed the candle and bottle on the tile outside the shower and flicked the light off. My wife let out a soft yelp of surprise as I slipped the glass open. "You scared me," she giggled.

"I'm sorry, my love," I chuckled. "I was trying to surprise you."

"Well, I was trying to lure you," she laughed, calling me forward with a finger pulling at the air.

I stepped into the shower. "That's not hard."

"It looks hard to me," she smiled, looking down. I shrugged awkwardly, suddenly embarrassed by my lust.

She pulled me close, seeing me shrinking.

"Did you think I'd let the rain spoil the first Star Night anniversary?"

"Never," I replied.

"I love you, Jamey. I'll always love you no matter what." She kissed me, pressing her mouth into mine, her hand wrapped around the back of my head. Our noses squished against each other's cheeks, and I pressed into her. She pulled my head against her neck and, panting, and whispered into my ear, "Relax."

She dropped to her knees, the water crashing over us, and I watched her by candlelight as she gazed up into my eyes.

Chapter 10

The Honda Element does not make for the world's best getaway car. I love the car for so many other reasons. It's rugged, has all-wheel drive, swinging suicide doors, a hatch, and a huge cabin that you can fit just about anything in if you remove the back seats. Some people use these delights of automotive ingenuity as mini campers even. But zero to sixty and sharp curves aren't the Element's thing. And stopping on a dime? Out of the question.

So we barreled into the apartment complex parking lot, yawing like a playground tire swing that had been shoved by an angry child, as we rounded the corner and slid to a halt.

"What the hell do we do now?" Melanie asked. "That was a total failure."

Throwing a knife at somebody? Hitting them in the head with a liquor bottle? Dumping them and fleeing? Had I really done all that?

"I don't feel good," I said. "I might puke."

"Ew," Melanie shuttered.

Sitting in my car in the parking lot, the slight smell of scorched rubber seeping up from beneath Melanie and I, I realized that the daylight was coming sooner or later.

I swallowed. "No payphone means no anonymous call. We're screwed," I admitted. "Sorry, I'm no criminal mastermind."

"Under different circumstances, I'd say that's a good thing," Melanie said.

Funny how alcohol and darkness give us false shades of time and possibility. We are magical, werewolf-sized liars hiding in the shadows, howling at the world. But the truth is, we rise and set with the moon. We shrink by daylight as the rest of the world wakes to the light's abilities and employs the full weight of its madness, its unyielding march against a universe which seeks to halt it every night in darkness.

Melanie must have been seeing the first peel of purple light tugging at the seams of night too, because she turned towards me and said, "What about the book, Emory's book? You said in your speech that you never went and found the three million Emory left for you."

"That's not my money," I gawked.

"Well, he basically said it was. He said there was money and he wanted you to have it as a way to apologize and to get you to publish his book, right?"

"He probably went back and got it. He said there was some money. If there was anything he left for me, it was maybe a few grand."

"How do you know? What if it's all there, waiting for you?"

I said I didn't know. I told her, sure, Emory didn't care about money. He never did. So he might have left it. But, of the thousands of people who had read the book, certainly some had gone looking for it, hadn't they? I told her that if Emory had left the money, then at some point it had certainly been found.

Melanie's response to my reasoning was, "Maybe they did go looking, but only you really know him well enough to find it."

I shrugged. "I don't know," I said. "I think we should just go home and face the music."

"What home? I saw the letters, James. You're being evicted," Melanie said. "I'm not letting that - I'm leaving. You were right. He'll do this again, just like, like, like Andrew." She crossed her arms and began to shiver. Then she stopped. "I'm going somewhere. I don't know where, but somewhere where I don't have to search anymore. Did you know that in Mexico City boys and girls stand in the city street with cars zooming by on either side all day? They sell cold mango juice for five pesos a cup. Breathing fumes, all day. Car pollution's not regulated like it is here. For five pesos a cup. All day. I read it somewhere. What can you know when you're standing in the road breathing fumes all day? Tell me I'm making sense." She grabbed the car door and opened it. "I'm not crazy."

I knew the property management company for our apartment was coming in a few hours to evict me. With classes having just ended, I knew my only income for the summer was working the drive thru at the restaurant. And I knew I would soon be living in my car, again. As for Nick? Well, he would be here soon enough.

"Who is Andrew?" I asked. "An old boyfriend?"

"The note is a sign," Melanie ignored my question, stepping out of the car. "It's like it came into your life. And it came into my life. This was fate. How else do we explain it? Maybe you're right, the money is gone. But maybe he's still alive. He's sending you a clue, James. I don't know what it is, but he wants you to find something, to know something more. Why are you afraid of looking?"

Fifteen minutes later we met back at the Honda. We decided to each grab what was important - cash, credit cards, clothes, gin, and other essentials.

On my way out of the door, I grabbed the book with the note in it and as many CDs as I could fit.

"I can't find Bruce" Melanie said, scurrying down the stairs. She wore her triangle glasses, masking her black eye. She had changed her clothes from red shorts and a torn white t-shirt into jeans, a black t-shirt, an army green jacket with lots of pockets on it, and black leather boots with silver shoelace holes.

As she came down the stairs, I saw that we both packed in hiking bags independent of any planning. I guess we were both in the same frame of mind and hiking bags gave us a false sense that we were heading out on a fun adventure. We were fleeing everything, even the truth that this was a desperate runaway, an insane hunt for lost treasure like we were characters in some twenty-first century bastardization of a Dumas novel.

"Who is Bruce?"

"My cat. The door was open when I got to my place. We must've forgotten to close it. Bruce is gone."

"Want me to go look?"

"There's no point. He's gone."

I told her I was sorry. But really, I didn't like cats.

"You got the book, right?"

I waved it at her, a CD case in my other hand.

"Wouldn't want to forget your 90s music," she joked.

I laughed. "Emory always said that the soundtrack to the ride is as important as the ride itself."

She shook her head. "Sure thing."

"Didn't get the reference?"

She gave me a roll of her thin shoulder, "Can't say anyone would."

"Fairweather," I replied.

"Is that a Drake song?"

"The university?"

"No, goof. The rapper."

"Fortunately, it isn't. It's a band. They've got a song titled 'Soundtrack to the Ride'."

"Never heard of it." She mock-yawned.

"That was a test."

"Oh? But I'm not your student anymore," she smiled.

I waved the CD case. "These are life lessons."

"We've got to catch you up to the decade, Old Man Birch," she laughed. "I've got dibs on the radio."

"If it ain't broke, don't fix it."

"Oh, it's broke," she laughed.

I laughed too. Suddenly, my wife's words came to me, "Cultivate a mind that clings to nothing."

"Wait here," I said. "I forgot something."

I ran upstairs to my apartment and headed for the junk drawer.

###

I wanted to see Emory. I hoped for years that he might show up late one night, off some bus from nowhere, his rucksack over his shoulders, his health intact. He'd need a place to crash and we'd stay up all night ironing out our past and in the end we would be friends, just as we had been as teenagers. But that didn't happen. I watched for mail from him, too. Every time I went to get the mail my heart would rev in anticipation until I'd finished rifling through every envelope and saw that there was nothing from him. Then, I'd feel an empty hole in my chest for a moment, my heart would stall, and I'd tell myself to stop expecting to hear from him so I would not keep getting disappointed. In time, the feeling slowly faded, like a DJ crossfading music to a new song, a song of acceptance that he was gone and I was still here with my problems.

Emory was like a fable in my life. When we were teens we were the best of friends. I have never had another friend since.

Years later, when he asked me to publish his book and I agreed, we became like mangled, entwined bodies in an automobile accident. I gave my talks and collected my fees. I took the money from speaking and selling the book and paid the bills, put food on the table, and kept the banks appeased. People said I got rich off of everything. They said I was famous. I guess I was famous. I guess I still am on some level. But the fame never felt the way I imagined fame would feel like.

I always thought that if I was famous it would be because I cured cancer or saved a bunch of kids from a bus that was hanging off a cliff. Instead, I got famous for what someone else did. And it's hard to be famous simply because you knew someone once. What do you do, offer people an autograph? I tried. I can tell you, they don't want my autograph. They just want to ask me about Emory. They want answers I don't have. And, as the keeper of all things Emory Walden, I swallow their questions down and hold them in my gut and no matter how much time passes, the acid in my stomach cannot break them down.

When I got back down to the apartment parking lot, Melanie and I hopped in the Honda. I don't know if you will believe this, but she took out her phone and snapped a selfie.

"What are you doing?"

"Letting my followers know I'm hanging out with Professor James Birch," she said. She adjusted in her seat so that I was in the background and snapped another selfie.

"Do you not remember what just happened?" I asked, incredulously. "And what the hell are you going to write in the post, 'Heading out to look for big dollars and a wanted man after conspiring to have my boyfriend arrested'. Hashtag imafuckingmillennial?" I snatched the phone from her hand.

"Hey. I was only going to share it on Snap. That shit disappears after a day. And only my besties can see it anyways."

"Look," I ground my teeth. I took a breath and tried to stay calm. "No tweets, no snaps, no nothing from here on forward. I can't believe I have to explain this to you. The goal is for people to not be able to find us, including Nick. Remember? We're not here to livestream a fun little adventure like some wannabe outlaw Kardashians. If you want to do this," I bellowed, waving the book in her face, "then you have got to know that this is some serious shit we're getting into. Emory is gone. He disappeared. I've been hassled by feds. You don't know the half of it. The last thing I need is more attention brought to me or this story. And I certainly don't need some lunatic boyfriend of yours wacked out on who-knows-what Hulk shit hunting us down because you wanted to snag a few likes to boost your fragile little approval-whoring ego!"

"That's a savage thing to say," she shot back, reaching for her phone. "I'm not an attention whore."

I pulled the phone away so she couldn't reach it. Then, feeling bad about what I'd said, I tossed the phone on her lap. "No posts. None. Got it?"

"I'm sorry," she said. "I guess I just wanted for things to feel normal."

"Say it. No posts."

"Okay. No posts," she allowed. "I won't post anything. Let's go."

"Good. Now, where are we going?" I asked, turning the engine over. "Where do we start?"

I WOKE UP IN A CAR

Chapter 11

Melanie and I began our adventure by sleeping in my car at a truck stop off of Route 81 in Virginia, about thirty minutes from campus and the town we had lived in just a few hours before.

I needed the sleep. But the bruises and scrapes from the night before woke up with me. It took some time before I could open my eyes and face the road before us and all the things lurking in our rearview mirror.

"Do you realize the magnitude of what we've done?" I asked Melanie over gas station coffee and a variety box of granola bars.

"It happened to us. It's not like we did it," she said. "We were victims. We can't think about it like we did something. We have to look forward from here on out."

"But it's the past that got us here."

"I'm sorry," she frowned, biting into a chocolate chip granola bar.

"No, I'm sorry. If my mail hadn't shown up to your place, then -"

"Ok, so we're both sorry. Now what?"

"He said he left the money on a DC awning right?" asked Melanie.

"I think it was a rooftop. It's in the book."

I grabbed the book from the car dashboard and flipped through. "Here it is." I began reading aloud.

On a rooftop near 2nd Street, behind a gas station where Congressmen's aides fill up cars, is a black garbage bag twisted sealed, buried under a mound of snow. Inside the bag is my rucksack. Inside it is a black case with my passport inside and twelve or thirteen envelopes pressed with Fletcher Spivey's pen. Maybe I will come back tomorrow and get them. If I can get to northern Idaho and trickle across the border through the wilderness, maybe it would be worth it.

I closed the book. "Okay," I said. "He said maybe he would come back for the envelopes."

"Yeah, yeah, the envelopes filled with Fletcher's money."

"We can only assume that they were filled with money."

"Well, it seems obvious that's what's in them."

"True. But, I'm just saying, we don't know for sure."

"True, we don't. But, based on the evidence," Melanie pointed to the book in my hand, "we can make an educated guess."

"You mean, a hypothesis."

"You're such a professor."

"Sorry."

"Don't apologize," Melanie said. "It's just kinda funny, that's all."

"Sorry. I mean, I won't," I sputtered. "I'm not sorry. I mean. I don't mean. Okay. Anyways. Okay, so that's our first hypothesis. Our second hypothesis is that he didn't come back for the money?"

"Yeah, yeah. Or if he did, he only took what he needed, which wouldn't have been much, right?"

"I don't know."

"Well, because in his original letter asking you to publish his memory he said there was money for you."

"True, and that original letter and the one follow up letter he sent me said where to get it. But the amount of money he might have left, I don't know."

"So he must have assumed you'd go get the money after reading the manuscript and realizing it was on the rooftop on 2nd Street. Then, once you had the money, you'd publish the book."

"But I never went and got the money."

"So we find a gas station on 2nd Street and climb up on it and ta-freaking-da," Melanie said. "Case closed."

"Yeah, I bet no one's thought of that," I mocked.

"Well, maybe they thought of it. But they didn't act on it because, like you, they figured someone else already did. So why bother, right?"

I perked up. "Ah, exactly! It's like the lonely hot girl theory."

"The what?"

I laughed. "I guess that's something only guys talk about."

"Well, regale me professor."

"Ok, Emory used to talk about this in high school. There was this really hot girl, Larissa Meyers. I wanted to ask her to freshman homecoming. But I was afraid. I figured there's no way she'd ever go with me. She was too perfect. She had teal eyes. I mean, literally teal. It was like she used those teal eyes to see things the rest of us couldn't. And she had this curly blonde hair cropped at her chin, a little longer than your hair. If I remember, she had cut it off and donated it to cancer survivors. She was smart, and had this dorky sense of humor I adored. She loved good music; I mean real indie stuff, before everyone knew about it. She was the girl you wanted to show off to your parents. The kind of girl you could spend the rest of your life with. So, anyways, I put off asking her."

"Wait. Is this the girl Emory stole from you?"

"So, I put off asking her. And I kept figuring someone had already asked her. So, I guess I used it as an excuse and never asked her to go."

"And she went with the school quarterback?"

"No," I said. "She didn't go. No one asked her to the dance."

"Oh, because everyone did what you did, assume she'd already been asked?"

"Exactly," I said. "People are afraid to go after the biggest prize of all because they assume that in a rational world, someone else would have already snatched it up."

"So the money is the lonely hot girl," she nodded.

"Maybe. It's worth finding out."

"And what happened with the girl, Larissa?"

"Well, after the theory proved right, I asked her out knowing I had no competition."

"And she said yes?"

"She said yes."

Melanie nodded. "So we're going to DC to find that bag of money."

"Yep," I said, starting the car. "And I'm picking the music from here on out."

Melanie waved dismissively. "Yeah, yeah."

"Here's a theme song for you." I sifted through one of my CD cases. "Put this in. Go to track four."

"What is it?"

"'Your Boyfriend Sucks', by the Ataris."

Melanie rested her elbow on the passenger door, plopped her chin in her hand, and stared out the window. "Let's not talk about him."

Driving down Route 66 East towards Northern Virginia, I remembered why I left and moved to the countryside.

The cocktail of self-absorption, self-loathing, and tyrannical desperation with which the Northern Virginia citizen lives is on full display in their trademark frenetic, seemingly murderous driving style.

With every mile we raced closer to the city, I felt the serenity of solitude being choked from me.

Sartre wrote in *No Exit* that, "hell is other people". If that's true, then cities are the lowest level in Dante's inferno. The outlying areas of DC are the upper levels of his inferno as concentric circles such that someone approaching the city is increasingly tortured by the unsustainable magnitude of pure, authentic Other People.

In every city I've ever had the bad fortune of having visited, it's as though the pulp of humanity is crammed into an espresso machine and shot through as concentrated hell. And what's worse, the closer you get to the city, the more you're restricted in movement. The arteries of roads and metro tracks clog. So there's little you can do to not feel trapped. The unbeating heart at the center of it all lives on, surely the work of another world where humanity has no place.

Anyways, in time, we crept up to the Roosevelt Bridge and petered across the Potomac River, past the stone monuments to a fallen civilization of noble men, and into the hell itself. That place called Washington.

"I'm looking up 2nd Street," Melanie said.

"It looks like there's a Northwest and a Northeast, which is it?"

"What do you mean?"

"There are two different streets in different parts of the city."

"Check the book."

Melanie flipped through the book.

"It's in the back."

"I know," she said swatting at me.

"Okay, found it," she read aloud.

gas station on 2nd St.

"That's all it says."

"Shit."

"We'll just check them both," I said. "Navigate me to Northwest."

###

Row houses. Rich people homes. That's all we found on 2nd Street Northwest.

One of the homes was for sale and Melanie hopped out and grabbed a flyer. When she got back in the car she said, "One point one."

"What?"

"One point one million dollars. That's what this old gray one will cost you."

"I'll contact my agent."

She laughed.

"Ok, let's go to 2nd Street Northeast."

Melanie tapped on her phone. "Okay, it looks like there are two different streets named that."

"This is a city for the deranged," I muttered as we drove to one of them. That street was but another residential street with trees and row houses. At the end of the one way street I turned to Melanie, "Okay, to the other street."

We turned left. Then right. We fiddled through a neighborhood and passed a cemetery. There we found the other 2nd Street Northeast.

The other 2nd Street Northeast was also residential, though arguably not as nice. Still, row houses, older homes, and a few small apartment buildings sat back off the tree-lined street. A few BMWs and Infinity SUVs stood proudly parked, shining in the spring sun.

"No gas stations here," I muttered as we rolled to the end of 2nd Street. There the road turned in an L shape and became MacDougal Street. I pulled the Honda over.

"Can you read that passage again?"

"Sorry, I lost the page. Let me find it." She flipped through *Discontents*.

"What's taking you so long?"

"I can't remember what page it was. Sorry," she grumbled. "Jeez."

I drew a deep breath and waited.

"Oh, I found something." She read aloud,

a gas station near 2nd Street NE.

"Oh, so it is 2nd Street northeast," Melanie said. "Sorry, I didn't notice that before."

"Okay, but the important thing is the word near. So it's near 2nd Street. We just got to –"

"Yeah-yeah" Melanie interrupted me. "Wait, but this isn't even the same passage. This one says something about dumpsters behind a gas station near

2nd Street NE. But there's another passage, the one I read a minute ago, that references a gas station on 2nd Street. It doesn't say near. It says on."

"This doesn't make sense, let me see that book."

I read the passage. I flipped through the book, heading from back to front and found only two other reference to 2nd Street. One mentioned a gas station on 2nd Street. One mentioned gas station near 2nd Street NE. And the last one - the one I first found back at the truck stop off Route 81 that talked about Emory's rucksack and the envelopes which we had hypothesized were filled with money - mentioned a rooftop near 2nd Street, "behind a gas station".

"Shitty shit," I yelled, flinging the book at the windshield and slamming my fists in the steering wheel.

"It's got to be a typo or something," she said.

"If this is just a typo, then what the fuck is the rest of this book? We can't rely on it for - look, this was a waste of time," I sulked, plopping my head on the steering wheel and folding my hands over my head.

I could hear Melanie tapping away on her phone.

"Now is not the time for selfies," I groaned.

"I'm not taking a selfie," she sneered. A minute passed. "James."

"What?"

"Drive around the corner."

"The only place I'm driving is home," I grunted.

"Just do it." She gave me a shove. So I drove left around the corner onto MacDougal Street.

"What? Look, more houses," I said, pointing across her body and out the passenger window.

"In front of you."

And there in front of us, maybe two hundred yards across a busy street, stood a green gas station. Its front faced towards us, and we could see the roof of the gas station building as it cast its gaze down MacDougal Street towards 2nd Street and us, and some distant memory of Emory Walden.

"I searched my maps app for gas stations near me," Melanie grinned proudly. "And James,"

"What?"

"Stop giving up so easily."

Chapter 12

"You're seriously going?" my wife asked. She stood in the kitchen. I stood by the front door.

"We could use the money."

"Seriously? Tonight?"

"I'll be back by 8 o'clock."

"But it's Star Night."

"We'll still go. I'll be back by 8 o'clock, just like I said."

"How much are they paying you to speak?"

"Three hundred bucks. It's just a few hours."

"All you think about is money," she grunted.

"I just feel like we never have enough."

"We've gotten by so far. Haven't we? It's all in your head."

"If it's in my head that we need more money, well, then doesn't that make it real? You know, I think therefore I am."

"What I'm saying is, you're always feeling like you got to do something. You can't handle sitting still. It drives you nuts. Your mind starts churning, and begging, and hoping for something to keep you busy."

"I can't help that."

She shook her head. "It's like you need a constant wheel to run on, a puzzle to solve, a problem to fix."

"What about you and Jessie? I heard you on the phone earlier. That was her right? You're trying to fix her."

"I'm not trying to fix her. I'm just offering her an ear."

"She needs drug counseling. She needs detox. Let them listen to her. They're the experts."

"You didn't mind it so much when she hooked up that bag of weed for your birthday last year."

I put my keys on the keyring by the door. "That was different."

"Different?"

"I felt bad about it afterwards."

"Felt bad? She knows people. She didn't mind. It was just weed."

"What I meant is, she was doing better then."

"You're right," my wife sighed. "She's slipping again. But I'm not trying to fix her. I barely talk to her. She called, for what, the first time in months? So I answered and we talked. That's all." My wife walked to the kitchen table and clenched the back of a chair. "I'm just being her friend. It's her life, her choices. I'm not obsessing the way you do. I'm not churning and churning and churning."

"Listen to me," I said, my voice rising and slowing. "I hear what you are saying. But I cannot help it. I've always been this way."

"Yes you can. Just let it be. Stop trying to fix everything. If you stop worrying, the problem will go away."

"The bills won't go away. The car payment won't go away."

"Jamey, we'll be fine with or without a nice car."

"Then how are we going to get ahead?"

"Ahead of what?"

"In life. How are we going to get ahead in life if we don't have money?"

"Look, if you want to go make some money, then go make some money. But I don't care about the money."

"I'm trying to do the best thing for us."

"It's Star Night."

"You said that already. And I told you I will be back in time. So what is it really?"

My wife pulled the chair out, its legs scraping across the tile. She sat down. "It's Emory. I'm tired of it. It's all you think about, all you talk about. Emory, Emory, Emory. I'm so sick of Emory."

"People want to hear about it. It's easy money."

"Don't shit me, Jamey. You love to talk about it. You're obsessed. You're an obsessive person. You get a little idea in your mind and it sprouts and takes root and you cannot let it go. You ruminate. You hold it there and stare at it from every angle. And you live in the past. You live in the past and you do not move on. You're in your thirties for Christ sake."

"I know how old I am," I said.

"You're entire life is stuck in this, this, whirlpool of Emory, and Ella Alice, and Fletcher Spacey, and —"

"Spivey. Fletcher Spivey."

"See!"

I walked over to the table and sat down across from her. "I'm sorry."

"All you ever talk about is Emory Walden."

"That's not true. I talk about music, and movies, and books I've read. And we go hiking and we talk about other stuff."

"Well, it feels like it. I know your whole life story."

"That's not true."

"Well, you're high school years. I know everything. You have literally handed me your diary from high school and told me to read it."

"Journal."

"What?"

"It's not a diary. It's a journal."

"Whatever."

"I just wanted you to, I dunno, to know about this stuff. I thought you were interested."

"I was," she said. "But I don't want to read your way-too-detailed journal and read about all the places you and Emory would go and hang out and pull juvenile pranks and how in love you were with Larissa and all that protracted girlfriend drama."

"I'm sorry. When we first were dating, you seemed really interested in Emory's memoir and how

I published it. You read it and asked me to tell you all about it and stuff."

"I did," she muttered. She plopped her elbows on the table and dropped her chin into her hands. "I did want to know. I'm sorry. I was interested. I still am. I just…It's too much. Seriously, your journal?"

"The high school girlfriend stuff was weird, I'm sorry. I didn't think about it like that. But when you explain it that way, it sounds, well, creepy. That's not who I am. I wasn't trying to make you jealous or something. I just thought you really wanted to know everything about Emory and me and how our friendship fell apart. Like, maybe it would help you solve the mystery in your own mind as to why he contacted me and asked me to publish his memoir for him."

"Don't apologize. I'm sorry I said it like that. You're the least creepy guy I know."

"Can I tell you something I've never said before? Something that scares me to death?"

My wife pulled her head up from her hands and sat back. Her eyes peered into mine. "Of course."

"I guess I just thought, maybe the Emory stuff was what got you interested in me. And if I kept feeding you more stuff, you'd stay interested." I looked down at my lap. The room was quiet. It felt empty. We were sitting across from one another, and somehow the sun had slid behind the trees and the room was growing dark. We sat enveloped in this darkness. "I know it sounds stupid," I said. "But really, I just wanted to keep you interested in me. I felt like, this is hard to say, but I felt like I didn't have a lot to offer you. Maybe all I had to offer you was this little connection I had to this big thing, this book. I mean, we met at one of the book readings I did."

"I remember how we met." She sighed. The room grew quiet again. Then she spoke. "That's why I became interested and wanted to meet you. But that's not why I fell in love with you."

"It's not?"

"No," she said. "It's your taste in music." A smile blossomed on her face.

I smiled back. "I love that we love the same music."

"It's your one obsession I'll never complain about." She reached her hand across the table and I took it. "Jamey, I fell in love with you because you're sweet, and smart, and considerate. You're fun, when you want to be."

"Thanks," I said. "I love you."

"I love you."

I glanced down at my watch. "Oh shit, I'm gonna be late." My wife let go of my hand. "I'll be back by 8 o'clock, 8:15 at the latest."

Chapter 13

Melanie and I pulled into the gas station near 2nd Street. We decided to case the place and figure out how to get on the roof. Plus, we needed gas.

Melanie wasn't so sure that the money was on the rooftop. She pointed out that Emory had written that the money was on a rooftop "behind a gas station". But the building behind the gas station, separated by an alleyway, was much taller. A quick look around made it evident that there was no way to get onto that rooftop unless one were to access it from within.

"I think he just meant behind the gas station pumps," I speculated.

"Maybe."

"Well, it's worth finding out," I said. I suggested getting some bottled water to go with our granola bars but Melanie said she was not eating granola bars for dinner. So I suggested it was time to do an accounting of our funds. Combined, we had $4.71, two credit cards with a combined $3500 in credit - yet neither of us was sure how much of that we'd already used, though we decided it was probably at least half - and we both had debit cards. We decided we should each check our balances at the ATM inside. But first, we filled up the gas. There went thirty two dollars of my credit.

While filling up, I gazed around a bit. The building was your average mid-sized gas station with a multi-bay repair shop on the left and the entrance to the convenient store directly in the middle. The roof had a shingled, slanted veneer all the way around that was maybe five feet high. Above that, the roof was flat. I ruled out the station overhang directly above me, and the one to my left, as they were standalone structures probably fifteen feet in the air with no way to get on top of.

Inside, Melanie strolled to the ATM. I shuffled to the counter to grab the bathroom key. Two gas station employees argued at the register. The younger one, with creases running down from either side of his nose past the corners of his mouth, complained to the other, saying, "I'm freezing, *jeffe*."

"I told you amigo, my name is not Jeff," the older one grunted. Bald with circular glasses, he waved his hand as if staving off gnats and said, "We wait until the men come and fix it. But you're complaining? I may have to fix that myself." He made a fist. They both laughed.

"Easy to say, *abuela*. Give me the sweatshirt, eh?"

"Holy hell, you Mexicans can't take a little *frio*."

"I'm from Honduras."

"Same difference, *amigo*."

"*No se, presidente*."

"Um, excuse me," I interrupted. "Can I borrow the bathroom key?"

Wet toilet paper lay in clumps on the bathroom floor. I tiptoed around it and peed. On my way to the ATM, I got us a few waters and looked around a bit. I'm not sure what I was looking for, but it seemed important to look. Nothing special caught my eye; just rows of stale chips and squished clear-wrapped single-serving desserts.

"I told you, I'm not eating granola bars for dinner," Melanie groaned. "I'm heading outside to look around."

I checked my balance, bought the waters, and headed to the car where I found Melanie.

"There's a roof access ladder around the building on the right," she said. "It's in plain sight of the street."

We added up out bank balances: $576, most of which belonged to Melanie. It was more than I expected and I didn't want granola bars again either. So we went to get dinner and waited for it to get dark.

After dinner, we parked on 2nd Street and walked to the gas station. We hatched a plan to get the money off the roof, have Melanie hide with the money behind a dumpster crammed between the station and a fence, and have me go get the Honda. Then, I'd drive by all nonchalant and scoop up her along with the money.

The access ladder hung under a spotlight in clear view of anyone pumping gas at the closer of the two station bays, about twenty five feet away. The ladder was visible to drivers on Michigan Avenue which ran adjacent to the station.

We walked up and down the sidewalk as the traffic flowed and the cars swept through the station, trying to figure out what to do.

"Why are some of the roads in DC named after states?" Melanie asked pointing to the Michigan Avenue street sign.

"I dunno. Pandering, I guess. There's an avenue for every state."

"Is there a District of Columbia Avenue?"

"This place loves itself so much, there probably is," I joked.

"I'll admit, that music on the ride down was pretty good," Melanie said.

"Ah, Melanie actually likes good music. There is hope for your generation."

"Thanks Old Man Birch." She pinched my arm. "Who was it again?"

"Jimmy Eat World. We listened to the *Bleed America* and *Futures* albums."

"What's next?"

"Well, we could listen to their album, *Clarity*. It was my wife's favorite."

"I think I'm ready for a new band," Melanie said.

"Have you heard of Something Corporate?"
She shook her head. "Of course not."

For two hours we paced around under the streetlights outside the gas station. Twilight approached. This antsy feeling swelled in me.

"We just gotta climb up the ladder as fast as we can," I said, tapping the sole of my shoe on a dandelion that grew through a crevice on the sidewalk. "I go first. Then, you follow me at a lull in the traffic."

"How will I distract them?" Melanie asked.

"Flirt," I said.

"What if it's a woman?"

"Then give her a compliment. It's the same thing."

Fifteen minutes passed. The traffic let up. I started to make a go for the ladder when a minivan rolled up to the nearby pump.

"Now. We got to do it now," I instructed. "Go distract them."

Melanie scurried towards the van as I paced towards the ladder. I grabbed the ladder rung and threw a look back over my shoulder. Three shoeless kids shot out of the back of the van, while their parents with matching 'I Heart Washington' t-shirts plopped out of the front.

Melanie swiveled towards me, mouthing, "Now what?"

I shrugged, waving her on.

The kids ran inside. Melanie darted towards the parents. The three of them chatted. But the parents faced right at me. So I leaned down and did the only thing I could think of. Pretend to tie my shoe. It was some B-list acting.

When I looked up, Melanie had somehow gotten the parents facing the other direction. So I hopped on the ladder and climbed. A pack of cars prowled down the street. I scurried the rest of the way up and fumbled over the top.

This little act induced a clarity within me. The last time I trespassed was back when I was a high schooler, when I was a common nuisance. A little vandal, bouncing around my hometown with Emory, stealing beer from neighbor's garages, stealing beer from convenience stores, pranking friends' houses, riding along as Emory drove my old truck on rich people's lawns across town, and drinking and smoking pot under bridges and behind shopping centers.

Emory would scream, "We're free to be, we're free to love, we're free, you and me!" And we would laugh and high five. He would beg me stay up all night with him. "Let's never go home," he'd say. "I can't face my parents. We'll never be like them, miserable and greedy." And I would nod, promising, "People like us don't end up like that."

Here I sat on a gas station rooftop, a taxpaying, fearful little adult. Fully conformed. Fully neutered. Somebody driving by on their merry way with a head full of worries and two kids kicking the back seat wasn't about to swerve across two lanes into a city gas station and pull some citizen's arrest crap for some crime they didn't understand. They weren't going to tattle on me. An adult climbing a ladder at a gas station was normal. I was normal. There was a lot that adult James could do that teenage James couldn't. I could hide in plain sight. How sad.

I poked my head up to see Melanie praying with the two parents, all three of their heads bowed.

When they finished, she hugged them. The kids returned. And she rubbed their scruffy fat heads. She said her goodbyes and walked away. She looked up, saw me, and gave a little wave. I waved back, urging her up.

When Melanie climbed over the top, I made some trite religious joke. She pinched my arm, and simply said, "They had a bumper sticker from my old high school."

The rooftop wasn't too big. It was rectangular in shape, with the front of the station to our left. A wall about two feet high framed the edge on all sides. In the dark, I made out a few pipes and odd workings jutting up out of the tar paper roof. A bag could be easily stashed behind some of them, or maybe wedged underneath. In the far left corner, an electrical box protruded from atop the service garage. In the far back on the right side of the rooftop, more or less in front of us, stood a large, tan HVAC.

"Okay, we'll spread out," I whispered. "I canvas this half to the HVAC and you canvas the front half to the electric box, so the top is split like two triangles. We meet at the electric box."

"Okay."

"Stay down, don't say anything if you find something. We'll talk at the electric box."

She nodded.

We crawled around, looking behind abutments and under pipes. The blackness of the roof swallowed our sight. I felt around and jammed my hand under objects. Here and there, I watched Melanie's silhouette, her curved bottom rising and falling like a caterpillar as she scooted over the rooftop.

We met at the electric box after maybe fifteen minutes.

"Find it?" I asked, rubbing a sore knee.

"No," she whispered, wiping her hands. "You?"

"Nothing."

"It's gone?"

"I don't know. I can't barely see anything."

"Me neither."

"Why don't we use the flashlight on our phones?"

"No way. Let's wait through the night until the sun starts to come up."

We lay down. We waited. Hours passed. I must have fallen asleep, because the next thing I knew Melanie rustled my shoulder.

"It's getting light. Let's look quickly and get off this roof before someone sees us."

Just then, I heard two voices. The one voice said something that sounded like, "No more wait, *jeffe*. I know the fix. I do the fix."

"Chopra will have your Mexican ass," said the other.

"No worry about Chopra, man. He freeze here? No. He no here. He no freezing. We freezing."

"Crap," I whispered. "It's the workers from before. How long are these guys' shifts?"

"What workers?"

"The gas station guys. The one was complaining about the air conditioning."

The sound of their voices followed them around to our left towards the back of the building where the access ladder was.

"Shitty shit," I whispered.

"What do we do?"

"You tell me."

"Let's just lay low and crouch behind this metal box thing. It's not like he's gonna come over here, right?"

The HVAC perched maybe fifteen feet away with a large, spinning fan facing towards us.

"I guess not," I replied.

"You checked around the HVAC really well, right?"

I nodded. "Yeah, there's nothing there."

The ladder clanged. Was one of them climbing up?

Melanie and I squeezed behind the electric box. But together, our shoulders stuck out to either side. "Duck your head down," she whispered. "It's poking up."

"So is yours," I replied.

"This isn't gonna work."

The clangs grew louder.

Melanie leaned forward, peeling away from the box.

"What are you doing?"

"Center yourself on the box."

"Why?"

"Just do it."

I scooted to the center. Melanie scooched in front of me so that her back was to me. We pulled into tight balls, our knees up and our feet on the roof.

"Spread your legs," she whispered over her shoulder. I spread my legs. She scooted back into me. Her butt pushed against my crotch.

"Squeeze your knees to mine, wrap your arms around me and duck," she whispered. So I did.

My ear pressed against hers. My cheek against her cheek. Her skin felt soft, softer than I imagined given her boney features. But her skin, elastic, soft, translucent, felt like a warm outer layer to an angular, fragile body. A woman's skin. It is a calming thing to feel. How little we touch others nowadays except to shake a strangling hand. Strands of her hair fell on my face, tickling my nose. I pulled her scent in and held it in my lungs. The sensation of another human being. I closed my eyes. I dialed into to her breath as it whisked gently across my lips.

The young worker breached the top of the roof. He climbed over. I heard him walk along the roof to the HVAC. He muttered to himself. It was too far away to hear.

A bang ran out. Then another one. The metal HVAC casing vibrated, the sound crashing against the metal of the electric box causing it to vibrate.

The young worker started yelling in Spanish. The bangs grew louder. The electric box against my lower back clanged harder, and harder.

A voice called from below, directly in front of us. "Hey Mexico, Chopra's here."

Footsteps pounded towards us from behind. "Why?" the young worker called just over my left shoulder.

"Oh no," Melanie whispered.

A new voice called up from below, "Alberto, get down from the roof."

The footsteps ceased.

"Senior Chopra, I, um -"

"Now!"

"Senior. The store. We freezing -"

"Shut up your mouth! Superior Heating and Cooling's gonna be here by 9. No *bueno*? Then go get your ass a new job. Whatever you do, get off of my roof. Now!"

A step landed just behind us, like a hammer smacking the roof. I squeezed Melanie close. She pushed into me. We leaned together as forward as we could.

The footsteps faded. I listened closely, Melanie's panting crowding the air. Above her breath, the clang of the ladder receded until I heard it no more.

Melanie's body rose as if taking in the air she couldn't quite collect moments before. She sunk, her shoulders falling, hands loosening, legs peeling from my legs. Her tenseness vanished and with it, her touch. When I opened my eyes I noticed that I had slipped my hands over Melanie's hands, my fingers woven between hers. I yanked them away. "I'm sorry." A slight upward turn of her bottom lip gave me a sense that the moment was gone.

We scooched forward, completely peeled apart. And again we were two people, two strangers on a rooftop.

"I'm sorry," I repeated.

Melanie turned toward the ladder. I looked out over the neighborhood, the tree tops beginning to take strands of light from the reddening sky, the light they worked so assiduously to collect all their lives. The light they would stretch and reach for all day and each day to come until they were axed down for some new development sure to rise when this neighborhood grew old and out of favor.

"What's that?" Melanie whispered. "James, what's that?" She pointed behind me. I turned. I saw something painted on the electric box. It was a crude little graffiti cartoon of a troll, it's upper half missing the left side as though the artist didn't finish it. Its one eye gazed off somewhere. On its right side, I saw an exposed breast.

"I dunno," I shrugged.

"I want off this roof."

Sweat dripped down Melanie's neck and off shoulders, the same neck, those same shoulders that first drew me to her.

"Stop giving up so easily," I said. "This is a clue."

"A clue?"

"Yeah, there's something else here. There's got to be. Look around."

"You think Emory painted this?"

"Well, he was a graffiti artist," I said.

"Yeah, yeah. Who else would've done it?"

"Exactly," I said. "Let's look around."

We crawled around but couldn't find much. Back at the electric box I looked at the cartoon graffiti again. I looked at its face. Its one eye, which glanced off to the side, seemed to peer around the corner.

"Come on," I waved. I crawled in the direction of the HVAC, Melanie in pursuit.

I hadn't gone a few feet before I felt Melanie nudge me. "There's a little spray paint here," she said. "Right under you." On the floor by the electric box I saw a half circle painted.

"What is that?" she asked.

I shrugged. "Keep looking."

We crawled to the HVAC. Melanie turned to me, "What?"

"The eye, it was looking this way."

"The graffiti eye?"

I nodded. "Look around. There's got to be something."

We crawled around some more. Soon I felt another nudge. Melanie pointed to the ground under a lip where the HVAC jutted out. "Drops of paint," she whispered. She got on her back and looked under the lip.

"Take a look," she said. I got on my back and looked and I saw "4/15/18" sprayed in black on the underside on the lip.

"What's today?"

Melanie checked her smartwatch. "April 29th."

"Interesting," I said.

"He's alive," Melanie gasped. "Emory's alive."

"Could be," I said.

"What does it mean?"

"Wait, wait. I need to see that graffiti one more time," I said.

We scurried back to the electric box.

"Yep," I whispered.

"James, what does it mean?"

I pointed to the missing side of the graffiti cartoon, "We've got to find Ella Alice."

Chapter 14

Ella Alice wore pearls[1]. Emory always said to never trust a girl in pearls because she thinks too highly of herself and not very highly of you.

I knew that she only had one hand, the other a prosthetic. But I didn't even notice it at first. It looked so real and she hid it so adroitly. She wore a red sleeveless dress. A light shawl hung around her elbows, cloaking the point where Ella Alice ended and her paperweight hand began. Her face was betrayed by scars that ran in little folds, as if a toy car left tire tracks on her left cheek just below her left eye. She covered it artfully with makeup and dark glasses. But the little folds could not be ironed out by Maybelline or masked by Ray Ban. And I could see a redness like a permanent blood stain in the white of her left eye. That empty eye seemed to be looking at nothing, as though things it once saw were all it ever would see.

Despite these things, or perhaps because of them, she stood tall and regal. She walked on heels like it was a lost art form and her hips swayed from side to side as though bobbing in some lake the rest of us couldn't see. And I had the feeling of her entire

---

[1] The name Ella Alice is used to refer to a person who is known as Ella Alice in *Discontents: The Disappearance of a Young Radical,* though she is no longer known by that name. In point of fact, she has been known by several names. However, to avoid confusing the reader, I have elected to refer to her only as Ella Alice.

body swinging like a pendulum a half a foot in each direction at the ass as she walked. And that ass. The stuff of royalty. And it knew it. When it all came together, the walking, the swaying, the ass, it drew every man in the room towards her like an erotic vortex. She was the kind of woman who could actually pull off those pearls. And the pearls probably wondered if they were regal enough for such a woman as Ella Alice.

But I'm getting ahead of myself. Because locating Ella Alice wasn't simple. Do I expect you to believe that we just looked her up and, bam, went right to her?

So let's backtrack a bit.

After sunrise on the day we found the graffiti on the gas station roof, Melanie and I spent the day trying to think of how we could find Ella Alice. We lounged on the Washington Mall and watched tourists doling about, snapping photos, looking at maps, and buying 'I Heart Washington' t-shirts from street vendors.

"Well, I have this friend Penny who lives in the city," Melanie said, looking up from her phone. She wore a white tank top and orange shorts in the early-May sun, her eyes glazed behind soda-can shades.

"So?"

"Well, it doesn't sound like we have a clue where Ella is. You've been reading Emory's book all day and, unless there's something you haven't shared with me, I'm not hearing that you're finding any clues in there."

"Yeah," I sighed, rubbing my eyes. "I got nothing. I mean, Ella liked to cook and wanted to make money. But, that doesn't really help her stand out from most women around here."

"You're lucky."

"Why?"

"Most women would call you a sexist for saying that."

"I'm not trying to be sexist. It's just that I grew up not too far from here, remember?"

"Yeah, yeah. Where was it again?"

"Let's just call it Fairfax County." Melanie nodded. She tapped on her phone. I think she was looking up where Fairfax County was.

"So it's just what people are into," I said. "And I don't mean just women. Men around here too. They like food and money. And, well, anything else that makes them seem cultured or successful."

"Aren't those kinda the same thing?"

I shrugged. "I guess. I mean, I always thought that education, reading, travel, those kinds of things made you cultured. Not buying food."

"But food is a part of culture. So, wouldn't knowing about food make you cultured?"

"Look, if you traveled to another country and tried the food then, yeah. But if you just go to an Indian restaurant and say you like Indian food and then you think that makes you cultured, well, that's a bunch of crap."

"Jeez, I didn't know you felt so strongly about anything," Melanie mocked.

"What does that mean?"

"I dunno," she rolled one exposed shoulder, it's creamy softness pink in the sun. There was something about Melanie's skin; its elasticity, its youth. Something missing from my own life, my own skin. "You just always came across as very, um. Hmm. I don't know. Detached maybe. When you taught, you never expressed any opinions. You were just nice and always respected what everyone said. And you never tried to persuade us to think any which way. You just presented the information and told us to make up our own minds. Most professors don't do that. They try to convince you of how smart they are and that their view is right."

"I guess I didn't realize. I just want people to make up their own minds about things, about life."

"Yeah, but what do you think?" Melanie asked, pushing her sunglasses down and peering into my eyes. I gazed off towards a child in a green hat running by, a yellow balloon like a kite dragging behind him. "You were so hard to read," she continued. "I took, like, four classes with you and I don't know a thing about you."

"Well, now you know one thing," I smiled.

"True," Melanie smiled back. "Remind me not to suggest Indian food."

We both laughed. "Sorry," I said. "I just, I never felt it was my place to try and influence others; like I didn't have the right."

"Stop apologizing for living," Melanie said, her mouth a frown. "Of course you have the right."

"Yeah," I shrugged. "I guess that's what this adventure is all about." The running boy tripped and tumbled, losing his grasp of the balloon. It floated off towards the sun and disappeared, its yellowness swallowed by the sun. "Anyways, what about your friend?"

"Well, I'm thinking maybe we can stay at her place for a night or two while we figure out where Ella is."

"Who is she?"

"Her name's Penny. I messaged her and she said it's cool," Melanie said. She stood up and waved to me to get up too. "She was my best friend growing up. Then she came to the city for college and we kinda lost touch. I don't know much about what she's into now or anything."

"If I was a betting man," I said, standing, "I'd say she's into food and money."

Penny seemed to be making good. We met her and her boyfriend, Clark, at one of those Argentinian meat-orgy restaurants that are advertised on NPR podcasts.

The only way that I can describe Penny is to say how noticeably unnoticeable she was, except for one thing. She had a massive head of hair. Thick and dark brown, it sprouted in waves from her head and seemed to pour down her back like water over rapids. Her bangs billowed up out of her forehead. They hung down past her eyes as though she was some kind of human-sheepdog mix. But other than that, I couldn't tell you anything about how she looked. She owned no distinguishing nose, eyes cheeks, mouth, or chin. Nothing. She wasn't tall and she wasn't short. She wasn't thin and she wasn't fat. She offered no curves, no shoulders, no thighs, no butt that could catch a person's eye. Take away that hair, put her in a lineup, ask me to pick her out, and I couldn't do it. The same could be said about her boyfriend, Clark. Except he was balding. They were like melted cheese, intermingled in every sense in their personalities, attitudes, and self-assurances, but entirely commonplace among the dishes of everyday life.

It turns out that Penny and Clark worked for some startup that was trying to upend one long-standing business model or another. I didn't quite catch its angle, but I think it had to do with political fundraising from private corporations.

"It's called Politifuel[2]," Penny announced.

Melanie's eyes lit up as if Penny was telling us about a cure for colon cancer.

"In the valley," Clark followed, proudly, "there's a mantra: Break things." It was the kind of thing people read in pop business books.

---

[2] This is not the real name of the company. But I can assure you that the real name is as equally stupid.

"This is Washington DC," I cracked. "The whole place is broken." That got a laugh.

So they told us all about their lives. They were tech people. The savior kind that the news says will solve all our problems.

"Were closing an investing round this week of two million actually," Penny said. "That'll sustain us for six more months."

"What do you do after six months?" I asked.

Clark looked at me like I had raised my hand and announced that I didn't know what an automobile was. "Raise more cabbage," he said.

"Yeah but-"

"That's just how Silicon Valley life is," Clark declared, sipping his wine. "In startup life, you're constantly pruning cabbage."

"Again, we are in DC," I said, sipping my wine. No laugh this time.

Melanie said that she liked Penny's shoes or something.

"No, seriously. What happens if you don't get this round of funding?" I asked, putting my glass down and leaning forward.

"Politifuel would be finished and everything we've worked for-" Penny began confessing, but Clark interjected saying that they would get the money. He was sure of it.

"So how long you crashing with us?" he wanted to know.

We assured him it would be just a night or two.

"And you got some kinda project?"

"I told you Clarkish," Penny said, putting her hand on his lap. "They're doing research for a book Professor Birch is writing."

"Ah, the *proffesaur*. It got something to do with that Waldo guy?" Clark asked.

Penny shook her head, her mass of hair waving side to side. "You mean Walden."

I told Clark it didn't have anything to do with "that Waldo guy".

"I read that *Discontents* book. Killer stuff," Clark said. "What you do with the cabbage that guy left for you?" Funding this research trip of yours?"

"It is," Melanie nodded, smiling.

"So why you staying here? What are you, Jewish?"

"For real, Clark? His name is James Birch. Does that sound Jewish?" Penny withdrew her hand from Clark's lap. "You're so 20th century. They're crashing here because I wouldn't have it any other way."

"I'm just playing with my man here," Clark laughed. "Why so serious, Penny?"

"No worries," I shrugged.

"But seriously my man, why you drive that ratchety old toaster car? You could do better. Hundo P." Clark declared as he stood up, "This feminist wine is weak. I need to attack some whiskey."

When he came back with a drink, I got up and got another bottle of wine from the bar. When I came back, Penny, Clark and Melanie had turned to their smartphones. I sat down, took out my seldom-used phone, and tried to find something worthwhile to do on it. I peered up at Penny, Clark and Melanie from time to time as they tapped into the void, sedated by that blue light. I tried to find that same peace in the glow of my phone. But somewhere amid the wine sloshing in the dark of my stomach a dim feeling stirred.

Chapter 15

Penny and Clark wanted to take an Uber back to their place, but I refused. Melanie pinched me, saying she always wanted to ride in an Uber. But I was pretty bombed.

Their condo was smack dab in the middle of The Land of the Gentrified. They lived five stories above an even more expensive incarnation of a Whole Foods just across the way from the 9:30 Club. None of this part of the city looked like this when Emory was here back in 2009. Not one of these buildings was here. When we were growing up and coming in to see bands like Reel Big Fish and Zebrahead, you didn't walk around at night by yourself in this neighborhood. Now, twentysomethings weaned on Mom's engorged tits, drunk on broad-spectrum encouragement, coalesced outside a taco truck singing what I imagine was the 2018 version of pop music. The neighborhood natives must have been petrified.

This was what I imagine Emory Walden's nightmares were like.

At the condo, I crashed on the floor while Melanie curled onto a fold out couch.

I woke up as the sun sliced between the curtains the next morning, my head banging like a middle school drummer. I got up. Melanie slept, her arms tossed across her body, the bruises on her face cast against the peace in her expression. I tiptoed to the balcony and slipped behind the curtain. I gazed through the sliding door at the dirt-covered facade of the 9:30 Club and the nearby intersection that collected people the way a pothole collects water.

"No, no. Don't pull the plug. She'll come out soon. There's still time," said a voice on the other side of the glass. "I'm her daughter and I'm directing you. She'll wake up."

I peered around the corner to see Penny standing on the balcony leaning on the railing. She cradled her phone on her shoulder. "I don't flipping care. Tell them if they pull that plug I'll sue their balls off. Put dad on the phone. He's not there? Where the crap is he? Jesus on a bike, I can't even. I have to do everything myself. Listen, tell Mom - I know she's in a flipping coma, William. She can still hear things. Listen, tell her I'm so close with Politifuel. Tell her I'm gonna make it. She'll see. Well, yeah I'm gonna flipping come see her soon. Hundo P, like I said yesterday. I just got - soon. Do not let them pull that flipping plug. There's still time." Penny peeled herself from the railing. I stepped back. "Okay, I gotta go. Hey, any word about the other driver? Oh, oh. Okay. Okay. Jesus on a bike. Hey, William, do not let them pull that plug. I gotta go."

I tramped to the sink. I filled a glass with water. I heard Penny slide the door open behind me. She stepped inside. The sound of her feet ceased. I lifted the glass. I drank the water.

"How much did you hear?" she asked.

Facing the kitchen backsplash I said, "Nothing."

"Listen," she said. "Please."

"Sure," I replied.

"Clark's in the shade on this."

"Okay," I said, turning around.

"Please, do me one."

"What's that?" I asked.

"Vault whatever you heard. Especially from Melanie. Please. Just, do me this kindness." Penny rubbed her palm up her nose and screwed her palm against each eye.

I took a sip. "I won't say anything."

"Thank you, Professor Birch. You're kind. You really are."

"Hey, I think it's cool, you know, what you're doing. You and Clark. The startup thing."

"Yeah?" Penny sucked a wad of snot back. "It's just a lot of pressure right now."

"What happened with your Mom?"

"God-fumble," Penny sighed.

I nodded. "I know it doesn't." I stopped. "When I was 17 -"

"I'm sorry. I got a lot on my mind," Penny said. She turned and walked down the hall to her bedroom. She paused, opened the door, and slipped inside.

We borrowed Penny's computer while she and Clark were working at one of those office sharing places that had sprung up after the Recession. When they asked us why we didn't have a computer,

Melanie told them that I accidentally left it on the roof of my car and drove off.

And so we began our search for Ella. I knew that she now went by a different name, but we couldn't find anything on either that name or the name Ella Alice. The day ended with nothing. So the next morning we took the metro to the public library. But I don't know much about searching records and we didn't turn up much. We spent the next week puttering between researching in the library and wandering the city hoping for some divine inspiration. We told Penny and Clark we were out conducting interviews for my book.

On the eighth day of our search we sat at a computer in the library. Melanie threw up her hands and groaned, "You'd think with Google and Facebook and all that, that we'd hunt her down in no time. I can't believe this."

"Really," I grumbled. But Ella didn't seem to be on social media and we found nothing when it came to things like property, arrest records, or traffic tickets.

Melanie tossed Emory's memoir on the table. "According to the book, Ella said she earned her bachelor's at nearby GW."

"Yep," I nodded. "Emory called it a school full of Congressman's kids. So what?"

"Well, let's call the school and ask them for Ella's contact info."

"Smart," I said. "You know, you're turning out to be quite the detective."

Melanie smiled.

We called up the registrar and pretended we were old classmates trying to get in touch with Ella. But the registrar ducked behind privacy laws. Some lady on the other line said the school couldn't even confirm that Ella had ever attended.

"I'm starting to lose hope," Melanie said, thrusting her arm across the table and dropping her head onto her elbow.

"What about that whole not giving up so easily thing?"

"That was over a week ago," Melanie groaned. "Penny is really getting on my nerves."

"She seems nice enough," I said. "You the jealous type?"

"Me? No way."

We laughed.

"I love that bitch, I really do. But, why does everything always have to work out for her? She gets into a great school and lands a startup job right out of college. Then, get this, last night she tells me she's thinking about writing her own memoir. Her own memoir? Seriously? What's it gonna be about, how luck falls from the sky?"

"Hey," I shushed.

"What?"

"We're in a library."

She leaned over and pinched my arm.

"Seriously, James. If something doesn't happen soon-"

"Look, why don't you head back to Penny's place," I said. "Seems like you're eager to catch up."

Melanie faked a laugh. "Well, she did mention going to a whiskey bar on H Street." Melanie perked up. "But what'll you do?"

"I think I just need to just go for one of my walks and clean my head," I said.

"Don't you mean, 'clear your head'?"

"Yeah," I said. "Sorry, I'm just tired. But I could use a clean head too."

We laughed.

"Okay, go for one of your evening walks. And then meet us for a drink?"

I nodded.

I tumbled out of the library as orange wisps of light illuminated a few cirrus clouds high above the city. Were there no buildings to box me in, I bet I could have seen the beginnings of a magnificent summer sunset.

As I walked, I thought about Emory being all alone in the city, scaling buildings or whatever it was he did to get up on rooftops to make his graffiti. I wondered what he looked like and how he had aged in the years since we were teenagers and friends. Emory wasn't the kind of person who would ever age. I couldn't see his hairline receding or gray hairs sprouting around his temples. I stopped and caught my own veneer in a window and saw how my hairline had gotten lazy, lost its foothold, and had let the claws of time scrape it back across my skull. I saw the wrinkles around my eyes and the dark circles that had shown up one morning when I lost my first home in the Recession. Was Emory too, if he was alive, being weighed down by time the way I was?

If Emory brushed by me on the street, I knew I would recognize those bony cheeks atop the corners of his madman smile, that tousle of brown hair he never combed, and that jagged way he walked, his head always out ahead like his mind had somewhere to go, if only the rest of him could keep up. But if Emory brushed by me today on this city street, would he recognize me?

I held this same conversation with myself every evening for days and days as I walked down R Street past the Oak Hill Cemetery. And each night I heard a different answer as to whether he would recognize me. I turned right on 30th Street Northwest as I had done every night and ambled towards Q Street.

My thoughts shifted to Nick clawing at my feet as I ran off, leaving him in the gravel and dust behind the abandoned building. Where was he? Was he looking for us? I could hear him hollering. I walked and walked, passing Dent Place Northwest.

A little girl with choppy brown hair perched at the corner of Cambridge Place Northwest. I stopped and scanned the tree-lined street. American flags hung from the doorways of freshly painted brownstones. The girl was swallowed by an orange shirt. Her skin pressed through the holes in the knees of her jeans. A mutt poked around at her feet, its tail dragging on the bricks. She yanked at the mutt by a yarn of twine. The mutt sniffed on.

"Mr." she whispered to me.

"Who, me?"

She put her fingers to her lips. "Quiet."

"Sure thing," I said, drifting into the crosswalk.

"Mr. Help me."

"Look, I don't have any money," I said.

"Help me."

"I said, I don't have any money."

"There's bad people," she said. She came up to me with her hand out.

"Kid. I don't have any money."

"Pretend," she said. "I need help." She folded her fingers in, her thumb out, and jerked her hand towards her stomach. I peered over her shoulder and down the street. A few cars parked along it. A Porsche. A Tesla. An old white windowless van. A BMW. A Cadillac SUV. A red Audi.

"I'm trapped," she said.

I stopped. I reached into my pocket and grabbed a $20 bill from my wallet. I handed it to her. Then I reached in again and grabbed two more $20 bills. "Aren't we all?" I said.

I turned and crossed the street.

"Heya" I said, crashing into the stool beside Melanie at the whiskey bar. "I just had the weirdest experience. This little girl. She needed a haircut. Dirty. Out of place. And I didn't get it at the time, but I think she was in trouble. Like there was someone she was trying to get away from. I don't know. Maybe I'm losing it. But she said she was stuck, or trapped or something. And she pointed somewhere. But I couldn't tell what she wanted me to see. Stupid. I gave her money. I can't stop this feeling. I should've done -"

"I think I found her," Melanie blurted.

"You what?"

"Ella. I think I found her."

"How?"

"I just. I thought about what you said," Melanie shrugged.

"What I said about what?"

"Food and money."

"What about it?"

Melanie pulled out her phone and tapped on it. She held it before me.

"What's this?"

"It's where we'll find Ella Alice."

I looked at it, then at Melanie. How had she found her? When? She sipped her drink, some brownish-orange concoction with an umbrella. "Do you know that bitch is microdosing?"

"What? Ella's doing what?"

"Not Ella. Penny."

"What's microdosing? What are you talking about?"

"Seriously?"

I nodded. "Yeah, I'm old, remember?"

"You're not old. You're out of touch. Microdosing is when people take tiny amounts of psychedelics to enhance their productivity."

"I don't think people on mushrooms are notorious for getting things done," I laughed, trying to wave down the bartender.

"No, it doesn't work like that. You don't get high. It just helps you focus."

"Well, cool people take mushrooms to get high, not to do work."

She laughed, sipping her drink.

"I guess I should have expected this," I said.

"Expected what?"

"That Silicon Valley would find a way to ruin magic mushrooms."

Melanie spat her drink in laughter. "Yeah, I forgot she used to take Adderall back in high school. I guess uncool shrooms are her new drug of choice. No wonder that bitch is so successful." The bartender came over and I awkwardly ordered a drink I knew nothing about.

"Enough about Penny," I said, paying the bartender. "What about Ella? How'd you find her?"

"Sherlock's got ways," Melanie smiled.

"I'm sorry, you were saying something about a kid begging for money?"

"Yeah," I said. "Weird stuff." I waved my hand. "So, Ella Alice?"

Melanie raised her glass in toast. "Well then, to finding that money."

I tapped her glass and kept my mouth shut.

"Sup, mom," Penny called, sliding up beside us. Below that mass of hair was a scrunched nose and a pair of lips pulled tightly over teeth. "I need a drink. Make it two." Penny took Melanie's glass from her hand and sipped through the straw. "Sorry Mel, this day was rough," she said, handing back the drink.

We said our hellos. Clark waltzed in. He ordered two more drinks for himself, declaring, "Time to attack." We headed to a table in a quieter part of the bar.

"How's things with bae? It's Nathan, right?" Clark asked Melanie.

"Clarkish! You mean Nick," Penny corrected.

Clark shook his head. "The army guy? I thought his name was Nathan?"

"BAE?" I laughed. "What kind of word is that?"

Clark shook his head.

Melanie stood. "I got to use the restroom."

"Me too," Penny said.

They disappeared into the back. Clark turned to me. "So my man, you attack that yet?"

"Attack? Attack what?"

"Melanie. I'd plow that dainty little ass," he said, his drink held up in front of his face, his eyes glaring over the glass at me. "And those lips." He tipped his head back and swallowed, his Adam's apple firing like a piston in his neck. "You're plowing her, right? Some little student of yours; now that's some easy prey shit."

"I'm not -." I cleared my throat, my own Adam's apple rattling. "We're just working on a project."

"Let me lay down some knowledge, my man. Most guys, they dart on a hot girl and plot how to get with them. Not me. I dart on the guy they're with. That shit tells me all I need to know."

Just then, Melanie and Penny returned.

"So," Clark said, turning to Melanie as she and Penny sat down. "Where were we? Oh yeah, the army BAE. How's that rolling?"

Melanie drew a protracted sip from her straw, ice the only thing left at the bottom of her glass. "Oh, it's gold. Everything's gold," she said.

"Hundo P, okay?" Penny asked, wiping her hand across her forehead. The effect was like a windshield wiper and for a brief moment I saw her eyes for the first time. But the moment passed before I could make out their color or see their shape. Melanie nodded, clutching her drink. She picked at the straw and shoveled the ice cubes around. "Tinder," Penny pronounced. "Just make a Tinder profile, Mel. It's revolutionized dating. High key, there are buckets of guys out there now."

Melanie put the straw in her mouth, her lips squeezing around it.

"How's about my man?" Clark said, pointing at me. "He's a professor. And you're doing research." He winked.

"Me?" I asked.

"No one else," Clark smiled.

"I'm not joining Tinder," Melanie blurted. "I don't need love."

"Clark and I are just salty," Penny apologized. It turns out, the money didn't come through on their fundraising round. The largest investor pulled out, causing a cascade of withdrawals.

"So what are you gonna do?" Melanie asked, her face hidden behind her glass.

Penny shook her head. "Shit's basically canceled. We got a few weeks of runway left before we're dry."

"Aren't there other investors?" I asked.

"Once investors pull dick on a round, no one wants to touch that startup," Clark said, sinking into his chair. "We could probably slam another round in three months, maybe six, once people forget. But our runway's too short."

"We need that flipping money," Penny repined, a shakiness in her voice. She bit her thumb, her teeth showing. "We're in this one hundred percent. No bullshit." She shook her head, her tongue pushed between her teeth, her nose scrunched. "What timing! That weak ass Jackson, that spidery son of a bitch. That spineless shit bag."

"There's got to be something," I said. I thought about Penny and her Mom.

"We're fucking leveraged, Robert Fucking Reich," Clark barked. "Jump out of your ivory tower."

"Hey, I understand," I said, shifting back in my chair and turning my body away.

"You don't, *professaur*. I took out a reverse mortgage against my condo to start this company."

"Our condo," Penny corrected.

"Whatever," Clark snorted, kicking at the short table in front of him.

"Maybe we can help." Melanie suggested.

"Well, unless you're holding two million clean," Penny cracked.

Melanie said she wasn't.

"Politifuel is basically finished," Penny melted into tears. "That spineless shit bag Jackson. That spidery son of a bitch."

"What about this guy?" Clark asked, pointing at me.

I swallowed, ducking my chin and rolling my shoulders forward, pulling my spine back in my chair, trying to make myself small. "Who, me?"

"Well you got that cabbage that Waldo guy left you right?"

"Walden," Penny corrected. She turned to me, her eyes widening, the color returning to her cheeks. "Yeah, James. You could become an investor and get some stock in the company. It's a win for everyone."

"Think about it *professaur*, you could multiply your money ten times over."

"Diversification," Penny nodded, pushing the palm of her hand up her nose and wiping the snot with her drink napkin. "Even, like one hundred thousand, or one fifty would buy some time."

"Put that cabbage to work," Clark urged. "Attack."

I looked down into my lap, unsure of what to say. I started thinking about ways to disappear.

"Listen," Melanie said. "He doesn't have the money."

"How would you know?" Penny quizzed. "You just want to see us fail."

"No," I said. "It's true. I don't have any money to invest."

"You for real? You blew it all already?" Clark snorted. "No wonder your whip is such a joke."

"I didn't blow it," I sputtered. "I never took it." I looked at Clark. "But I'm gonna." The words spilled from my mouth. I don't know why. But something compelled me to say it. It was as though a pressure squeezed me in on all sides. As much as I tried to shrink away, I couldn't squirm out from between the three of them. Unable to make myself any smaller, I turned to the thing swollen inside of me and expelled the words trapped within. I thought that with my chest empty, I could shrink further. And maybe I could slip out. But once I let the words escape and float out into the air between us, they lingered there naked. And I was no less able to escape.

The next morning we left Penny and Clark's condo. We got up early to sneak out before the sun threw light down the cracks between buildings. But

Penny came in from the balcony with her phone and a nitro coffee in hand.

"Good luck with Politifuel," I said. "Sorry to hear about everything."

Penny waved her hand. "I'm a survivor. Don't worry about me."

Melanie and Penny hugged.

"Hey, I got this old computer," Penny said. "You guys can have it for your research," she said, pointing to a small bag on the counter. "It's just a PC. But it works."

"Bouncing?" Clark asked, emerging from the back bedroom. His last clump of hair clung to the side of his head.

"We can't take that," Melanie said.

"Please. Take the computer," Penny said. "I know how much it blows to rely on just your phone for work."

Melanie picked up the computer bag. "Thanks for letting us stay. Sorry it was so long."

"No worries," Penny said. "Clarkish and I were happy to have you."

"One hundred percent," Clark yawned.

"I hope everything works out," Melanie said, hugging Penny.

I shook Penny's hand. "Good luck," I said. "With —"

"Thanks," Penny cut in.

We stepped out into the hallway.

"What you researching for again?" Clark asked.

"A book," Melanie said.

"Right," Clark nodded, rubbing the scruff on his face. "You never said. What's it about?"

"Hey," I said, shaking his hand through the door threshold. "Next time, I'll tell you all about it."

"Next time. Exactly."

"Mel, don't forget," Penny said, raising a finger. "Tinder."

Clark, still looking at me, mouthed the word "attack".

James Wallace Birch

ONE FOR THE KIDS

Chapter 16

This brings us back to Ella Alice and those pearls.

Melanie and I stood on the sidewalk as we peered in through the glass at a fundraising event held at a high end restaurant situated inside a hotel a few blocks from the Capitol.

There, Ella Alice swayed down the aisle between circular tables. Men in suits and women in elegant dresses sat erect, chatting and drinking while servers bustled about.

"That's got to be her," I pointed.

"Yeah, yeah," Melanie agreed.

I eyed Melanie at the edge of my vision. How had she found Ella Alice? She still hadn't said and I didn't want to let on to my curiosity. But her vague answer at the whiskey bar the night before didn't sit well with me. Then again, most of my troubles in relationships had come from assuming things. That's what my wife said to me once.

How could Melanie suddenly manage to track down someone we seemingly hadn't been able to locate in over a week's time?

But could I really ask her?

What if she thought that I knew how to find Ella Alice this whole time?

But why would she think that?

But what if she did?

Would an imperceptible crack in the foundation of our relationship begin to form, just as had happened between my wife and I? And what damage would that do towards the reason Melanie and I were together? Would I really be here, standing beside a beautiful woman with triangle-patterned glasses, vulnerable lips and soft shoulders, if that book with the cryptic note hadn't landed in her mailbox? If Emory Walden hadn't done what Emory Walden had done? Would I even be on this adventure?

So I swallowed my doubt about her story and how we ended up here. And out of the corner of my eye as we stood at that hotel restaurant window, I saw that I had lost some control of the narrative of this whole adventure by allowing the detour with Penny and Clark to occur. And I saw that in allowing Melanie to be the one to find Ella, I was risking losing the whole thing. And I saw that maybe that was for the best.

"We need to go confront her," I blurted.

"Yeah, I know," Melanie said.

"I mean, right now."

I scuttled to the front door, shoved it open and charged into the hotel lobby. I sloped around the concierge and up to the restaurant door. I pushed through, pacing towards Ella Alice. Melanie scurried in behind me like a bug-eyed secretary trying to keep up. Suddenly, I stood in front of Ella Alice as she swayed between the round tables.

"Excuse me," she said politely, trying to squeeze by. She paid no mind to the fact that I wasn't wearing a suit, or to the fact that the young woman scurrying in behind me wasn't in an evening dress.

"Ella," I whispered. She looked at me from behind her dark glasses. "I'm sorry. I'm Mrs. Fisher.[3] You must be looking for someone else."

"Ella Alice," I spoke up.

"Is that David Alice's wife from Alice Steel? I'm sorry, they wanted to be here given the tariffs and all, but regrettably weren't able to make it."

I tried a different name that Ella Alice went by and got the same deft deflection.

Frustrated, I asked, "Can I see your hand?"

"Excuse me, but I'm occupied," she dismissed. "Can't you see that? Who let you people in here, anyways?" She spun towards the door and waved at someone. A linebacker type in a suit that burst at the seams lunged in our direction.

"Your hand. Your paperweight hand," I fumbled, pointing. She turned away and slid her arm from view. "How'd you get the scars on your face there?" I blurted. She ignored me. It was as if I wasn't there, as if she had a talent for making people feel that they were nothing.

---

[3] This is not the name she gave during our conversation. She gave me her current, legal name. At the advice of my counsel, I am using the pseudonym Mrs. Fisher in this book to protect her identity for fear of legal reprisals from her lawyers.

Melanie reached into her shoulder bag. She pulled up the top of our copy of *Discontents* just enough for the woman in pearls to see it. Melanie whispered sharply, "Listen you slithering, Gucci-wearing excuse for a human being, we," she pointed to me and then herself, "we know who you are."

The woman in pearls turned towards Melanie, slid her dark glasses down revealing that empty eye of hers, and gnarled, "Well, look at you, you chewed up little pencil. You turn sideways, ain't nobody gonna see you. I know your momma couldn't afford the library card to get you that Nancy Drew fiction book, so don't run in here playing junior detective." She leaned in close, the peaks and valleys of the tread-like scars on her face seeming to pulsate. "Take your pre-teen book and your incipient boyfriend here, and run back to whatever nowhere town you're from." She slid her glasses up, stepped back and cast her good hand up elegantly, turning at the wrist the way I imagine a ballerina would, acknowledging the bustling room and the cacophony and chatter of wine glasses clinking. "If you'll excuse me, I am in the middle of hosting a fundraiser for people who fucking matter."

She turned to walk away, then stopped and glanced back over her shoulder, "And hunny, some advice. No one cares about a cute face after middle school. Grow a bottom or a chest if you want to land something better than this." She pointed her finger at me when she said 'this', letting a heavy jeweled ring drag her hand downward, the light glistening off the ring as if it were a knife blade. And with that, she walked away, her ass swaying along with her pearls.

###

The linebacker escorted us outside. The sun peeked over the edge of the earth just high enough that some of the passing cars and busses left their headlights off.

"I guess I wasn't expecting that," I said, scuttering across the street.

"That's her. It's got to be," Melanie groaned.

"Maybe it isn't."

"James, seriously?"

"Okay, what do we do?"

"Wait her out and follow her home?"

"We could. What if she still denies it?"

"She doesn't even know who we are. Maybe if we just got a chance to tell her."

"Maybe."

We found a bench and plopped into a silence. I peered at the opulent hotel that, not too long ago, would have seemed out of place in Washington. Soon, darkness won the sky and the new building stood illuminated as if light was cast up towards it from below the sidewalk. It moved upward in the way those who would be forever outsiders to it were drawn to look in awe - for I certainly did. The cream facade glistened in the light under a warm drizzle that began to drip from the gray canvas above. All the while, the baby trees out front remained erect before a crowd of American flags, which hung garishly above the entrance. And so we remained, waiting for Ella Alice.

"I've been wondering something," I finally said.

"What?"

"What drew you to *Discontents*?"

Melanie shrugged. "Sounded interesting, I guess."

"Why'd you come to watch me speak that night?"

"Because."

"Because Nick hated it?"

"No. He didn't hate it. But he didn't understand it. And I think he hated that."

"Understand what?"

"Why I liked it."

"Yeah?"

"I told him. He told me I was making excuses. He said I was crazy. He called me Christopher Columbus."

"Told him what?"

"Well, I told him my theory."

"Theory?"

"About people who know. I think Emory was one of those people."

"Know what?"

"Know. The stuff the rest of us never figure out."

"Like what?"

"I don't know. That's the point. But I plan to find it, one day." Melanie grew quiet. She rocked her palm on a wood slat on the bench. "Remember when I told you about the kids standing in the road in Mexico City selling the mango drinks for five pesos? All those fumes? Like, maybe when you know it's like you get out of those fumes. And maybe you see the sky and it's not like everyone says it is. It's just the fumes you were seeing. That's what everyone else is seeing, though, so that's all they know how to describe it."

"Interesting. So, how do you know? And how do you know when you know?"

"You just know." Melanie danced her fingers across the slat. She watched them as they crawled like a spider. "It's like, you get there, to that place in life where things are clear. You've got to get out of this state of knowing and into that other state of knowing. No fumes, get it? That's how you know the things Emory really knew but he didn't put in his memoir."

"How do you know he knew them, if he didn't write them down?"

"It's not the kind of thing you can write down because people won't understand. But if you're looking for it, you can read it between the lines that someone knows. And I could see that Emory knows because I'm looking for it. Most people aren't looking."

"Oh," I said.

Melanie looked up. "Look, I'm not crazy."

"I don't think you're crazy."

Her fingers stopped. "You sure?"

I nodded.

"You can tell me if you think so," she said. "It's nothing new to me."

"I don't think you're crazy."

"Okay, well, I think that's why he wrote the memoir, to say that he knew to those of us who are looking."

"Oh," I said. "Am I supposed to be looking?"

Melanie's eyes combed over me. "You're looking, you just don't know it."

I glanced down at my lap. "Those kids really stand there all day?"

"All day. What a way to live, breathing fumes." Melanie shifted on the bench, "You're close to it, but still really far. And that's my other theory."

"What other theory?"

"That the reason he asked you to publish his memoir is because he knew you were looking. He knew you were closer to knowing than most people. He knew you could know one day."

"That's more like a set of hypotheses."

"See, you think I'm crazy."

"No, I'm just saying that those are hypotheses you have about me, not a theory."

Melanie poked me. "Ever the professor."

I smiled. "So, fate huh?"

"Yeah, fate put the book with the clue in my mailbox."

"What a word," I said.

"Anyways, it's somewhere out there," she said. "When we get that money, we'll be halfway there. The rest of the way is just having the money to go somewhere way away where no one is looking for anything, where we can be the only one's looking so all the energy to look is ours."

"What do we do when we find it, when we know?"

"Nothing. We'll never have to look for anything again"

We sat. We watched the cars.

"I hope he's okay," Melanie said.

"Who?"

"Nick."

"Oh," I said.

"He's not all bad."

I scrubbed my feet on the wet concrete. "Do you regret what we did?"

"I don't know." Melanie scrubbed her feet too. "He wanted to get married."

"Yeah?"

Melanie stopped scrubbing. "I told him I wanted more."

Soon, Ella Alice emerged, a step ahead of a handsome man with thinning hair that was cut expertly to make this follicle misfortune appear distinguished, almost enviable. He wore a well-tailored tuxedo, the kind you can't rent. And he popped an umbrella and held it over himself and Ella.

"That's the only man under fifty who still uses an umbrella," I cracked, giving Melanie a little poke.

But the truth is, I could see no flaws, no
shortcomings about him.

As if electrified by my prod, Melanie leapt up
and raced out into the street dodging between cars,
their headlights all on now. A black SUV pulled up in
front of the hotel. Ella and the man stepped out in
unison from under the hotel awning. Melanie drew
the book from her purse and waved it in the air,
yelling, "Hey, hey!"

Ella and the man looked up. Ella's face lost its
smile. A horn blared. A small car swerved. Melanie
must have tripped or something because she fell out
of view as the car hopped onto the curve an arm's
length from where I sat. I yanked my feet up, the car
careening towards me, its wheels trying to pull it back
onto the road. I can't tell you much about physics, but
for some reason the term kinetic energy popped into
my mind from high school science class. I don't even
know if that applies here. But the car caught its
footing just as the left blinker light scraped the bench.
A crack rang out. The bench kicked out from under
me. I think I was tossed into the air a moment. Then
suddenly I felt a scrape across my back like a giant
wand smacking it, then yanking away. I rolled, falling
forward. Somehow my hands got out in front of me
as I crashed to the sidewalk. I rolled to my side. I
remember seeing my bloody hands in the blue-white
LED glow of car lights cast through the rain. I could
make out the pebbles dug into my skin. I pulled my
hands away and I could see the road again. Melanie

lay sprawled diagonally across the road. Ella Alice and the man kneeled over her.

Someone asked me if I was okay. I'd like to think it was the driver of the car, but I don't know. I leapt to my feet. I raced into the road. Cars stopped on both sides of the street, the road lit with a cocktail of blue-white headlights and red brake lights.

"Melanie!" I yelled.

She rolled towards me, grabbing her ribs.

Ella and the man looked at me, their clothes and hair matted with rain. In the glare of the car lights, I could not see if the makeup on Ella's face was running, though I hoped it was. It was a strange thing to be thinking amid all that chaos. But I guess I wanted to see behind the mask.

"Are you okay?" I gasped as I arrived. My back pulsed with fire, and I felt a wad of flesh hanging as if peeled from my back. I had this vision of a cheese grater being run across the skin along my spine and capillaries lighting up red like electric pulses, spitting blood like sparks from a frayed wire.

Melanie coughed. I could see her face gashed below her eye and down her cheek. A spot of blood clung to her lips. I looked up at Ella and stumbled back at the irony of the situation. Both these women, who were so different, suddenly had something in common.

"Call an ambulance," I yelled, bending forward to let the rain extinguish the sensation of fire on my back.

The man leapt up. "Let's get her out of the street," he suggested.

The woman in pearls grabbed his sleeve, pulling him down towards her. "Let's not move her, in case," she said, shaking her head. We were a car width from the curb. "We don't know these people."

"I think he's right, we need to call an ambulance," he said, reaching for his phone. He stood up and began dialing. She stood too.

"He can call an ambulance," she said, motioning at me.

The man looked at her as if she had rolled sideways and her body was parallel to the city street where Melanie lay. I glanced down at Melanie and realized that her glasses had been thrown from her face. They lay before her. I kneeled down, grabbed them, and leaned towards her.

"Here you go," I said, brushing her hair away. I started to place them on her, but thought better of it. The man and the woman in pearls stepped to the sidewalk and out of the rain. Melanie motioned something. I leaned in.

"Where did they go?" she asked.

"They're talking on the sidewalk."

"The driver. Get their address from the driver while they're distracted." She smiled. So I got the address while the woman in pearls and her escort with the artisan's haircut argued. She wanted to leave and he couldn't make sense of why, as she offered no rationale for her cause.

Eventually they got in the car and left after I told them I would take care of everything. And wouldn't you know, once they were out of sight Melanie sat up. I helped her to her feet.

"Did you get it?"

I nodded. "Your face." I reached towards her face.

She rubbed her cheek and eyed the blood on her hand.

"Well, a cute face no more," she sighed.

"That's not true," I said. And suddenly we were both blushing.

"Sure thing," Melanie frowned. "So, did you get it?"

Chapter 17

"It doesn't feel right –"

"What doesn't?" my wife grunted from across the bed.

"This."

"This what?"

"This. All of it."

She didn't respond. I stared into the darkness, the little red light on the smoke detector blinking above. Had the light on the smoke detector always been red?

"Nothing seems right. Nothing looks right."

"I'm sorry," my wife said, climbing from the bed. "My stomach is killing me." She disappeared into the bathroom.

I watched the red light blink.

"Are you okay?" I asked when she finally returned.

"Ow," she yelled.

"What?"

"I bumped my shin on the bed."

"Bumped your shin?"

"That's what I just said."

"How?"

"What do you mean how?"

"Are you okay?"

"My stomach hurts."

"I hope you're not dying."

My wife grunted, crawling into bed. "What kind of thing is that to say?"

"I was just making a joke."

The red light blinked.

"I'm sorry."

"Don't joke about stuff like that. Maybe I should go see a doctor."

I rolled onto my side, facing away from her. "If we had health insurance," I said.

"It's just a doctor's visit," she said. From the distant way her voice sounded, I could tell that she was on her side, facing away from me.

"What does it feel like?"

"It just really hurts."

"Where?"

"Near my waist."

The red light blinked and blinked.

"I love you," I said.

"I love you too."

"Hey," I said.

"What?"

"Is something wrong?"

"No."

"It just seems like something's wrong."

"If you choose to see things that way."

"You always do that," I called across the void. "You always discount my feelings, my reality."

"I'm not discounting anything. But you let things take over you rather than taking over them. If you think we have a problem, then we have a problem."

"No," I said. "If we have a problem, then we have a problem. I don't have to think it. I can sense it."

"Maybe you're not sensing things right, Jamey. There's no problem."

"I just have this gnawing feeling."

"So what's the problem?"

"I don't know," I said. "This."

"This what?"

"Well, it's Star Night."

"Is it?"

"Yeah." I rolled onto my back. The red light blinked above. "Yeah it is. It's our fourth Star Night."

My wife didn't move. She didn't speak. I must have lain there for ten minutes staring at that red light as it blinked, blinked, blinked.

"Are you angry?" she finally asked.

"I'm afraid," I said.

"Afraid?"

"Afraid of what's about to happen."

"What's about to happen?"

"Another fight."

"Why would we fight?"

"We're always fighting."

"Is that what you think?"

"I don't think it," I said. "That's what I'm talking about. I sense it. I remember the fights."

"There are not that many fights, Jamey."

"Why do I remember so many then?"

"You're choosing to see things a certain way."

"I told you, I hate when you say that."

"It's true," my wife said. "You get stuck in these traps. And it stops you from living. You're overthinking things."

"God, please stop."

"Are you trying to provoke a fight, Jamey?"

"I'm not trying to provoke one. We're fighting."

"Okay, so we're fighting."

"Good, at least you admit it."

"Good? Good? Why are you talking like that?"

"Never mind."

"Never mind what?"

"There's something I wanted to talk about with you tonight. Something important to me. To us."

"Why are you sabotaging this?"

"I'm not."

"You started a fight before telling me something important you want to talk about?"

The red light blinked. It blinked and blinked. And I began to blink with it.

"I thought that light was green?"

"What?"

"Nothing."

"I'm sorry," I said. "I'm just. I'm nervous."

I felt my wife roll onto her back in the darkness. "What, what is it? You can talk to me, Jamey."

"It's really dark in here tonight."

"It is?"

"That's a red right," I said. "I thought it was supposed to be green."

"Enough with the light," my wife sighed. "Tell me."

I leaned towards her. I could see her outline in the dark. "Children," I said.

"What about them?"

"I want to have children. With you. I want to be a father. I want a family."

Darkness. Silence.

"Did you hear me?" I asked.

"You've told me that before."

"That's what I want."

"Is that what you want?" my wife asked. "After last time?"

"It'll be different," I said. "Can we turn the light on? I can't see you. I can't read you."

"Is it that important to you?"

"Yes."

"Then turn on the light."

"No, I mean, children. Children are important to me. I've always wanted a family."

"You didn't have to go through it."

"I went through it."

"Not like I did." My wife got out of bed. "I'm sorry, I have to go get something for this pain."

"Aren't children important to you?" I called.

"After last time?" my wife asked. "I'm shrugging."

"What?"

"You said you wanted to see me. I'm shrugging. That's what I'm doing."

Chapter 18

With nowhere to go, Melanie and I retreated to the Honda. We bandaged one another up with an emergency kit I kept under the seat.

I rolled up my shirt and bit my forefinger while Melanie dabbed my back with hydrogen peroxide. Her touch felt both far and near, and I wasn't sure if it was the touch of a woman or of a nurse. I did my best to keep a blank look while cleaning up her face for fear she would look for clues in my eyes as to how bad it was. The truth is that I didn't care how the cut might affect how she looked that day or anytime in the future. She was beautiful in ways that no cut or scar could blemish.

Finally, we slept. I opened my eyes sometime in the night to see Melanie's knees pulled up tight to her chest. It was hot and clammy but she was shivering.

The next morning we drove to the address that I got from the driver. Before us stood a handsome brownstone near the Oak Hill Cemetery in what constitutes a neighborhood in a city. That is to say that the houses had little iron-fenced yards about the size of a bathroom stall. Each yard had been turned into an outdoor living space for the summer with a few chairs crammed inside the iron fences.

We sat in the Honda across from the brownstone in question. We sipped coffee and watched a little girl with long blonde hair that ran down her back. She filled up a plant pot from a hose and poured it down the chair backs of the metal gray chairs that stood like tombstones in the little yard.

"You sure this is it?" Melanie asked.

"Yes. Cambridge Place. That's what it says. This is it," I said. I knew where we were. Cambridge Place was the street where the girl in the orange shirt had asked for my help.

"The one with the American flag?"

I pointed. "Yep. That one."

We finished our coffees and headed for the house.

"Are you here for mother or father?" the little girl asked as we arrived at the gate.

"We're looking for your Mom," I said.

"She's inside with Scotty," the girl said. "I'm Aubrey and this is my garden."

"And what are you doing with your garden?" I asked.

"Washing away the chairs. Making room for my plants, of course."

"Of course," Melanie nodded.

I smiled. "You're doing a great job."

"I'll make room," Aubrey said. "Mother is angry when I block the way." She pushed two chairs a few inches and we came inside the gate, thanked her, and took the steps up to the front door.

The woman in pearls answered the door. But now, there were no pearls. She wore skinny jeans and a long-sleeve t-shirt, the collar of which hung off her shoulder. Still, earrings hung and her face remained obfuscated behind dark glasses and a canvas of makeup.

She sipped coffee, her fake hand on her hip. "Can I help you?"

Melanie looked at me.

"Um, yeah. We, uh, we met last night."

"Oh." She pressed the mug to her temple and closed her eyes. "Yeah, I remember now. The losers with the book or something."

"Or something," Melanie sneered.

"Yeah there was an accident. Ring a bell?"

From inside the house we heard a male voice call out, "Mailman."

"Look, I don't know what you journalist types want, but… wait. How did you find me?"

"Mailman." The voice grew louder. "Mailman. Mailman!"

"Can we come in?" I asked.

"Mommy, look," the little girl called from behind us. "I'm making my garden."

"Aubrey, shut up. Can't you see mommy's tired?"

I lurched back. "Hey, that's your child."

"You got kids?" the woman snapped.

I shook my head.

"Then screw off." She sipped her coffee. "Aubrey, did you pour water on the chairs?" The woman looked past me, her eyes squinting through the sunlight crashing into her foyer. "God dammit. I told you not to do that."

"Mailman." The voice grew louder. Feet pounded the floor like hooves in a rodeo.

"Why do you do this to me, Aubrey?" the woman scolded.

"Lady," I said. "Seriously?"

The woman turned to me. "Get off my porch."

"Mailman! Mailman for Scotty!" A hefty man with rounded shoulders shuffled towards us. His knees were bent inward, as if out of alignment.

"Mommy, am I allowed inside yet?" Aubrey asked.

The woman told her daughter no. Aubrey could come in "when the nanny arrives". She spun back into the foyer and scurried towards the round-shouldered man. "Scotty, it's not the mailman," she sighed, reaching him.

"Hello mailman," Scotty called over her shoulder. We waved back.

"Scotty, it's not the mailman," the woman said.

"No mailman?"

"I'm sorry, Scotty. Not the mailman."

Scotty's knees crumbled. He fell to the floor. "No mailman? No mailman?" He screamed. The woman bent down. She slid her butt to the floor, her leg bent out. She wrapped her arms around Scotty and muffled his screams.

"It's okay, it's okay," she comforted.

"Mommy, I need to potty," Aubrey pleaded. She stood on the porch with us, her hands on her crotch.

"Seriously, Aubrey? Why must you put yourself at the center of everything? Can't you see that Scotty's sad?"

"I can take her," I offered.

The woman looked up at me, then at Aubrey. Scotty wailed. "Okay," she said. "It's down the hall, first door on the left."

Melanie and I waited outside the bathroom while Aubrey went. I heard her singing to herself, "Happy faces, happy places, I can see happy faces."

The woman shoveled herself up off the foyer floor with her fake hand dangling. She looked into the kitchen, which opened up to a family room. The home was utterly modern in decor. It was evident that the decorating had been precise and laborious, with the interaction of each painting, furnishing, and appliance carefully considered and cross examined to ensure a seamless, effortless flow from one room to the next.

This was not a series of rooms linked by proximity. No, it was a masterful weaving of spaces into a centrality. Everything was white and black. A remodel had taken place here with the finest dollars spent. Materials were probably flown in from Italy, Spain, and God knows where else.

This was a place of judgment, cast down on everyone from the chandeliers above. I lifted myself onto my toes as I stood in the hallway by the kitchen.

My old shoes on the marble floor might bring down resale value.

The woman coaxed Scotty to his feet. She patted his head, led him past Melanie and I, and into the family room. She guided him into an old rocking chair. All the furniture was white leather, and here was this rickety old wooden rocking chair.

"No mailman," Scotty muttered in defeat.

"Not today," said the woman, sitting down on the couch next to him. She placed her hand on his.

I watched Scotty rock forward and back as he settled down. He wiped his nose and hocked back a wad of phlegm, his feet and eyes now both pointed inward until they crossed, so that they focused on the small world he lived in within arm's reach. The confusing world beyond was now out of focus.

Ella turned in towards Scotty's simple little world. She sighed. She asked me to bring over a tray and she asked Melanie to heat up some oatmeal in the microwave. "The nurse maid quit," she said. "I can't find anyone who isn't some immigrant qualified enough to help Scotty."

"It's okay, Ella," Melanie said.

We watched the woman spoon feed Scotty, oatmeal dribbling down his chin as he muttered something only Ella could understand. Whatever it was, she didn't bother sharing it with us. Only the two of them occupied his world. We might as well have been invisible.

Finally, the woman seemed to remember we were standing awkwardly in her home.

"So what do you want?" she asked. "I'm not doing interviews."

"We're looking for Emory Walden," I said.

"Why?"

"Because he's missing still."

"Is he?"

"Yes," I said.

"Oh well," the woman sighed. "Maybe he shouldn't have written that book."

"What does that mean?" Melanie asked.

"What he said about me isn't true."

We didn't respond.

"He made everyone look like shit but himself. Trust me, there are some things he left out. And if you knew them, you might think a little differently about your little hero boy."

"So you read the book?"

"No." She shook her head violently. "I read the reviews online. I found some essay some college kid wrote about it for his class. Everything made me look like the bad guy. Would you read a book where you were the bad guy?"

"You never read it?" Melanie asked.

"Look at me," she said, pulling down her dark glasses. "Do I need to read that book to know what really happened?"

I could see now that she had a glass eye above her scar. "I had to change my name. I had to see a fucking therapist for five years. Thank God I met Geoff or I'd probably be relegated to some trailer park back in Troutville. Look at my face. Look what

Emory did to it. Emory tried to take from me the one thing he couldn't stand, my beauty. Of course, Geoff wanted me to hire a lawyer and sue your ass."

"Who? Me?" I asked.

"Yeah, I know who you are," she said. "You published that hack job of a book. You went around giving talks about it like your some somebody."

So she was Ella Alice after all. I should have yelled out "I told you so" like a barking dog. Instead, my face flushed with blood. Here was a woman who I had seen as pure evil all these years. She existed only on paper and in my imagination. In a sense, I forgot that she was a real person with real feelings. I never thought for a moment about the consequences that the book must have had on the people Emory wrote about. My mind raced to the others he included in his book. Pat, Carolyn, Brock, Fletcher. There were so many.

"I'm sorry." The words fell from my lips like the drool from Scotty's mouth. "So why didn't you?"

"Why didn't I what?"

"Sue me."

"My therapist said I needed to let everything go. She said I needed to move on. She said the law is not the answer to my problems."

"I'm sorry we came," I said.

Ella stood. She thrust her head high and waltzed into the kitchen, leaving Scotty to rock gently in that closed, safe world of his. She grabbed a bottle of white wine from a small refrigerator and opened it. She poured herself a glass and took a sip.

"I'm not sorry," Melanie said.

I looked at Melanie. She glared at me.

"So what are you really looking for?" Ella asked.

"The truth," I said.

Ella sipped her wine. "There are no truths left," she said.

"Did you kill him?" Melanie asked. "Is that what you mean?"

Ella laughed. "You child."

Aubrey cracked the bathroom door and slipped out. She watched her Mom maneuver through the kitchen. She sprinted over to Scotty and climbed onto his lap in the rocking chair. Scotty wrapped his arms around Aubrey. He smiled as she burrowed her head into his chest.

"Ella, can you help us find him or not?" Melanie asked.

"No, I can't," she said. She took a gulp of wine. "And even if I could, I wouldn't."

"So you did kill him," Melanie accused.

"I'm no killer," Ella said. "I'm just a trophy wife."

"Do you know where we can find anyone else?" I asked.

"Yeah," Ella said. "In a cemetery. Poor Fletcher died, of course."

Of course he had. Why didn't that occur to me?

"Brock's dead too." Ella swirled wine in her mouth. "I lost him."

"What?" I coughed.

"He and another officer were shot dead. They were working a protest after one of those black kids got killed by police a few years back. Of course, no one saw a thing. No video, either; not when it's a cop that gets killed. But some gang banger dies and there's video from every angle."

"You're such a lying racist," Melanie barked.

"Google it, you fuck," Ella spat. The 'k' sound shot from her mouth, as though the memory was a bad taste she wanted off her tongue and out of her life. "They were good people, Brock and Fletcher. They saw my ambition, my potential."

I realized in that moment that in our myopic quest for Ella Alice, we hadn't thought about a lot of things. We hadn't bothered to look up Fletcher Spivey, Carolyn, Brock Grismore, or even Pat Drassel.

"Things were supposed to turn out differently," Ella said, taking another swig.

"Looks to me like everything worked out for you," Melanie said, running her hand across the kitchen counter.

"To have it all," Ella's voice trailed off. She faded into her own world, a realm separate from ours and distant from the one she sometimes visited Scotty in. When she emerged, she said she had a question. It dawned on me that she might want to know how we found her. And I didn't know how to answer her. I didn't know what Melanie might say.

But instead she asked Melanie, "How's your face, hunny?" as she touched her own.

Melanie touched the bandage on her face, and with a tightening of the skin on her cheeks, she said, "Oh, it's fine. Just a little scratch."

We hopped into the car across the street from Ella Alice's brownstone.

"What's up with you?" Melanie flung the words at me.

"What?"

"You're soft."

"What are you talking about?"

"You backed off," she accused, her mouth full of razors.

"She doesn't know anything," I shrugged.

"Fuck her sob story," Melanie lashed. "I don't feel bad for her. Spoiled. Rich. Oh what a trash life she has sitting around with that retard. How can you take pity on her?"

"If she knew something, she would have said so."

"Like you could see that? You're blinded by that, that, that ostentatious bubble of hers. I saw her shaking it for you."

"What are you saying?"

"You were staring at it last night too."

"No I wasn't. Don't be crazy."

"I'm not crazy. Don't call me that. Don't you ever call me crazy."

I shook my head and began to say something before choking it back. A silence settled in the cabin and it felt like concrete feathers on my shoulders and thighs.

"That cum dumpster," Melanie barked, the words gashing through the silence. "She's hiding something."

I gazed across the street at Ella's house. Aubrey played outside, filling her cups at the spigot. A girl with choppy brown hair and an orange t-shirt that hung nearly to her knees walked up to the low iron fences where Aubrey poured a cup over the deck chairs. The girl stood about the same height of Aubrey but somehow she seemed smaller, less noticeable. She said something to Aubrey, who came over to the fence. They talked for a minute and it appeared Aubrey was showing the girl in orange what she was doing. The girl climbed inside the fence and began pouring water on the deck chairs with her. The two played like this for a bit. Then, the girl climbed back outside the fence and pointed at something down the street. She motioned Aubrey to follow her. Aubrey looked where the girl pointed and then back at the front door to her house. She looked back towards the girl who kept motioning towards something. Aubrey took a step towards her house, stopped, and stepped towards the iron fence door. She pushed it open and stepped out.

The girl in orange grabbed her hand and pulled her down the street. A white van sat parked under a tree at the corner of the block.

"That's the girl."

"What?"

"The girl with the dog. The girl I was telling you about."

I jumped from the car and skittered across the street. "Aubrey! Aubrey!" I called.

The girl in orange spun towards me and so did Aubrey. The girl in orange tugged at Aubrey's arm. Her little legs started pumping faster, her bare feet kicking up.

"Aubrey," I called "Wait!"

The orange girl, dragging Aubrey behind her, ran faster. She pointed to the van just a car length away. The van's engine rumbled to a start. It lurched forward. It rounded the edge of the curb and halted. The engine chugged. The cabin rattled. The sliding door flung back like a steal gash slicing open on the side of the van. An arm shot out.

I lunged at Aubrey. The girl in orange yanked. Aubrey reeled forward just out of reach. I stumbled as my arm swung, my weight swaying with it.

I missed and crashed to the sidewalk. My chin skidded across the asphalt.

The girl in orange stretched for the arm. The arm latched onto her and the chain was complete. The van held the arm, the arm held the girl in orange, the girl in orange held Aubrey. The van jolted forward. The arm pulled the girl in orange up and into the van.

I flailed my arms. Aubrey's little feet evaded my grasp. Up into the air they went.

A bang erupted. The back of the van jolted into the air as though something had burst behind it. Aubrey was jostled free. She plunged to the earth simultaneously with the thud of the van's back tires.

Melanie had slammed the Honda into the van from behind. She jumped out, staggering and screaming something I couldn't hear. She threw her fists on the rear van window.

"You child molesters. You sick pedophiles. You-" She drew her phone like a cowboy draws a gun and snapped a photo of the license plate.

The van jerked forward, careening into the street. It swerved back into the lane. The girl in orange flew out, her legs above her, her choppy hair fanned out like a broken umbrella. Her head smacked the running board. Her legs, arms, and frail torso spilled like vomited noodles to the asphalt. She did not move. The van stopped. It lunged back, its tires screeching. The arm shot out from the van. It grabbed the girl by her orange shirt. It heaved her in, her limp-noodle legs and arms dangling beneath her. The tires spun, smoking as the van raced away. I hopped to my feet and ran to Aubrey.

Chapter 19

"We're taking the kid," I blurted. "To protect her."

"What?" Melanie turned with wild eyes towards me.

"Look at her there. Her life sucks. Her Mom doesn't love her. She's playing with rocks in a yard the size of a cigarette carton. And this is what she has to put up with? Some city creep tries to kidnap her and her lush Mom doesn't even know, probably doesn't care? What chance does this girl got of having a happy life?"

"You don't kidnap a kid to protect her from being kidnapped," Melanie rebuked, her eyes darting between Aubrey and I. "You call the cops and report it."

"We're not kidnapping her. We're liberating her. Besides, what are the cops going to do? File a report? Ella's neck deep in her own life. The girl will be back outside tomorrow. And these human trafficking people are relentless."

"That kid is like seven years old. What do you know about seven year old kids? What do you know about kids, period?"

"I know more than you think," I jabbed. "I love kids."

"Great, you love kids, so what? I love beaches. That doesn't make me a lifeguard."

"So I don't have any qualifications. But neither does Ella. And I know I can do a better job than her."

"James, you can't change the past."

"You're right," I said. "But I can affect the future."

We stood by the Honda, the front bent in, the cover on the right headlight shattered. Little bits of orange plastic littered the street. The hood of the Honda jutted up a few inches. It bent back. Now, I am no mechanic, but it was clear to me that I would never get the hood to completely close again.

"Look, you already made the decision that drastic action was needed to help this girl when you crashed my car into that van" I said.

"Yeah, sorry about your car," she frowned, the piercing glare fading from her face.

"You okay?"

"I think so. At least I didn't mess up my face anymore." She chuckled in a way that seemed to point inward, like an awkward girl first seeing a woman in the mirror.

I nodded. "You look fine."

"My ribs hurt a little."

"Want me to check them out?"

"Nice try," she smiled.

"Hey, we got to go before the cops show up and drag her off."

"We need to bring her home," Melanie protested. "You know, to her mother."

"Do you see her mother coming? Look down the street." I pointed towards Ella's brownstone. "Do you see her? Do you think she has any clue where her daughter is and what just happened? Do you?"

Melanie looked down the tree-lined street, the street full of people but empty of the one that mattered.

"That is not a mother," I declared. "Let's just get her in the car and go. We can always bring her back if we change our minds. But we gotta get out of here now."

"What if this thing doesn't start?" Melanie asked, pointing to the front of the car.

"It's a Honda," I said. "Of course it will start."

146

NOTHING GOLD CAN STAY

Chapter 20

"Here's your long black," I said, placing my wife's coffee down on the small wooden table at the One Drip coffee shop near campus. She nodded her thanks without looking up and continued to doodle on a napkin.

"What're you drawing?"

"Nothing," she shrugged. She put down her pen and blew on her coffee. "I always wished I'd learned to draw well. Or paint. Or something creative. I have no artistic talents."

I blew on my coffee and braved a sip. "Well, you do crafts. You're good at it. Look, you've built a whole Instagram following. That's creative."

"That's not the same." She palmed her coffee and looked up at me. "Do you think I'll ever be a good drawer or painter?"

"You've got a whole Instagram following."

"Thanks for being honest," she frowned. She sipped her coffee and put it down. "Why are some people born with talents that they don't want and other people are desperate for those talents and they don't have them?"

"Oh no," I gasped, leaning in. "Did it happen again?"

My wife nodded, her shoulders slumping forward, her body sinking. "I lost it," she whispered. "I'm so sorry."

"It's okay." I slid my hand across the table and folded my fingers into hers, her fingers cold, bloodless.

"We'll try again," I said. "It happens all the time."

"Jamey. There's something we need to talk about."

"We can go back to the doctor. Maybe she can help."

Just then a voice shot between us. "Hi Professor B." I looked up to see Melanie standing at our table, holding a to-go coffee cup, the metal wrap around her thumb tapping the cup.

"Hi Melanie," I said. "This is my wife."

Melanie extended a hand and my wife eyed it a moment before accepting it. "Nice to meet you Mrs. Birch."

"Likewise." A smile sprouted from the blank, sullen landscape that had been my wife's face just moments before. "I like your haircut. It's bold."

Melanie touched her head and blushed. "Thank you. My boyfriend hates it. He says I look like a boy."

"He's nuts." My wife shook her head. "I think you stand out and it's pretty. Be you, girl."

"Thanks," Melanie grinned. "Well, I'm sorry to bother you both." She turned to me. "The assignment is due tomorrow, right?"

"Yep. Monday at noon." I sipped my coffee and smiled awkwardly.

"I'm almost done. I'll have it in," Melanie assured me. She turned back towards my wife. "Your husband is an amazing professor. We all love him."

"That's so nice to hear," my wife smiled.

Melanie gave a little wave. "Anyways, better run. So nice to meet you. Have a great day, both of you."

My wife lifted her eyebrows as if to wave back and said, "Have a great day, Melanie."

"Good luck with the paper," I waved.

I turned to my wife. "Sorry about that. Students."

My wife brushed it aside. "I like her. She's cute, she's got spunk."

"Yeah," I nodded.

"Her boyfriend sounds like a real dick. She needs to do herself a favor."

"Maybe," I shrugged. "So, I'm sorry. You were going to tell me something?"

The smile shriveled up and my wife's face returned to an ashen state.

"What? What is it?"

My wife shivered. She leaned in. "Cancer."

"Who? Your mom?"

My wife shook her head.

"Dennis, your dad?"

"Me," she said in an airless voice.

"What? You? What are you talking about?"

My wife cast her lips wide. But she did not speak. She rolled her jaw and popped it forward as if trying to reset her voice box. "I went to the doctor after this miscarriage and… I don't know. All of the sudden they're doing these tests and -"

"Why didn't you call me?"

"I - I didn't know. I didn't know something was wrong. I just thought - it all happened fast."

"What did they say?"

"Cancer. That's what they said."

"How? How long have you had it?"

"They don't know. A while."

"How long?"

"It's stage four."

"Okay, that's not bad. It's not even halfway, right?"

"No, Jamey. Stage four is bad. It's the bad one."

"Stage four? You're sure? Sounds like early stages."

She nodded. "It's the bad one." I nodded with her as if without choice, as if to say that I already knew that, but I didn't know that I knew that and yet now I did know and so I also knew that I knew that. It was confusing. Everything was. The coffee shop was flooded with customers and we sat in the bay window by the entrance. People fluttered in and out. And it felt like the table might tip over and we might fall on our sides and no one would notice. They would just keep walking in and the staff would just keep taking orders, and the customers would just keep drinking coffee, and laughing, and chatting, and working on their school assignments, and then they would just get up and walk out and we would just be laying there on our sides. They would be walking down to leave and more customers would be walking up to come in and the laughter would come from above us and nothing would change for anyone but us and yet everything had changed for us and no one else.

"How long?" I managed to put the words together. But I didn't want to ask them.

"Couple of months, they say. Six at best."

I looked around. Was I already on my side? Was my wife on her side? Were we lying on the dusty floor? Were people walking by? Did they notice?

"Six at best?"

She nodded. She was on the floor next to me. And she nodded when I asked the question. "Six at best?" Yes. She nodded. She nodded. She nodded. She nodded when I asked, "Six at best?"

"What are you thinking?" I think that's what she asked me. But it was as if the words came in like puzzle pieces thrown onto the floor beside us. I spoke and the words came out like a nonsense riddle. But somehow she heard them and understood.

"It's okay," she said. "I'm not afraid of dying Jamey."

"You're not afraid of dying? Of dying? You're not afraid?"

"I'm afraid for you."

"For me?"

"Jamey, are you listening to me?"

"Why are you afraid for me? Am I dying too?"

"Because this is what you do. You obsess. You're mind gets in these loops, and it clicks and clicks round in circles."

"We're going to need money for these hospital bills," I said. "I'll do more talks. I can get a third job. But, then, well, who would take care of you? Your parents?"

"This is why this is so hard to tell you."

"I'll do more talks. I'll get a third job."

"We'll figure it out, Jamey."

"You're not going to die," I said. "I won't let you."

"I am, Jamey. You're going to have to let go."

My shoulder was pressing into the floor and beginning to numb. "I can't let go. I can't let go. Why would I let go?"

"You have to."

"There's so much we have to figure out. We have to have the best care. We have to get the best doctors. I'll start applying for jobs in the morning."

"What about the Emory money? Why don't you just go get that and be done with it?" I never thought she would say that. But lying on our sides, well, that changed everything. "If we're desperate for money for the bills that are going to come, why not go get the money Emory left for you and be done with it? I don't want you saddled with debt when I'm gone. You know where the money is. Hell, it's written in the book. Anyone who has read it knows where it is. Get the money, pay the bills, let it go and we can focus on other things."

I shook my head. "I don't want that money."

"But you're happy to take money for talking about him?"

"So long as that money is there on that gas station rooftop, there's something we can look forward to."

"You mean, look back at?"

"Not now," I begged.

"You've never wanted to go find that money?

"I haven't had a good enough reason yet."

"This might be it, Jamey. So you're not left with more debt. So we can focus on what matters."

"We'll see. But I hope not. We'll get by." I tried to sip my coffee but I couldn't do it lying on my side.

"The money is sitting right there," my wife said. "You're the one who is always talking about money."

"How do you know it's sitting there? Maybe it's gone."

"Maybe. And maybe it's worth a look."

No. I don't want to talk about that. Not now. It makes me sick. I'm sick."

"Maybe he left something there other than money. Maybe he tells you how to contact him or something."

"I don't want to contact him. I'm better off not knowing any more than I do."

"And lingering like this, always wondering?"

"I'd rather just wonder."

"Then how can you let go and move on?

"Maybe I can't."

"Jamey, I don't want that for this."

"Want what for what?"

"For you to linger. For you to obsess like you always do. This is cancer. It is what it is."

"That's all, just cancer? Nothing to worry about?"

"Nothing to worry about."

"Are you serious?" I asked. "We got a tornado heading for us and you're as calm as a clam."

"Promise me you'll let go of Emory and this book stuff when I die. Promise me you'll let go of me."

"I can't let go of you," I protested. "I love you too much."

Was my wife sipping her coffee? I couldn't tell. I looked at her but it wasn't clear. Her face and her body seemed to be on two different planes. Everything appeared like a shapeshifting dream. My attention stretched in several directions. I struggled to stay present. I saw my wife's face. I saw her body. But I couldn't see them both at once.

"Meet someone new," my wife said.

"You met someone new?"

"No," my wife said.

"Have you had your coffee?" I asked.

"Yes, Jamey. It's all gone."

"Did it spill?"

"I don't understand. Are you okay?"

"Six months?" I heard the question drop from my mouth but I didn't feel myself ask it.

My wife got up from her side across from me and fixed her chair. "At most," she said sitting down. "What was that young woman's name again with the cute haircut?"

Chapter 21

It's hard to explain to someone who lives in a city how insane cities are. I feel like the only thing, living or mechanized, capable of being quiet for miles in every direction. It's as though not one person in a city ever shuts up.

I guess it's all about pain threshold. The insanity of a city drives the psychic pain threshold up for its residents. As an outsider, I was worn down and glad to finally be leaving.

I had not seen the stars in weeks. Every time I looked up at night, an orange glow emanated from the buildings and street lights and this umbrella of haze hovered over us like a specter. It was like a UFO invasion of our own making, and the weapon of attack was not the sudden burning of a death ray, but the protracted suffering from tiny pollutant particles that slip into our lungs and cling to our cells and quietly grow into cancers.

I once read an article that the inability of many humans today to see the stars was causing a disconnect between people and the universe to which we are a part. This, the author argued, was giving humanity a bloated sense of importance. After all, we humans are but specs in an ever-expanding universe. And we seem to have lost our sense of proportion.

We are a tired people in these frantic times. Rush here. Rush there. Fill every moment and don't live a second of it. We suppress our exhaustion. We bow at the altar of so-called progress. We are easily wowed but never satisfied. We are spinning, falling, and terrified to find that the Earth that will one day swallow us all is the same Earth that swallowed our ancestors. We have made a lot of progress with little improvement.

Yet even as I rally against the poverty of now, I wonder to what end I lived those bygone moments I pine for - those long, youthful days of childhood or the warm, wild nights of my teen years. Was I really there? Or was I longing for something else then, too?

What is life but a chance to run away from happiness?

What are these sprawling places we have rushed to build without making plans for escape?

In *Travels with Charley: In Search of America*, John Steinbeck wrote that progress and destruction look a lot alike. His words should be tattooed in reverse on the foreheads of every city planner and developer across this country so they can read it every time they brush their shiny little teeth.

Anyways, on the highway out of the hellscape that is Washington DC, I watched the traffic pulse through the arteries of the city. The traffic poured into the urban sprawl that surrounds the city and I was overcome with the mindlessness of it all, the motions that seemed senseless and constant. And I saw something on my reflection in the windshield that felt familiar and worth continuing to drive away from. Maybe I'm the one who needs Steinbeck's words tattooed on his forehead.

Where to now?

Forward. To find Emory Walden. To find evidence of him. To find money.

To rush towards the past and away from it at the same time.

There was no point in looking for Carolyn. The rereading I had done of *Discontents: The Disappearance of a Young Radical* made it clear to me that Emory didn't want anyone to find Carolyn. He only used first names when referencing any person associated with her. Adia, Gabe. Perhaps it was because he loved her. Perhaps it was because he gave her some of the money.

Pat Drassel would be of little help. Fletcher Spivey was dead and so was Brock Grismore. Trying to hunt down apparitions from Emory's book was a time-intensive and fruitless task. It was time to try a different approach. I told all of this to Melanie and she agreed except for one thing. "But what about the graffiti on top of the gas station, the one with the missing arm and stuff?" she asked.

I shrugged.

"Wasn't that a clue to find Ella Alice? Come on, James. I think she knows something she isn't telling us."

"Well, if she did, we can't go back there now," I said, motioning towards Aubrey who was in the back seat of the Honda staring out the window. She would point to different cars on the road and call out their license plates as if everything was normal and this were a family road trip. "California. Did you know their state flag has a bear on it? Wyoming also has an animal on its flag. It's a buffalo."

Melanie chuckled at Aubrey. "The kid is cute," she said. "I want to have two someday, a boy and a girl."

"Kids are great," I smiled.

"Promise me we're going to bring her back to her mom."

I nodded. "Okay. We will. Let's just get through the next few days and we'll bring her back."

"Okay," Melanie said. "Okay. Deal."

"So, the graffiti on the gas station. I mean, as things go, Ella Alice has identifiable features."

"I know she's got a great ass, James."

"I was talking about her fake arm," I said. I looked over my shoulder. "Hey, let's not cuss in front of the kid."

Melanie nodded. "That's why I think it was a clue to go find her. Graffiti of a person without an arm, what's the chance that's not a hint about Ella?"

"I dunno, maybe the graffiti was just Emory's way of telling me he was alive and that's all it means. Like, he knew I'd recognize it was a portrait of Ella."

"Yeah, possibly," Melanie nodded. "Or maybe someone else made that tag on the gas station roof."

"Maybe one of Emory's fans did it."

"So what now?"

"I guess we got to brainstorm."

"How about some of that music you're always playing," Melanie asked. She flipped through my CD wallet.

"What's this?"

Almost all of my CDs were burned copies of MP3s I had downloaded off Napster or Limewire in high school or copies of original albums by friends. I didn't always do the best job of labeling the CDs and my horrible handwriting often made it so I had to decipher a CD's contents.

"What does it say?" I asked.

"Looks like it says H.E.A.D. The title is, Through Bring Quiet. Er, Being. Through Being Quiet."

"Ah. It says, H.F.A.D. *Through Being Quiet*. Put it in. That's one of my all-time favorite albums."

She popped it in and the CD revved to life.

"I'm hungry. Can we have pancakes?" Aubrey called from the back.

"Why not," I said. "I think I know a place."

As we exited the highway Melanie turned to me, "That exit says Fairfax. Isn't that near where you're from?"

I reached for the stereo and turned the music up.

###

"Where are we going?" Aubrey asked as we waited for our food at a chain restaurant made to look like a 1950s diner.

"We're going to see my friend."

"Where is he from? Maybe I saw his car. I saw license plates from Vermont, Minnesota, North Carolina, New York - no New Jersey - , Pennsylvania, and of course Maryland, Virginia and Washington DC. Minnesota is the furthest away of all those states. But I've actually seen a Minnesota license plate before. Correction. I saw California too. That's the furthest state. It's also the biggest of the states I saw."

I smiled. "You're pretty smart."

"My mother says I'm educated, not smart."

"Oh," Melanie said, looking cross.

"You know who else used to say that?" I asked.

"No," Aubrey said.

"My friend," I said.

"The one we're going to go see?"

I nodded.

"Where is he?"

"Well, we don't exactly know."

"If you don't know, how can you find him?"

"Well, we're not really sure."

"It's a mystery. I love mysteries."

"Well, yes. It's kind of a mystery we're trying to solve."

"I'll help you. I bet I can find a license plate from every state. I've seen plates from 37 states. Did you know that?"

I shook my head smiling.

We ate in silence. Aubrey asked Melanie to cut up her pancake for her but I offered to do it. She poured half the jar of syrup on her pancakes and sipped her orange juice from a straw.

After we ate, Melanie told Aubrey that we weren't sure how long we'd be gone or where we were going.

"Is this an adventure?" Aubrey asked. "I love adventures."

"Well, yes. It's an adventure," Melanie said. "But it's more of an adult adventure."

Aubrey clapped her hands excitedly. "It's a mystery and an adventure!"

"Well, yes. But, maybe you miss your Mom and would like to go home now," Melanie suggested. I turned to her and gave her that "what the fuck" look. You know the one. Melanie shrugged at me and mouthed the words, "She's a child. We have to think of her best interests."

"I don't want to go home," Aubrey pouted.

"But aren't you homesick? Don't you want to sleep in your own bed with your own things?" Melanie asked.

"I do miss all my teddy bears. And of course I miss," Aubrey's voice fell away. A slouchiness overcame her. She stirred her fork around on her plate, carving a little wake in the remaining syrup. She grabbed the salt and shook some on the syrup and stirred it up. Then, she looked up. "I think Scotty will understand why I left."

"Yes, but school. What about your friends? Won't they miss you?"

"I go to school at home. Miss Ana comes to our house."

"Well, won't you miss her?"

"Maybe."

"Oh," Melanie said. She stopped a moment. "I bet your Mom is worried about you."

"No she's not," Aubrey declared.

"Why do you say that?"

"Because my mom is the worst kind of person."

"That's a horrible thing to say," Melanie said. "All moms love their children. I bet she's worried sick."

"You don't know my Mom," Aubrey sighed.

"What's the worst kind of person?" I asked.

"A grown up."

I laughed. "Yeah, they are the worst."

"Yes, but we're grownups," Melanie said. "We just want to do what's best for you."

"No you're not," Aubrey replied.

"We're not?"

"Nope. Grownups only care about money and themselves. You helped me. And you drive an old car. So you don't have any money. Yep, you are definitely not grownups."

###

We slept in the Honda Element that night, parked next to a dumpster behind a Hispanic market.

Aubrey thought the whole experience was like camping out and barely slept from her excitement. I kept hearing her rolling around in the back, kicking her little feet and sometimes talking to herself. Eventually, we found sleep and woke up the next morning unsure of what to do and where to go. I emerged from the Honda to stretch and in the light of day I saw my hometown.

For the sake of this book, because I don't want you to be able to go find these places, I'm going to refer to my hometown as Progressville[4]. But just know that it is somewhere in Northern Virginia[5].

Melanie climbed out of the Honda and took a place beside me.

"I could use some coffee," she said.

"I could use some gin," I laughed.

"Hard to be home, eh?"

"Yeah," I said. "I never thought I'd be back here."

"Yeah?"

"Too many memories. You know that saying about how you can never go home and all that."

Melanie draped her arm across my shoulder. She was touching me. I shivered in the morning chill. A fog had settled in overnight and the damp grass had looked like wet splinters when I emerged from the car

---

[4] Note that all street names, store names, park names, and other location-based references will be changed to maintain the anonymity of my home town.

[5] It's not like it matter what town it is because these Northern Virginia towns are all the same.

a few minutes earlier. But now the blades looked again like grass, still wet, but not so menacing.

"Maybe this is actually right where we need to be," I suggested.

"Beside a dumpster?"

"No, where Emory and I grew up."

"What do you mean?"

"How better to find Emory than to go to the last places I knew him."

Melanie's hand began to rub my shoulder. "You think so?" she wondered.

I nodded.

We stood, gazing out at my hometown, or at least the part we could see from behind the mercado. "Now let's go get that cute kid up and give her a granola bar or something. She's gonna be hungry."

"Yeah, yeah. Cute, maybe," Melanie said, "but I barely caught a wink of sleep."

"It wasn't so bad," I said. The work day was beginning in my hometown, the traffic pouring into the main roads from the neighborhood streets.

"She's going to want something more than a granola bar," Melanie said.

"That's all we got."

Melanie shook her head.

"We'll go somewhere for lunch," I conceded. "But we got to conserve money."

Unsure of where to go or what to do, we drove around town. A sign on Main Street read 'Progressville Historic District'. I laughed, glancing around at the shopping centers, hotels, and gourmet burger restaurants. What was historic about this part of town? Nothing. The sign simply meant that this was once a nice place to live before all these people moved here and all this development came and all of these roads were widened and all of these buildings made taller and all of these cars got nicer and all of these people got meaner and all these peoples' dogs grew more vicious and all of these people stopped saying hello to one another or waving or being patient to let another person pull out into traffic. That's the only thing I can think of that would have made it historic. That several decades ago, it was a nice place to live.

After wasting the morning, we drove to the grocery store to buy cheap food and a few gallons of spring water.

"What do you want for breakfast tomorrow?" I asked Aubrey.

"I like pancakes," she smiled. She took my hand and squeezed it. "Do you make pancakes?"

"I do," I said, squeezing back. "It's just that, well, it's hard to - well, we're living in the car. I don't have a griddle."

"No pancakes?" Aubrey turned her feet inward. Her nose pointed down.

"I'm sorry. But, we'd need a portable butane griddle to make pancakes. It's just hard to make pancakes living in a car. How about some cereal?"

"Why do you live in a car?" she laughed. "That's strange."

"I didn't always live in a car," I said. "I used to live in a house."

"Was it nice with lots of windows and a big yard?"

"Yes. When I was a kid, I lived in a house with a big yard and lots of windows near the ocean," I said.

"I want a house like that."

"You have a very nice house," I said. "It has many nice things I didn't have when I was a kid."

"I don't live in a house," Aubrey said, scrunching her mouth to one side.

"You don't?"

"I live in a car, silly," she said. "With windows and my own seat." She nodded, her mouth straightening. "With you and my new, totally rad mom, Melanie."

"Melanie's not your mom," I corrected.

"But you and Melanie are married."

"No," I said, crouching down. I took a hold of Aubrey's other hand and turned her so that she faced me. "Maybe this wasn't a -"

"Why do we live in a car?" she asked, swinging her arms up and down, my hands flowing along as I held onto her hands.

"Well, because we're traveling so we can find my friend."

"Why don't we stay in a hotel? People who travel stay in hotels."

"That's a good question," I nodded. I let go of one of her hands and her arms stopped swinging.

"Come on," I said. "Let's go pick out some pancake batter."

"Really?" she squealed. She let go of my other hand and ran ahead. We found a big bag of pancakes and a bottle of syrup. "This is the best day ever," she exclaimed. "Can I carry the syrup?"

"Of course." I handed her the bottle. She grabbed it with both hands and raced ahead.

"Just don't run too far," I called.

Aubrey turned around and waved. "I won't," she called back. "I'll wait at the end of the aisle." I stopped and watched her run. She put life in each light step as she scurried. She swung the bottle of syrup side to side, needing both arms to carry it as though it were the biggest thing in her life. When she got to the end of the aisle she stopped and turned around. I stood there looking at her. "Come on slowpoke," she yelled, hoisting the syrup bottle in front of her. "Come on, come on, come on."

I smiled. I took my time lumbering down the aisle, enjoying how eagerly she wanted me to hurry.

"What's that for?" Melanie asked when we met her by the checkout line. Aubrey picked up a magazine and began fanning herself with it.

"We need to find a hardware store," I said.

"A hardware store?"

"I gotta buy a portable griddle."

That afternoon we took Aubrey to the park to let her stretch her legs on the playground. Melanie and I sat in on a nearby bench and I faded into the past. The empty sky stretched out, pushing aside a few thin clouds that clung at the horizon. It looked as though the moon ran a rolling pin across the clouds. The sun, beginning its odyssey towards the horizon, blasted light from its ancient wick. The light with its billions of tiny, imperceptible pulses crashed into the clouds from the far side, their wide bottoms burning a fiery orange. On their near sides, the clouds emanated a pastel violet light like an Easter egg painted from the inside with a torch.

How determined the sun is. How powerful that even after a long day of feeding the plants, helping the animals see, and pacing time for humans, it fires just as optimistically at the end of the day as it did when it started. It's as if the Earth must turn away from the sun to protect us all from the sun's endless, scolding light. If you believe in God, then you must believe God knew we were no match for the sun. I wish He, or someone, had bothered to tell us.

Maybe that's the problem. We humans take our cues from the sun, a 4.5 billion year old plasma ball one hundred times the size of Earth which, as you know, holds the entire fucking solar system together. And here we are, aimless and insignificant. And we see that sun working day after day, commanding everything. We see all the other humans pointing at the sun, saying, "Now that's important". So we decide we too want to be important. We spend thousands of years trying to be. How? We invent this thing called progress. Each generation has to "leave their mark", has to "make progress" over the generation before it. It's not good enough to let the good things that someone who came before us made remain. It's not good if we don't have our sweaty little fingerprints all over it.

The sun comes up. And we say "It's a new day". And we think that if the sun is going to work then so should we. After all, the sun made the world we have today. It's important. Without it, there would be no life. So we must be like the sun. And we say, "We're important. Without us, there will be no life." But there's a difference. The sun is selfless. It knows it will one day fizzle out and still it burns as brightly as it can. All we humans do is shift dirt around, thinking that if we move enough of it, we will live forever.

The evening was dry and clear. The air above was thin, the grass below crisp. Were a day to go on forever, this should have been it. But there I go being human, hoping to change the order of things.

"Can I tell you something about this park?" I blurted.

Melanie nodded.

"This is where I first made out with Larissa."

"Really? How suave. A park."

I laughed. "Yeah, over in that baseball field dugout."

"What a typical high school guy you were," Melanie laughed.

"Hey, it was the only place we could go to get away from our parents or adults we knew."

"I know how it is," Melanie said. "I had boyfriends before Nick, you know?"

"Yeah, Nick. I forgot about him. You don't think?"

"I don't know," she said. "Let's not talk about him."

"So who were these other boys?"

"No one you knew," Melanie laughed, poking me.

"Well I know that."

"What, are you jealous?"

"No," I said. "Why would I be?"

"Right," she said. "So don't worry about it."

We sat and fidgeted.

"So what was your line?"

"What do you mean?"

"Like, how did you start making out with her?"

"I don't know," I said. "I just went for it. It was the weirdest thing. It was broad daylight."

"I thought this was at night."

"No. It was the middle of day. And the funny thing was, these parents were at the playground over there with their kids. And there Larissa and I were just making out on the bench in the dugout. Totally going at it."

"You brazen, horny little -"

"Hey. It was a passionate affair."

Melanie laughed. "Sure thing, Fabio."

"Well, if it makes you feel any better, I never did that again. Not in public. You know, it's the first time you're making out with someone there isn't anything that's going to get in the way of that."

"What, you had a sudden sense of self-awareness?"

"Yeah. After that I felt bad. Like, she was a girl and, well you know, girls get called all kinds of things. I didn't want someone to see her just making out like that. They'd call her a lip slut or something."

Melanie laughed. "A lip slut?"

"You didn't have those at your school?"

"Oh, we had lip sluts," Melanie laughed. Her body leaned towards mine as if she had lost her balance and her shoulder pressed into mine. She righted herself as if nothing had happened." "For all you know, maybe I was a lip slut," Melanie laughed.

"Maybe," I laughed along.

"I just didn't realize that you were a lip slut," she snorted.

"I didn't say I was."

"You were going at it on a dug out bench in a dug out that was just a chain-linked fence in the shape of a box, totally, completely visible to little kids on a playground, their moms standing around gawking." She laughed harder now. "The moms probably grabbed their kids off the slides, covering their eyes, and ran to their minivans and sped out of there. But you were too busy sucking face to notice."

I hollered with laughter. Melanie did too and the two of us nearly fell forward off the park bench.

"So, anyways, where did you go to?"

"Where did who go?"

"You and Larissa. If you didn't want to make out in front of other people, then where'd you do it?"

"Oh, just down the hill from her house. There was this little path between her street and another street. No one ever went down there."

"Down the hill from her house," Melanie laughed. "You like to make out outside, huh?"

"Under the stars and all that," I smiled. "Girls like that romantic stuff."

"Do they now? Getting their thrills outside, in the dirty grass?"

"Thrills are thrills when you're young. Anywhere will do."

"Getting thrills on hills," Melanie shook her head.

"Down hills," I said.

"So sorry. Getting thrills down hills," Melanie mocked. "So where would you go now thrill seeker?"

I thought a minute. "I don't know. The ballet."

"Making out at The Nutcracker?"

We laughed.

"I think you better stick to getting your thrills down hills," she joked. She leaned into me.

Was that a hint? Here we were on a park bench. Outside. There was no hill. But, maybe she was trying to send me a hint. A hint to lean over and kiss her. To have the confidence and the gall I once had way back in high school to just lean in and kiss a girl, to show her I wanted her.

"Wait a second," Melanie said. "Just down the hill."

"Yeah. Behind Larissa's house. We've established that."

"No." Melanie shook her head. "Just down the hill, James has his thrill. Or something like that."

"Exactly like that. It was just down the hill from her house," I said. "Wait a second. It wasn't just me, of course. She had her thrills too. I'm not selfish -"

"That's not what I'm saying," Melanie leapt to her feet. "Where's the book?"

I glanced up at her. She stood erect, her bare shoulders back, the violet and gold sunlight perching like little flames on each shoulder as though she had struck a deal with the sun.

"It's in the Honda," I said.

She took off in the direction of the parking lot, her feet kicking behind her.

"Why?" I yelled. But she didn't turn back.

Chapter 22

As my wife grew sick, her energy turned towards meditation and mindfulness. My energy folded inward, closing in on itself like one of those Russian dolls in reverse. We both grew numb, distant. She became wrapped in the present moment in a way that she was nowhere else but focused on sensing the breeze or the sensation of the doorknob in her hand. I wasn't in that moment. I was elsewhere, walking among the questions in my mind.

I watched her sit in meditation, and all I could see was time, inaction, decay. And she saw me pacing, angrily scrubbing dishes or yelling at the dying plants in the window sill. And she looked at me and I don't think she saw much of anything but time, inaction and decay.

In the morning as I headed out the door, my bag slung over my shoulder, my coffee mug in hand, I would tell her that I loved her. Sitting on the couch, she would turn to me with this blankness in her eyes and paleness in her cheeks and say, "Cultivate a mind that clings to nothing."

I would smile and nod, unsure of what she was expecting me to say. I felt like she was telling me to leave or that she no longer needed me. So one night I didn't come home. And then I stayed away the next night too. I wasn't cheating or anything. I would just pass out on the couch at a drinking buddy's place. My wife didn't call or text. When I finally returned home, she said not a word about it. She just asked me, "What's for dinner?"

"Aren't you mad at me?" I pleaded.

"Stop putting yourself at the center of the universe," was her response.

I began to wonder if she had even noticed I was gone. That made it easier to disappear for longer periods of time.

Chapter 23

"Take us to that hill by Larissa's house," Melanie called. After she had gotten up and ran to the Honda, I got up and trotted after her. As I arrived at the car the passenger door was open and she was waving my copy of *Discontents: The Disappearance of a Young Radical* in the air.

"Why? What is it?"

"The poem," she called.

"What about it?"

"It's not a poem," she declared. "It's a riddle."

"A riddle?"

"I'll explain in the car," she said, jumping into the Honda. "Just go get Aubrey."

I hustled over to the playground and scooped Aubrey up.

"I'm playing," she cried.

"You can play later," I offered. "We've got to go." She kicked her legs in protest against my thighs. "It's the mystery," I said. "Don't you want to solve it?"

"I want to play."

"You did play," I replied, legs pumping in the direction of the car.

"But I want to play with you," she pouted.

"Maybe later." I stopped and looked into her eyes. "Not maybe. Definitely. Definitely we will play later. I promise."

At the car, Aubrey climbed in and put her seatbelt on. "It's not fair," she insisted. "You said you were going to take us to get pizza."

"We will," I promised.

I hopped into the car and shut the door. "What's going on?"

"I got a hunch," Melanie declared, her face stiff with anticipation.

"What is it?"

"I'll tell you when we get there." I started the engine. "Well, let's go," Melanie begged, flicking her wrist side to side as if trying to build the momentum to will the car into motion.

"Just a second." I pressed my palms against my temples. "I'm trying to remember how to get there." Giving myself over to instinct, I pulled the Honda out of the parking lot and onto the street. We weaved through traffic, making our way across town, navigating by dusty memories. And as though awaking from a coma, I found us turning onto a main road not too far from the house Larissa grew up in.

A new apartment building was under construction on a lot where an auto body shop once stood. The road I used to drive to Larissa's house vanished, erased from history. And a new road was thrown down; an afterthought, it's path branching off the old road in an abrupt right turn so that it ran parallel to the apartment building, and then with a sharp left turn, snaked alongside the apartment building and behind it, like a river built around a city rather than the natural order of things. We followed this road as it carved a fresh path through what was once a wooded area. Finally, the road flowed into a larger road that I recognized as Progressville Parkway. Soon, we passed new office buildings and I found us driving in front of my Dad's old building.

We moved to Progressville when I was in sixth grade from an ocean town and this building was where my dad worked in pre-boom Northern Virginia. I had no idea how close his job was to where Larissa lived because no roads ever connected the two locations until now.

"Sorry," I muttered. "Wrong turn." I backtracked through the new road. And after retracing our tracks I took a succession of different roads that I knew had also once led to Larissa's house. Fortunately, those roads were still intact and we found our way to the neighborhood where Larissa grew up.

New multifamily residential buildings sprouted up on every available blade of grass surrounding Larissa's neighborhood. These condos and apartment buildings, four and five stories high, took on the jagged shape of the lots on which they were built, like 3D Tetris pieces masterfully dropped into place by the hand of some hidden real estate developer. Everything crowded and crammed. The roads felt narrower than I remembered them, or maybe cars are bigger now. The houses in Larissa's neighborhood looked miniature. How much smaller were we back then, I wondered.

As we pulled onto her street, the sun slipped behind the tall buildings at the edge of the neighborhood, casting a dim red on the houses so that they shone velvet like a blood moon.

Finally, we settled in front of Larissa's house. I heard that her mother and step father moved away some years before. The house was as I remembered it, a gray split-level with a one-car garage the family never opened. Like all the houses we passed on our way in, the shingles on the roof peeled, the siding cracked, and the paint on the front door and window sills faded in the nearly twenty years since I graduated high school. The grass was long and the bushes unkempt. Had they always been like that?

The walkway to the front door came off the driveway, the front door right of center. On the left half of the house, overgrown bushes lined the front. Larissa's bedroom window sat on the top level, just reachable if you stood between the bushes. On the bottom level, hidden behind the bushes, crouched two low windows which looked into Larissa's family room. I remember her mom called that room the 'den'. I had never heard that word before until the first time I met her. At my parents' house we called the room with the TV in it a 'family room'. I'm not sure why I'm telling you this. After all, Larissa's mom didn't seem to care when I muttered this little factoid as I stood in her claustrophobic foyer for the first time, gazing down the half flight of stairs into the den as I waited for Larissa to come up.

The memories plowed through me like a subzero gust. The next memory that came to me was of the time when Larissa was grounded on Valentine's Day and I left a box of roses under a tree in her neighbor's yard. I drove to a payphone and called her and told her to tell her Mom "I'm going to go take the dog for a walk" so she could go get the roses.

Larissa was always getting grounded. She would sneak out at night and we would meet up. I would park my car down the street. And all I ever wanted to do at that age was make out and hopefully get a little action. I would show up drunk after hanging out with my friends until 10 or 11 p.m. and Larissa and I would go down the hill behind her house and we would make out and, with any luck, do other stuff.

Larissa's father lived in Indianapolis, having moved away when she was just a girl. She was the product of a one-night stand and her mother, who drank coffee as though it was water and grazed on cigarettes as though they were salads, was a saggy lump with a big curved nose and a wart on either cheek. Those warts were like brown, bulbous eyes that looked out at the world as if the world too were a wart. How someone like that gave birth to Larissa remains one of Progressville High School's great unsolved mysteries.

Her house smelled of smoke and dog vomit. Larissa's mom was a pack rat and little paths had been shoveled through her house by stacking boxes on either side of the path. You had to follow these paths through chest-high junk to get from here to there, from the front door to the kitchen, from the kitchen to the bedroom.

Her mother kept four storage units spread across four different storage unit companies all over town. She filled them with stuff she bought at renaissance fairs, craft fairs, and yard sales.

"How embarrassing," Larissa admitted to me one of the few times she ever invited me in. She kicked at a box near the back door and slid the door open. "Junk, everywhere. Junk, junk, junk. It's driving me mad. Can we hang out outside?" It was cold out.

Larissa began to pull away from me our senior year. One night I was drunk and she hit me on the arm and I told her I didn't love her. It wasn't true.

I blamed Emory for stealing my girlfriend from me. But maybe our break up was really just a story about junk. I was out drinking and having a good time. And Larissa's mother would come home from work screaming and throwing things at her while her stepfather sat in his lazy chair staring into his laptop and chatting with people he couldn't see on the internet.

One day Larissa's dog died. She wrapped her arms around me, sobbing, and I tried to get some action. Maybe I was just the junk littered at her feet and she found herself shoveling a path around me.

That night when I told Larissa I didn't love her, maybe I was actually throwing the last of my junky self at Larissa's feet.

Anyways, it's hard to have something you haven't earned. It's even harder when it's worth so much. And Emory? All he did was scoop Larissa up amid the debris and try to help her. Maybe what I'm trying to say is that sometimes, things just need to be someone's fault.

"Where's the hill?" Melanie asked, shattering through that frozen feeling that comes from chiseling away at the ice around our regrets.

"It's down there," I said, pointing to the gap between Larissa's house and the house to the right of it.

"Aubrey?" Melanie asked, looking over her shoulder from the front passenger seat.

"Yes?" Aubrey said.

"Do you like riddles?"

Aubrey nodded.

"Good," Melanie smiled. "Because we're about to start solving one."

"I don't get it," I said. "What's down there?"

"I don't know what's down there," Melanie answered.

"Then why are we here?"

Melanie opened the copy of *Discontents* she clutching the entire car ride. She turned the book sideways, flipped through a few pages, and handed it to me.

"The poem," she said. "Read it." She was referring to the poem which had been typewritten onto the side of the page of the end of the foreword I wrote when I published the book. And there before me I saw the first line of the poem, its words staring up at me: "Just down the hill, James had a thrill."

The poem was about my past?

"Who knew about the bottom of the hill behind Larissa's house?" Melanie asked.

"Larissa did," I said.

"Did anyone else?"

"Well, yeah. All my friends knew," I said. And then, awkwardly I admitted, "You got to realize, this is the kind of stuff high school guys talk about. It's no big deal."

"So Emory knew?"

I nodded. "Yeah, he knew."

Melanie nodded back. "So maybe it means something."

"Yeah," I said. "Maybe something's down there."

"Exactly," Melanie said. "A clue."

The three of us climbed out of the Honda. "Be quiet," I said. "I don't want to be caught creeping around in someone's backyard." As the sky dipped into that purgatory between day and night, tiptoeing for a moment in purple twilight, I led Melanie and Aubrey between the houses and down a small hill where a path cut through a wood of trees separating the backs of the houses on Larissa's street with the backs of the houses on the street behind her's. The path, once wide and patted down by mine and Larissa's foot traffic, had been strangled at its edges by encroaching thicker bushes.

A little valley hid at the bottom of the hill. In that valley a clearing nestled beside a dribbling creek that seesawed to the far side of a hundred year oak. The oak cast a canopy much larger than I remembered it. Back in high school, Larissa and I would lie in the grass and stare up at the stars. We could hear only the sound of each other panting after what felt like hours of rolling and tasting the honey of our teenage sweat. There, we were alone. The houses, parents, teachers, and nagging college applications and future plans faded into the trees. Although Larissa's house and the houses on the other side of the clearing were no more than fifty feet away, the trees between us and that world felt like an impenetrable barrier that shielded us. We laid there deep into the night, never wanting to leave our cocoon, knowing just how fragile it was.

"It's getting dark," Melanie groaned. "Where should we be looking?"

"You're the one that brought us here."

I looked up into the sky to find the stars Larissa and I once shared. But the stars were not out and the oak tree obstructed much of the view.

"Maybe the tree," I said.

Melanie rushed over to it, Aubrey right behind her. A few minutes passed. I stared at the sky, hoping some familiar stars would make a cameo. I closed my eyes and reached out my hand, half expecting Larissa's hand to squeeze back. "I'm sorry," I whispered. But my hand was empty and the words lifted like whiskers of spring pollen and cast off into the sky unheard.

"There's something over here," a voice called.

I opened my eyes to the clouds and branches of the moment lingering above. "What is it?" I called back.

"I don't know, I need a light."

I raced over, brandishing my smart phone. Melanie and I turned on the flashlight apps on our phones. We waved them like wands and there it was, sticking under a rock at the base of the tree. A plastic zipper bag.

Melanie reached down and pulled the bag up and opened it. She drew out an index card from inside. The following was typewritten on the paper: "NF-871"

"What does it say?" I asked.

"NF-871."

"What?"

"NF-871." She shoved the card in my hand and threw the light from her phone upon it.

"Oh," I said.

"What does it mean?"

I shrugged.

"Maybe it's like his employee ID number from when he worked. Like maybe we're supposed to go there."

"That's a good guess," I said.

"Where did he work?"

"Blockbuster at one point."

"Well that's long gone."

"But the building might still be there."

"I'll look it up."

"Let me do it," I said. "Hand me your phone. I don't know the address, but I can find it on the map." I looked through Melanie's map app and found where the Blockbuster was located. It was gone. The whole shopping center was razed and a big box store, the one with the hypnotic red circles, stood in its place.

"I know," Aubrey exclaimed. "A decoder pen. Yup, that's what we need. Just like the Little Squirrels Detective Show."

"What do you mean?" I asked.

"The numbers are really just letters," she said. "So, like, the squirrel detective finds out that 2 is a B, and 3 is a C. Duh! Haven't you seen Little Squirrels?"

"Afraid I missed that one," I said.

"Oh my gosh, you're such a dork."

I nodded. "Right. Good thinking. I'll get on it."

"The squirrel detective used the code to find where he had buried his nut. It was near a tree. Just like this note."

Melanie shot me a look. I smiled.

"Are we done now?" Aubrey asked. "I'm hungry."

"Why don't we go get something to eat and we can think about what this means," I suggested.

We marched up the hill, using our flashlight apps on our phones to find our way. As we approached the back of Larissa's old house, we flicked off our lights. I led the way by memory, holding Melanie's hand behind me, with Melanie holding Aubrey's hand behind her. As we passed through the side yard between the houses, Melanie squeezed my hand. I turned back. She jabbed her chin through the air, pointing. I spun around to see the light of a flashlight molesting the Honda, darting side to side along the passenger windows. The figure holding the flashlight was a silhouette in the night. A ghost.

"Hey!" I yelled.

The ghost froze. I dropped Melanie's hand. I sprinted into the front yard and towards the Honda. A car pulled onto the street. It turned into Larissa's driveway. I dropped to the ground.

"Get back!" I called, waving over my shoulder. Melanie tucked herself and Aubrey into the shadow between the houses. The headlights swooped above me as the car rounded its turn and came to a stop. I lay still. Someone got out of the car. I rolled my head away. I didn't want to see if it was Larissa's mom, or worse, Larissa herself.

I told myself that her family sold the house and moved away. That's how I 'heard it'. But it was just another lie I told to keep myself wrapped in a makeshift cocoon, a cocoon that could never replace the real one Larissa and I had woven together on the wet grass down the hill from her parents' house all those years before. That same cocoon she had flown away from only to blossom and never look back to - her hand in Emory's as she soared. That fragile cocoon, broken open and no longer able to protect me. That lonely cocoon that a part of me was still lying in, alone, unable to drag myself away from.

Chapter 24

"Who was that by the Honda?"

"I couldn't see."

"Do you think it was?"

"Who?"

"I don't know. Nick? Or," she leaned it and whispered so Aubrey could not hear, "Ella Alice?"

"I don't know. I guess. I mean," I leaned in and whispered back, "could either of them have followed us?"

Melanie shrugged. "Your car does tend to stand out. It's an orange box on wheels."

"Don't forget the banged up front."

"How could I?"

"I was just trying to be funny," I said. "I didn't mean for you -"

"It was probably just a neighbor wondering why the car was parked out there," Melanie reasoned.

I nodded. "Have you heard from Nick?" So much had happened in the last few days that Nick seemed a distant memory.

"Yeah. He sent a text."

"When?"

"I dunno, sometime when we were staying at Penny's place."

"What did he say?"

"He asked me where I was."

"Anything else?"

"He said he loves me."

"He loves you?"

"He loves me."

"Do you love him?"

Her eyes averting mine, Melanie shook her head in a way that could have meant yes or no.

"Did you respond?"

"Well, I started to. But I didn't."

"Why didn't you tell me?"

"I dunno. I guess I figured it wasn't your business."

"Ouch," I said.

"Sorry."

"Look, you got to share stuff with me."

"The same goes for you."

"Yeah," I nodded. "Deal."

We sat in a chain pizza place having lunch. It was the day after we found the clue by the oak tree.

We had gone looking for my favorite pizza shop in a plaza shopping center a few miles from the house I grew up in. But when we got to the shopping center, we found that the pizza place had been replaced by a smoothie stand called 'Q.D.'s Fresh Fruit Palace'.

The parking lot was full, the storefronts all different now, and the people all different too. The people that once came to this shopping plaza, teenagers, parents with kids, and older folks putting their way across the parking lot, were gone. They were replaced by wealthier people in work attire scurrying across busy roads to grab lunch at the quick-concept veggie bowl eateries that had replaced the local spots. Giant buildings sliced through the sky at every corner. And off into the distance they spread like the steal fingers of that devil named Progress. Each finger shot up through the earth from some fiery hell. And on the Earth, the flaming names and logos of high-end companies tattooed the skyline.

Then there were the busses. There were a few busses when we were growing up with routes built around rush hour. Now, the development was built around the busses, with routes running everywhere at all hours.

Progressville was no longer a town, no longer a community where it was possible to know someone as a friend. It was a clamoring mess of people carrying yoga mats and slipping into glass doors, a sprawling grid of appointment and schedules. I felt bad for the kids and high schoolers growing up in this place that was once my hometown. What did they do for fun, where could they escape to, where could they truly be happy? Where was their hiding place for making out, their cocoon?

I thought of the pranks that Emory and I used to pull, like driving my old Mitsubishi SUV on rich people's lawns, stealing street signs, or getting drunk in the woods behind some shop. There were no woods left to hide in. There were simply places to spend money and feel alone at. This was no place for a child to grow up. Everything moved so fast and the stakes seemed so high, which is strange to say because the stakes felt high when I was growing up and now I could barely catch my breath. I know that makes me sound old. I know that makes me sound like someone that has no chance at survival. But I don't care. Because I think there are other people out there who, deep down, feel the same way. People that, for whatever reason, put on their nice clothes, put on their makeup, get their hair cut twice a month, and go out to grab a bite with their workmates at one of those chain eateries only to hide in their bedrooms and rock themselves to sleep at night the way Scotty rocks in his old wooden chair when the mailman doesn't show up.

For me, Progressville became a place of conflicting emotions, with the closeness of a few old streets and buildings but the distance brought on by vast change. And I was left with a nostalgia for something that I knew no longer existed because time only moves in one direction. This was a place that had once been a forest, and then was built up, and then was bulldozed down and built over again. And I could see the same thing too in my own life. I bulldozed over the James Wallace Birch that grew up in this town. And I built up this new version of James Wallace Birch. It was a beautiful facade.

I think that's why when Aubrey was over in the kids' corner playing with a giant tic-tac-toe table, I turned to Melanie and said, "My marriage collapsed."

She looked up at me and stopped chewing.

"I'm sure you were wondering where my wife was in all of this," I wondered aloud. "I'm not sure why you've never asked me. But I feel like it's something that I should say out loud even though I think you already know and we both know between us."

"Yes, of course I know," she swallowed. "You wouldn't be traveling around with me if everything was peachy keen at home, would you?"

"Why didn't you say anything?"

"I figured that if you wanted to say something about it, you would."

I nodded.

"Well, she's gone for good."

"I know," Melanie said. "I'm so sorry."

We sat and chewed without eating.

"James?"

"Yeah?"

"Can I ask a question?"

I nodded.

"What was your wife like?"

"She was great. We were so in love."

"What happened?"

"I don't know. Time, I guess." I sat with that thought in my lap a few minutes before continuing. "In time she stopped wanting to put the windows down when we were driving. Do you know what I'm saying?"

"Maybe I've never ridden in an Uber, but I know about car windows," Melanie joked.

"No I mean, she just wanted the air conditioning on. But the world is outside of your car. A car with the air conditioning running on a beautiful day? Why breathe that sterilized air when you can feel the breeze, the heat, the life all around you as you fly down some country road? The air conditioning isn't living. Does that make sense?"

Melanie nodded, telling me that it did.

"Well, that's what happened. She rolled up the windows one day and we never put them back down."

Melanie thought a moment, her eyes moving off and out of focus. "Why didn't you roll them back down yourself?" she asked.

I looked towards where her eyes were looking as if to find the answer there where she had found the question. "I don't know," I said. "Maybe I should have."

"Eh, don't worry about it," she said, taking a bite. "Look, I think deep down you're a good guy who is just a bit too hard on himself."

"You think I'm a good guy?" I hoped aloud.

"Yes," she smiled. "I do."

From under the table Melanie brought the zipper bag out that we had found under the rock at the base of the oak tree. "What do you think these numbers mean?" she asked.

I shrugged. "Maybe it's like Aubrey said, there's some kind of code we have to crack to get the next clue."

"Yeah, but how do we do that?"

I sipped my water. "Beats me."

We sat and chewed some more. I looked over to Aubrey, watching her spin the X's and O's on the tic-tac-toe table, her face aglow in wonderment. Her nice clothes were wrinkled, her hair matted, her cheeks smeared by pizza sauce. She saw me looking at her and smiled. I waved. She waved back.

"Let me see the book again. I want to see the note," I blurted.

Melanie perked up. "What, what is it?"

"Well, if the first line of the riddle was referring to a place - "

"Then maybe the second line is too," Melanie said.

"Right."

"Good thinking." She passed me the book and I flipped it open to the poem.

"What does it say?"

I read it aloud. "In the middle of May, James was a hero today."

"James was hero today?"

I nodded.

"How are you a hero today?"

"I don't know," I shrugged. "But it is the middle of May."

"It is," she said, checking her phone. "You're right."

"Who knows how I'm a hero today. I've never been a hero before."

"Maybe you already were? I mean, it says was."

"Were? Was?"

"It says, James 'was' a hero."

I nodded. "Possibly, I guess." I thought a minute. "Maybe I already was a hero by saving Aubrey from Ella Alice."

"So, if it's referring to a place, maybe there is a clue back by Ella Alice's house?"

"Maybe," I said.

Melanie took a bite of pizza. "As soon as we're done here we got to drive back to the city."

"Shitty, shit," I muttered. "Not the city again."

Melanie gave me a look as she chewed. "Well, wait a second," she said. "You weren't the hero, I was."

"What?"

"With Aubrey. I was the one that, you know, crashed your car."

"Yeah, I remember," I laughed. Melanie laughed too. "And that's what saved Aubrey. Because, you know, they were getting away with her."

"Yeah. I tripped."

"Yeah, yeah. I don't care about that. I'm not trying to take credit. It's just, well, re-read the riddle."

I read the passage aloud again. "In the middle of May, James was a hero today."

"So, if the clue was on Ella Alice's street somewhere, then wouldn't the riddle read, Melanie was a hero today?"

"Well, but, maybe I was supposed to be the hero and I didn't do it. After all, you just got my mail by chance."

Melanie shrugged, conceding the point.

"It's like *Back to the Future Two*, you know? You did that one little thing that changed the course of history. And now Biff's going to become the mayor," I jibed, pointing my straw at Melanie.

Melanie snorted. "I hope not."

"Melanie was a hero today," I said, reaching my arms into the sky as if the words were printed on a marquee.

"A hero today," Melanie nodded. "I like the sound of that. Maybe I'll start an emo band and call it 'Melanie was a Hero Today."

"But, like you said, was a hero. It was a few days ago, right?"

"What?"

"You aren't a hero today. You were a hero a few days ago."

"Well, maybe I'm a hero today too."

"Yeah, but what about tomorrow? Are you a hero tomorrow, too?"

"Maybe. Why?"

"That's a lot of hero work."

Melanie snorted and giggled.

"I don't know. But, grammatically it doesn't make sense. In the middle of May, James was a hero today? The word 'today,' should be dropped, right?"

"Okay. New band name, then." She took a bite of her pizza. "Well, how about, Melanie, Hero for Just a Day?"

"Nice," I laughed. "Too bad it's kinda already taken."

"What is?"

"There's a band called Hero for a Day," I said, dipping my straw back into my water. "We listened to it in the car."

"We did?"

"Yeah."

"Was that the CD you knew all the words to and were rocking out to playing the air drums?"

My face turned red. "That's the one."

"The one I thought said H.E.A.D.?" Melanie snort-chucked.

"Yeah, it's H.F.A.D," I said. "Hero for a Day."

"Badass album," Melanie said. "Cool band name."

"Favorite band of all time," I nodded.

Melanie dropped her piece of pizza.

"Wait a second," she said. She grabbed the book from me and read the line from the riddle out loud. "James was a hero today." She read it again. "James was a hero. Hero today. Drop today. But, still a hero."

"Mmhmm."

"And it's the middle of May right now."

"For a few more days. So?"

"So, in the present tense, it's hero today. But, we didn't find the clue until after you, or, I, was a hero. So, hero today doesn't last. What if we didn't find the clue until late May? Or June? Or July?"

"Hmm," I nodded along. "Yeah, but anything with the word today in it only lasts a day."

"Was that your favorite band, like, back then? Hero for a Day?"

"Yeah," I said. "It was my favorite band in high school."

"How many CDs did they have?"

"Well, at the time, they had *Faster, Still, Through Being Quiet,* and then *Don't Dare Change.* But I can't remember if *Don't Dare Change* came out when we were in high school or college. Maybe college. But *Through Being Quiet* was my favorite anyways. Still is."

"Did Emory like them?"

"Yeah, of course. We would drive around screaming out the songs while everyone else was listening to Mace and Ja Rule. Like I told you, music was the thing that brought us together."

Chapter 25

"I want to go home," my wife bellowed. It was a hollow, tired howl, like a toddler standing in her crib fighting but losing slowly to the sandman. I stood at the door to her hospital room, a coffee in each hand, peering through the slit in the door. My wife's mother, Eleanor, stood by her bedside with a hand on my wife's hand.

"I know," she said.

I didn't know what to do. The hot coffee throbbed in my hands.

"I want to die at home," my wife wailed, squirming in the bed.

I sucked in a breath, waited a moment, shot the hospital air out of my lungs, and pushed into the room. "I've got coffee," I announced. "Hey, did I tell you about that woman? The one I saw yesterday on my way in from the parking lot? I swear, hun, she looks just like your old roommate, Jessie. You talk to her lately? How's she doing?"

"James," my wife grunted.

"Yes, hun?" It was hard to look at my wife; hard to see her like this. I didn't recognize her face except for her ears. It is strange to say because ears are not the sort of thing we think we notice, that we think we would recognize. We don't much consider ears to be part of the face. Ears are just ears, protrusions on either side of our head that seem simply utilitarian. But only when the rest of something is unrecognizable do we recognize what we usually overlook. And the rest wasn't her face. So when I looked at her, I would look at her ears.

What was her face? It was the face of someone I had never known. Someone I wish I had never met. My wife, the woman I fell in love with so long before, could not be seen, but for her ears. The rest of the face and the gray, boney torso, and arms that were mostly elbow and skin, and legs that were like straws, were not my wife. They were a shell. And, like a crustacean, I had this feeling that she was in there somewhere trying to crawl out and find a new shell.

"James," my wife stammered. "At home I will be in peace."

"But there's still hope," I said. "The doctors are trying -"

"How's about that coffee?" asked Dennis, my wife's father. He sat in the chair in the corner reading some stupid hospital magazine. I handed him the coffee. He didn't say thanks.

"Like there's anything they can do. You have no idea," Eleanor said, glaring at me.

"Pumpkin, do you want me to pull the car around?" Dennis asked, sipping.

I looked around the room. These people have given up, I thought. They have no agency, no sense that their actions mean anything. They have resigned from hope.

"Can I talk to you in the hall?" I asked Eleanor. I knew Dennis wasn't about to get off his ass. Outside the room, I told Eleanor that we should let the doctors proceed with their plans. Her response?

"It is what it is, James." She wagged her finger at me, her head forward. She leaned at me as if to poke me in the face with that finger. "It's already done. Let it be."

I wanted to protest. I was sick of the fatalism that subdued her family. And that fake wisdom her mom spewed? That belief that trying or doing anything to change a current state of things was doomed to fail? Well, it was anathema to how I was raised. Birch's worked themselves to death trying to make any little progress we could. Birch's can spend an entire day and make an inch of progress on some project and the next day we'd get up and get back to work. That is living. That's what being human is. Just put one foot in front of the other until one day you collapse. Then get up again. And when you can't get up anymore, when there isn't an inch left of crawl in you, lay on your back and stare at the sun in envy as your body is dipped below the dirt by those Birch's who still have the strength to get up and march.

The way I saw it, my wife's family had developed this philosophy about life that was just an excuse to be lazy. But of course, I couldn't say anything to Eleanor. What could I say?

"Besides, who is going to pay these hospital bills if we stay?" Eleanor asked, almost spitting as she wagged her finger at me.

"I will," I replied.

"Really, James? Like you can afford it."

"I'll get another job, a third job," I said.

"Don't be ridiculous. The opportunity to do something passed you by. You missed it."

There are two types of people. Actors and reactors. And I was a reactor. Reactors live in response to the actions of actors. Their lives are dictated by the decisions of others because they don't have whatever is needed to take the initiative themselves and command a situation. So they react and grow unhappy with things while others steer the boat. Reactors are like flags blowing in the wind that actors make from their farts and belches. When reactors are in a room, someone else sets the tone and reactors observe and modify their behavior and language in response, always careful that they don't upset a balance or draw unwanted attention to themselves.

So what could I do? Not a damn thing but react.

Back in the room, I sat and waited. I wasn't going to do anything. Maybe I was a pushover and a meek little man. But I wasn't going to aid my wife and her parents in their quest for in-home hospice care. I got up and pretended I had to use the bathroom and sat on the toilet reading a book on my smartphone. My wife's parents were gone when I finally came back.

"Where's Eleanor and Dennis?" I asked my wife. She told me they went to find out who they needed to talk to in order to get my wife discharged.

I nodded and slouched into a chair.

"I don't love you anymore," my wife muttered from her hospital bed.

I looked up. "What?"

"I said, I don't love you."

But somewhere in that gray, limp shell of a body was my wife, whatever was left of her.

"That's not true," I said. "It's just the painkillers."

"James, stop clinging."

"But, but I love you." I stood up.

"It's not about you," she said, leaning forward and meeting my eyes with hers. "Let go," she said.

"But, what about everything? Our past? Our lives? Everything we've built?"

"I just want to be left alone," she sighed, sagging back into the bed. "At home. To die at home, away by from all this. Away from you."

GHOST MAN ON THIRD

Chapter 26

"Maybe it's a reference to a song title," Melanie suggested. "Or lyrics. Maybe it's a reference to lyrics from the CD." She was getting up to throw her paper plate in the trash can.

"You might be onto something," I said, standing.

"Let's go listen."

We gathered up Aubrey, who protested a little, and dashed towards the Honda. Inside I started the album *Through Being Quiet*. The song 'We Were All Stars' began, the amp kicking to life.

"What's your favorite song on the album?" Melanie asked, flipping through a case of CDs

"There are so many good ones. It's like they all explode out of the speakers and the lyrics cut you apart." I thought a moment. "But this song, actually, it's one of the shortest on the whole album but there's an energy to it. And the lyrics, I could recite them by heart."

"Yeah, yeah. What are they?"

I recited the lyrics.

This is how it happened.
Is it how we lost sight?
Those days we spent napping, and high on through the
night.

If You Find Emory Walden

*We climbed up on a mountain, and held hands on the
roof.
Ask me how we got here, promises don't change the
truth.*

*Ask me how.
Ask me how.*

*When we're there, ask me how.
Say, "Hey, look out past the ledge."*

*"I'm falling."
"I'm falling."*

I think of what I did.

*Even now, that I'm alone.
I think of what I said,
These houses don't seem to mind,
I climb them from my bed.*

*But when I hear you calling,
The sky's my only friend,
It's like a knife in my spine.
And I see it all in red.*

*The stars are out tonight,
And I see it all in red.*

We absorbed the music.

"Did you know that the drummer is the most important member in any band?" Aubrey asked.

"I didn't know that," Melanie smiled.

"What does the singer mean about climbing mountains?"

"Houses," I corrected her. "He's climbing up houses like they are mountains - Oh wait," I gasped. "Climbing houses. Rooftops."

"What about them?"

"Emory and I used to climb up on his rooftop. That kid always liked to climb on things, even then. He was like a chimpanzee."

"So?"

"That's where he told me he was dating Larissa. We were on his rooftop, drinking. And we got in this big argument." I reached forward and turned the music off. "And I shoved him," I admitted.

"You shoved him?"

"I was drunk and angry."

Melanie nodded.

"What does drunk mean?" Aubrey asked from the backseat. I had forgotten she was there and a sense of shame washed over me. I didn't like that she was hearing all these things, all these adult things, all these teenage things, all these shameful things. I wanted to protect her and was doing a terrible job of it. I had dragged her into my mess.

"He fell off," I finally mumbled, my voice barely audible so that Aubrey could not hear. "Landed on the deck. Broke his leg real bad."

"Wow," Melanie said. "It's almost like that song was written about you and Emory."

I nodded. "Except, the song came out before I shoved him."

Melanie put her hand on my neck and rubbed. "It's okay," she said. "You didn't mean to hurt him."

I didn't reply.

"Can we get on that roof?" she asked.

"Yeah," I said, my head sunk forward. "If we wait until it's dark."

After dark we drove to the house Emory grew up in. His parents had long divorced in that violent way that is reserved for divorces and the new owners painted the shutters a pale yellow. They put new siding up too. It was a hue that could only be described as baby blue, only tackier. LED walkway lights ran every few feet along either side of the driveway as if it were an airport runway and the garage was the hanger. A flag pole, yes a flag pole, stood in the front lawn and a green flag that read "Welcome" rippled in a lazy May breeze under the blue glow of an LED light which sat atop the flagpole.

I laughed. This was the last physical connection to Emory in the entire town, perhaps the entire world, and it looked like a family of cheery saps had turned what was once a house into some painted Easter egg.

We parked down the street in a cul-de-sac to wait until all the lights went out. Then, it might be safe to make our way up onto the roof of Emory's old house. The adrenaline faded. Aubrey grew tired. I manage to occupy her through a rotation of reading children's eBooks off my smartphone and a few cheap toys I bought her during a trip to a consignment shop earlier that day.

"Thank you," she said as I tucked her into a second-hand children's sleeping bag with what appeared to be a vomit stain on the built-in pillow.

"For what?"

"Playing," she said, closing her eyes.

"You're welcome." I brushed my hand through her hair and rubbed the back of her head until she fell asleep on the floor.

Melanie asked me to duck outside so she could change. I took a seat against a wheel and soon she came out in a tank top and jean skirt. She slid down beside me, her long, exposed legs inches away. We ate leftover pizza and passed one of the gin bottles I brought.

"Well done," Melanie said. "You're good with her."

"I'm learning," I said. "By the way, well done to you."

"For what?"

"Crashing into that van."

Melanie jabbed me playfully with her elbow.

"I mean it. It was brave and quick thinking. You saved that little girl in there."

Melanie smiled. "It needed to be done. You know, I'm starting to think it was worth it."

I smiled. "We'll return her to her mom soon, I promise," I said.

"I think she's been good for you," Melanie said. She passed me the bottle. "So how are we getting on this rooftop?"

"Half an hour after all the lights are out, we'll head over and I'll show you." I took a swig and passed the bottle to Melanie.

We sat and passed the bottle a while until I was transfixed on Melanie's legs. I caught myself and pulled my eyes away. I stared out at a patch of trees and watched the early season lightning bugs. I looked for the frogs as they moaned and the crickets as they sang. But my eyes found their way back to her legs the way a cold person instinctively turns to a fire. Those soft legs teased me. I didn't think anyone wore jean skirts anymore. They were everywhere when I was in school. Larissa wore one the first time we made out, the first time I ran my hand down a girl's leg and felt that buoyancy, that creamy warmth against my fingers.

"I'm so confused," I muttered. "It's like everything's going off in a different direction, and I feel like I'm losing control."

"What do you mean?" Melanie leaned her head back against the car, her long neck running down to that little divot between her collar bones.

How had Melanie known where to find Ella Alice? I forgot all about it with everything that happened in the last, what, twenty four hours or so? Then the question appeared in my head the way gas from a burp suddenly appears in your mouth. I looked over at her. How had she done it? It's the alcohol. You're always suspicious when you drink, I told myself. Do you want to ruin everything you've got going for you right now?

"I bet all this stuff brings back a lot of memories," Melanie mused, her voice elbowing in on the voice in my head.

"What?"

"I said, all this stuff. It must bring back a lot of memories?"

"Yeah," I nodded. "More than I could have realized I would want to remember."

"The past is like that, isn't it?"

"Just like that song by the Faces."

"What song?"

"You know, I wish I knew and all that."

"Oh yeah," Melanie snort-giggled. "I know that one." She hummed, "When I was younger."

"You're cute," I said, smiling.

Melanie smiled, the corners of her face turning up and though I couldn't see her mouth, I imagined her vulnerable lips opening to show her teeth.

"I'm sorry," I sputtered. "I shouldn't have-"

Melanie reached out and placed her hand on my forearm. She shushed me and said, "Stop apologizing."

I turned away. "What about him?"

"I want to be here with you," she said. "That's all I want."

"I don't know if that's a good idea," I admitted.

"Hey," she said tugging on my arm. I turned back towards her, her head still laying against the car, her eyes pointed skyward. "If you could do it all over again, like everything way back, like way back to puberty when suddenly everything is crazy, what would you do differently?"

I thought a minute. "I guess, be more confident," I said, swigging the bottle around in my hand.

"Yeah?"

"Yeah," I sighed. "I think I just realized that every problem I've had since I was thirteen years old was really just a problem of confidence."

Melanie peeled her head from the car and turned to me. "Interesting."

"You?" I passed her the bottle.

"Get my head around what love is." Melanie raised the bottle to her lips, then wiped the back of her hand across her mouth. "Then maybe I would be free to know the things Emory knows."

"Love," I replied. "That's a hard one."

Just as the question about Ella Alice effervesced from my gut into my mouth minutes before, my throat tightened and a pang lurched up from my gut. I sniffled to try and stop it, like a prideful counterpunch, but I missed and it leapt from my mouth. Then another. Then another.

"Why are you crying?" Melanie whispered.

I shook my head. "Nothing."

"James, open up. You can tell me."

I sniffled and turned away. She placed a hand on my shoulder and tried to roll me back. I gave in and rolled towards her.

"Stop guarding so hard."

"I messed up."

"Messed up?"

"Messed up love. I had it. Twice. I knew what love was. And somewhere along the line - it was my fault. Both times. It was no one's fault but mine."

"You'll get another chance," Melanie said.

I took a breath and let it seep out. "All the feels," I laughed with a choke.

Melanie laughed.

"Did I say that right?"

"You did. It's kinda old by now. But good job."

"I got all these feelings rushing back."

"Yeah, you said that earlier."

"Yeah," I said. "It makes me realize I haven't allowed myself to feel anything for so long."

"Do you feel that?" Melanie's hand slipped down my pants.

I nodded. She leaned down and kissed me and I touched her and slid my hand along the smooth skin of her thighs, down to her knee.

"Wrong way," she said.

"It's been that long," I smiled.

I woke up in the grass near the Honda, Melanie's arm draped over my chest. I laid awhile, taking her in, her scent, the soft touch of her arm. I ran my finger up and down that arm a hundred times and felt the warmth of her torso wrapped on my side and the cream of her legs against mine.

Melanie awoke, brushing the hair from her face. She smiled and I could see her tongue, the gin-drenched tongue my tongue had now touched before I had ever really seen it.

"Outside thrills," Melanie snort-giggled.

"Outside thrills," I smiled. "Romantic, huh?"

She giggled and pinched me and we lay in one another's arms.

"If you had had children, what would you have wanted for them?" she asked. "To be rich? You know, every parent wants their kid to have more than them in some way."

"To be happier than I've chosen to be. I've always just worked and hoped that something in the future would be better. So, yeah, to be happier."

"You?"

"The same," she said.

"Hey what time is it?"

Melanie checked her smartwatch. "Just after 1 a.m."

I sat up. "The lights are off," I said. "I bet they've been off at least an hour. I get the sense the people who live there are the early to bed type."

We crept down the quiet street and snuck into the backyard, which sloped down a hill. By the back of the garage I waved Melanie to stop.

"We just got to climb that," I whispered, pointing to the deck on the back of the house which hung above a walkout basement.

"Climb what?"

"The lattice on the deck," I pointed again. "In the corner. It leads to the roof of the garage."

We tiptoed up the deck stairs, setting our weight down on each step with the patience of a slug so as not to offend the wood for fear it would call out a painful creak. Once on the deck, we took the same inch-by-inch approach, passing by the French doors that led inside to the family room where Emory and I used to sit and play Playstation.

"Okay, you go first," I said.

"I don't want you looking up my skirt." Melanie scrunched her nose.

"I already have," I said.

She smiled in that embarrassed way that is only shared between people who have, for a few vulnerable minutes, put their embarrassments aside and truly been together. "Still," she said, "you go first."

On the rooftop we caught our breaths and looked out over the neighborhood. I could see the Honda down the street by the trees and the patch of grass where Melanie and I had been together.

"Weird to be up here?" Melanie whispered.

I nodded. "In ways I can't describe."

"It's pretty up here."

"I grew up on this roof looking out at these houses," I whispered. "I drank up here for the first time. I smoked weed up here for the first time. Man, the conversations we had."

"Yeah?" Melanie said. "Wish we had some weed."

"I didn't know you smoked,"

"I didn't know you did."

"I don't," I said. "Not in a while."

"My mind is blown."

"What?"

"You, smoking? Plus, I got the impression from his book that Emory hated weed."

"He sure loved it when I knew him."

Melanie giggled her snortish giggle.

"Anyhow, I'm going to show you where we used to stash it. If Emory left a clue up here, that's where it would be. Who knows, maybe we'll find a stale old bag of bud."

We shuffled on our rears up the shingles to the chimney. I pulled out a loose brick to reveal a cutaway where Emory had chipped a small pocket in some mortar. I reached in and felt around.

"There's something here."

I pulled it out.

"What is it?"

"A zipper bag, I think. I can't quite see. But there's something inside it."

"Hey, what's that?" Melanie said.

"Be quiet," I shushed.

She grabbed my arm and pointed down the street towards the Honda. A flashlight danced around the car. Then, it went out.

"Maybe it's just some nosy neighbor," Melanie reasoned.

"Oh shit," I said.

"What?"

"I can't remember if I locked the car."

Just then the cabin light burst on in the Honda. The scream of a child rang out, deafening the crickets' songs and the frogs' moans.

"Aubrey," Melanie gasped. She grabbed me, her fist clutching my shoulder like a kid on a rollercoaster, and pulled close. The brick shuffled lose from my grasp. It thudded on the rooftop, then toppled, and rolled, momentum building, until it launched off the roof. It dangled in the air a moment before falling out of sight. Glass shattered below us. A light popped on upstairs, its bright, long shadow cast into the backyard.

I shuffled down the shingles. Suddenly my feet slipped out from under me. I slid down. I kicked my feet out in front. I caught myself on the gutter just short of slipping off the side. The metal gutter groaned as it bent. "Come on," I called to Melanie. She shuffled cautiously towards me.

"Hurry!"

She turned onto her stomach and wormed her way down to me. I helped her onto the lattice. She climbed down. I climbed after her, leaping to the deck with a crash. We sprinted across the deck. We passed the French doors where the light was now on. We tumbled down the stairs, falling into the yard. We leapt to our feet and raced around the broad side of the house and up the hill. I overtook Melanie - I think on the hill - and accelerated onto the pavement.

The light glowed in the Honda. A few screams shot out of the open door like Roman Candles whistling through the night.

The cul-de-sac where the Honda was parked was a few houses down from Emory's old house. I was halfway there when something burst behind me. I spun around to see Melanie topple off the lawn. She rolled onto the asphalt. Behind her stood a man in a robe, his legs spread wide. The butt of shotgun was propped on his hip, the muzzle pointed skyward.

"The next shots coming atcha!"

So much for cheery, I thought.

I lunged towards Melanie. The man in the robe pointed the shotgun at me. "Not worth it," he yelled.

"You hit?" I called to Melanie.

"No," she called back. "I tripped." She waved me on.

I turned towards the Honda and ran. Something tumbled out of the open driver's side door. A person. But it was on the far side of the car. I could not see much more than it's jagged shape. It pogoed to its feet, froze a moment, turned and bolted in the direction of the woods at the edge of the cul-de-sac. I veered around the passenger side of the Honda in full gallop after the shadow.

The shadow broke the edge of the woods. I leapt from the asphalt onto the grass where Melanie and I had been together not twenty minutes earlier. The burn in my lungs pumped into my arms. As I tore down the hill to the edge of the woods, the burn rushed into my legs.

I spilled into the darkness of the woods. He, she, whoever, was gone. There was no way I would catch up. Still, I ran amid the trees, rocks, and fallen branches finding my way by the patches of pale light scattered like skipping stones along the forest floor.

Then, there was a thud up ahead. A male voice screamed out in pain.

I raced along the jagged ground. A shadow staggered to its feet. The man rubbed his head, his body bent forward as though preparing to vomit. I slowed. I drew closer. I was just behind him. He reached down and grabbed something. A bag. My bag.

I hurled myself at him, plunging forward like a man leaping from a bridge. I swatted my arms down on his, pinching his arms to his side as we crashed to the ground, my body landing atop his. The bag broke loose. He screamed, perhaps in pain, perhaps in fright.

We rolled over and back and he gained momentum and then leverage. A light flashed on in my face. I writhed. A fist clutched my hair, lifted my head, and slammed the back of it against the ground. A stick or jutting rock knifed into the base of my head where my neck started.

I swung my arms but landed nothing of consequence.

I stopped fighting back. He stopped. He felt for something at his waist.

He's going to kill me, I thought. I couldn't see. But I knew that whatever it was he was reaching for was not a white flag or a peace offering. It was an instrument of pain.

With a lurch I swung him over. His head must have hit something because he grunted like a bull stuck in barbed wire. For a moment I thought I heard a cry for help. I struggled from under him and rolled on top. I pinned his arms down with my knees.

A mask.

He wore a mask. I put my hand on my fist and struck him with the back of my elbow below. The eye holes of the mask and his head rocked to the side, then back. I struck him again and again. He fell limp. His head stopped rolling back to face me. The tension ceased beneath me.

I coughed. I coughed and coughed and gasped for air. When I finally caught up with my breathing I slouched, exhausted and victorious.

As the moon cast down upon us through the cracks in the canopy of trees overhead, I wondered aloud how I had become so violent, so willing and able to do all I had done these last few days. Where was that meek little boy I told you about on those first pages?

I reached down and pulled off his mask. The face was swollen and gnarled. A patch of blood smeared up from his nose and lips across his forehead and onto his head.

I couldn't believe who it was.

I got up.

He didn't move. His head rolled to one side as I stood.

Suddenly, I remembered the bag. I poked around in the dark until I found it. Still, he lay motionless like the sticks and rocks.

It was my bag. Why had he taken it?

I turned and headed back the way I came. I stopped to look back.

He was gone.

Chapter 27

Memory

Chapter 28

I found my way out of the woods and onto the grass by the Honda. The dome light was on and I found Melanie and Aubrey huddled inside, Aubrey wailing in Melanie's arms.

"Are you okay?" I asked, tossing the bag in the back.

Aubrey looked up with tears streaming down. She nodded. She pulled away from Melanie, crawled out of the car, and leapt into my arms.

"Why?" she cried.

"It's okay."

"I can't believe those perverts," Melanie grunted. "Sick fucks."

"You okay?" I asked.

"Yeah, just scraped my knee." Melanie showed me the dried blood, its harsh red crust against her smooth pale leg.

"And the shotgun man?"

"He went back inside after you ran."

I nodded.

I opened the back hatch and sat, sinking forward.

"Oh my God," Melanie cried. "There's blood on your neck."

"I'm fine. A little woozy."

"You think those perverts are coming back?"

"It wasn't them."

"It wasn't?"

I looked up. "It was Clark."

"Clark? Penny's Clark?"

I nodded.

"What the fuck? Why is he after Aubrey?"

"He's not," I muttered. "He's after the money."

"But we don't have it."

"He doesn't know that."

"Jesus."

I nodded.

"Did you catch him?"

I nodded again. "Yeah," I motioned to my bag in the back of the Honda. "But he got away." I tumbled from the hatch and vomited.

"You Ralphed." Aubrey pointed.

Melanie turned away.

"Sorry," I muttered.

"You okay?"

I nodded. "It's nothing. I hit my head."

"Should we bail?" Melanie asked. "He might come after us."

"He's not coming after us," I said, wiping my mouth.

"What, did he grab an Uber back to the city or something?" Melanie snorted.

"Yeah, probably," I tried to laugh. "We should go. The cops are probably - and I need to lay down."

"Where we going?"

"Let's get a hotel."

"Sounds good," she smiled. "I haven't showered in days. And a bed would be heaven."

"Oh crap," I said, patting my pockets. I suddenly remembered the clue. "Where's the bag from the chimney?" A volcano of anxiety shot up my stomach and erupted into my chest.

"You don't have it?" Melanie looked up. I shook my head. "Good thing I do," she said as she reached for her skirt pocket. She smiled. "It was in the street. You must have dropped it when the shotgun went off."

Chapter 29

People always say that they remember what day of the week it was when something terrible happened. "It was a Tuesday," they'll say. But that's a load of crap. Memory is a deceiver. We contort the past, twist it into tales we were never a part of and places we've never been. What we do remember is so clouded by our pain, our hopes, our sad and bitter attempts to make sense of a world outside our control that we may as well be walking through life blind.

What I do remember is that I drove all the way to her hometown in a black suit. The funeral was in California. No, not that California. It was in California, Pennsylvania. She grew up in a town outside of Pittsburg. It was a fall day and the orange leaves lit the air like fire.

I sat in my car outside the funeral home. Inside, my wife's family and friends gathered to say their goodbyes and tell reassuring stories and lies to one another. There would be crying, laughing, hugging. My wife would be in a box. The audience would stare at the box, or maybe a picture of her on an easel beside the box. I imaged the picture was in a sliver frame. The photo was probably her high school or college graduation photo. I'm sure it wasn't a photo from our wedding day.

I was invited to the funeral of course. But I was sure I wasn't wanted. So I stayed back in Virginia. Then I put on a suit and drove all the way there with every intention to go in and give a speech that I spent all night writing. I wanted to say that I missed her, that I loved her.

I could sense the needles in her parents' voices the one time we spoke after my wife's death. Her mother remarked simply, "Had she gone to a doctor when she first had symptoms, they could have caught it early. My little girl would still be alive."

So I sat in the car gazing across the parking lot at the funeral home. The lot was full. I was alone. I turned on the radio and spun the dial to some talk radio channel. I had my audience and I read my speech out loud, my notes on the dashboard.

When I was done, I looked up to see Roderick, her younger brother, standing outside my car door. I rolled my window down with the radio still playing. Handing me an envelope, he said, "She wrote this before she passed away. It's for you." He must have seen the sad in my eyes because he asked me if I felt okay.

"I don't know," I said.

"That's too bad," he replied. "Not going to the burial afterwards, eh?"

I shook my head. "I can't."

He turned and left. I turned off the radio and stared down at the envelope in my lap. It was white, like a bill you would get in the mail. I tossed it on the back seat and dragged my forearm across my nose, using my shirt sleeve as a handkerchief.

I drove to a big box store. I'm not sure what compelled me to do so. A tattooed older man who should have been enjoying his retirement years sold me a small handgun and a box of bullets. I didn't know a thing about guns but it was small enough to fit in my pocket and for some reason that made it seem less scary. I got back in my car and cried in the parking lot. Exhausted mothers and bad fathers walked by pushing screaming children in shopping carts. Each of us was somewhere else in our minds, numb, flaccid bodies unable to see the other.

Chapter 30

We awoke to banging on the door of the hotel room where we spent the night, the three of us curled up together on a double bed, the tire iron from the Honda in Melanie's hand and my bag on the floor next to the bed.

"What is that?"

"Cleaning lady," I mumbled through the last whisper of a dream.

The banging continued.

Then a voice forced its way through the steel door. "I know you're in there. Open up."

"Penny?" Melanie wondered aloud across the pillow. Her words wisped over Aubrey's hair.

"Don't answer it," I said.

"I'm not going away," the voice called.

"Let's just wait her out," I whispered to Melanie.

"What is she doing here?"

"I don't know. Let's just wait."

"But we have to check out by noon. What time is it?"

"We could stay another night. I can call down to-"

"Can we afford to?"

"No, but..."

"Who the hell does this girl think she is? She sends her clone after us to try to steal money we don't have and now she's tracked us down."

I shrugged.

"I mean, how could she find us?"

"Keep your voice down," I whispered.

"Then again, we're driving around in a bright orange toaster with a banged up front," Melanie whispered. "How hard is that to follow?"

We decided to let Penny wait. Aubrey was waking up and would be hungry. I couldn't cook pancakes in the hotel room because the griddle ran off of a small butane tank. But maybe Penny would leave if we waited just long enough.

Melanie and I crawled gently out of bed. At the desk, Melanie pulled the clue from her pocket and we examined it for the first time. Just as before, the clue was a piece of paper with something typewritten on it. It read: "Get some help."

"Get some help? From who?" I said.

Penny banged on the door.

"Aubrey's waking up," Melanie groaned.

I flipped the paper over. Another clue. On the back, typewritten as always, it read: "Three days ago."

"Shit," Melanie said. "We're three days behind him."

"How could he know that?"

"Maybe he's watching us."

"How?"

"I dunno."

I sat on the edge of the bed and rubbed my elbow. It was swollen. My head hurt at the base of my skull and my cheeks pulsated. Memories from the night before drifted up in little pockets, each passing by my eyes between moments of darkness.

"This isn't what I thought it would be," I said.

"What isn't?" Penny stopped banging on the door. Aubrey shifted in the bed. "All of this. I don't know if I can go any further."

"What?" Melanie grabbed my arm. "But the money."

"What about it?"

"We can get the money and get out of here. Don't you dream of escaping?"

I nodded. I looked at her and then away, my eyes peering towards the door where I could see two shadows in the light coming through the crack below the door. My mind shuffled back to how everything started. How Nick shoved me and how my head slammed the sticky linoleum floor. It skipped ahead to last night and Clark's limp, bloody face in the moonlight. "This isn't going as planned," I said. "There's too much collateral damage."

"What are you talking about?"

"Forget it," I said. "I just want a way out."

"There's a way out. Find the money. How can you quit?" Melanie dropped my arm and pushed away. She stood, leering at me. "How can you abandon me? Abandon Aubrey?"

Aubrey sat on the bed behind me, her legs crossed, her hair matted to the side of her head. She watched us.

"I'm not," I said. I smiled at Aubrey. "Everything's okay."

"I thought you wanted to be like a father to her," Melanie asked, pointing at Aubrey.

"You're the one who wanted to send her home."

Aubrey pulled her knees up, grabbed the blanket, and threw it over her. From under the blanket I heard little sobs, and those sobs grew and spread and soon they became wails and screams the way a little cough grows and spreads into pneumonia. "Happy faces, happy places, I can see happy faces," she sniffled.

Something about hearing Aubrey cry made me think about her little heart and the pain I was causing it. Then, I thought of my own heart, and my own sadness, and the pain I had caused it.

The heart has a mind all its own. It learns quickly at times and slowly at others. Sometimes it feels like the heart doesn't learn a damn thing. But that's not true. A child's heart is fearless, and loving, and in need of love. An adult's heart is like a corroded battery. All hearts move in the same direction, from loving, to fearing, from yearning to hiding. The problem isn't that the heart doesn't learn. The problem is that it must do its learning from humans.

"Okay," I said. "Where are we going when we find that money?"

Aubrey stopped crying. She pulled the blanket off her head and looked at me. "An amusement park in Florida?"

Melanie laughed. "No honey. We're going far, far away from any amusement park. And it'll be twice as magical."

"But amusement parks are the only place where there are no grownups."

"Yes there are. The lost kind."

"Lost kind?"

"Yes, but where we're going there won't be any grownups, I promise. They'll just be people who know."

"Who know what?" Aubrey asked.

"Know the secrets only special people know."

"But I like the rides."

"But don't you want to know the secrets?"

"I want to ride the rides."

"No, no. Not the rides. No, they're a distraction. Don't you see?"

"Rides are fun."

"No, they're a distraction. Don't you see?" Melanie sat on the bed next to Aubrey. "Did I ever tell you about the kids in Mexico City? I bet they're your same age. They stand out in the road between the cars. All day. They sell mango drinks for five pesos. That's all they do. And they breathe fumes. All day. For five pesos. They just see cars and breath fumes."

"Are they having fun?"

"No. No it's not fun to stand in the street like that."

"Then why? Why do they stand there?"

"That's all they know. That's all they ever get to know." Melanie put her hand on Aubrey's shoulder. "Trust me, it's better than some amusement park. We'll make our own magic, together. Won't that be nice?"

"Better than an amusement park," Aubrey said. "Promise?"

"I promise."

"Better than an amusement park," I echoed. "We'll make our own magic, together."

"Okay. I like magic," Aubrey said. "Is your friend in the place that's better than amusement parks?"

"He is," Melanie said. "And he wants us to come, too."

"You're going to take me with you?" Aubrey asked, her eyes big. "You're not going to abandon me?"

Melanie placed her chin on Aubrey's head and pulled her close. "No, baby. We would never abandon you."

Penny banged on the door. "I'm not going anywhere."

Melanie scuttered to the bed and grabbed the tire iron. She stormed to the door, the tire iron behind her back, and cracked it open.

"Mel," I heard Penny say.

"What?" Melanie asked gruffly.

"Where's James? I want to talk to James."

"What do you want?"

"Where's James? I know he's in there."

"Piss off."

"Where's Clark?"

"Oh you mean that thief that broke into our car and tried to steal money from us - money that we don't have?"

Penny didn't reply.

"We know it was you that broke into the car. You traumatized a little girl. Are you out of your mind?"

"Clark didn't come back last night."

"I'm sure Clark's okay," I called from behind the door. "He's probably just -"

"James?" Penny called. "What did you say?"

"Clark's fine. I'm sure he's fine," I called. I leaned against the wall and slid to the floor behind the door. "Just be patient. Go home."

"James, please. Do me this kindness," Penny begged. "Help me find him."

"He's probably waiting for you at home," I called. "Just go home."

"Maybe he left you," Melanie barked. "I bet you put him up to this and he realized how utterly insane you are. He probably ride-shared his way the hell away from you. Guy's probably halfway to Montana by now."

Penny swatted at the door. Melanie stumbled back into the room. She brandished the tire iron, raising it above her head. "Don't touch me," she warned. "I'll bust that mop head of yours wide open."

"Mel," Penny gasped.

"Your app is dead. Give it up."

Melanie shoved the door in Penny's face. Then she opened it. "Oh, and Penny, can I recommend something? Tinder. You can find a new loser on there to do your bidding." And with that she slammed the door.

###

We decided to get rid of the Honda Element. It was too easy to follow and Melanie didn't feel confident that Penny would give up. I can't say letting go of the Honda was something I wanted to do. I loved that car. But I knew it was the best thing for us.

While we waited Penny out, Aubrey watched cartoons while Melanie and I poured through the last chapters of *Discontents: The Disappearance of a Young Radical*. We snacked on what little food we had brought in from the car and drank water from the bathroom sink.

"Do you think Emory went to Idaho?" Melanie asked.

I looked over the passage that had her thinking that[6]. "Maybe," I said.

"Yeah," she said. "Maybe. Just maybe."

"Seems kind of obvious though."

"Yeah, maybe. But maybe it's one of those hidden in plain view kind of things."

"That was another band."

---

[6] I won't spoil it for those of you haven't read *Discontents: The Disappearance of a Young Radical* yet.

"What?"

"There was a band called Hidden in Plain View."

"You and Emory into them?"

"Not that I remember."

Melanie nodded.

"No," I said. "I can't see there being a clue about them. Jimmy Eat World, sure. Get Up Kids, a distinct possibility. The Starting Line, I'd believe it. But, no, not Hidden in Plain View."

"Okay," Melanie said. "What do you think these clues mean?"

We looked over the two clues we had found side by side. The first one read "NF-871" and the second read "get some help" on one side and "three days ago" on the other side.

"Maybe NF-871 is an airline flight number?"

"Maybe."

Melanie pulled out her phone. She tapped around on it a minute. "No, it doesn't look like it."

"What if you just Google NF-871?"

She tapped her phone. "There's some information about a luggage bag, a walkie talkie made in China, and a dishwasher."

"Doesn't sound too promising."

"Maybe the walkie talkie?"

"Maybe. I doubt it. We haven't found any walkie talkies. If he wanted to talk to us, wouldn't he just hide us a walkie talkie?"

"True." Melanie bit her bottom lip and thought a minute. "How about the other clues? Get some help? Who do we get help from?"

I shrugged. "Maybe it's not who we get help from, but what kind of help? Or where we get it?"

Melanie shrugged. "I wish I did better on those riddle questions on the SATs."

I laughed. "Yeah, me too."

I got up and poked my head through the curtains. "I still don't see her."

"Maybe she left."

"Maybe. I sure would if someone threatened to crack my skull with a tire iron."

Melanie chuckled. "I'm sorry. I kind of lost it with her."

"Don't apologize. We've both lost it a bit these last few days."

"What was that bullshit about Clark?"

I shrugged, turning away. "She's just looking for a way in."

We packed our stuff and ran to the Honda across the wide parking lot, our heads swiveling in every direction expecting Penny to jump out from behind each car as we passed it. I spun the Honda around to the front.

"Take the wheel," I told Melanie. "I'm going to run in, pay, and come out. I want you to drive around and come back in five minutes. I'll wait in the lobby and when I see you come up, I'll run out and hop in."

So I went in and paid. When Melanie came back around I hopped in and we took off, running a light as we sped away.

We drove around town, taking odd turns into side streets and erratic detours that led to nowhere. After about half an hour of this, our heads constantly swiveling, our eyes snooping for signs that we were being followed, we decided we were probably safe. We found a used car lot, the kind of place on a busy road between mini malls and fast food chains that no one ever seems to buy a car from.

We parked the Honda at the back of the small lot as far from the street as possible. The office was just a double wide trailer. Inside we grabbed a seat in a little lobby. It was just big enough for four chairs, a small coffee table which was loaded down with newspaper and magazines, and a few filing cabinets.

Whoever owned the place loved dinosaurs. The walls were covered in dinosaur posters. There were posters that showed the size of different dinosaurs, like the kind of thing you would see on a children's placemat for sale in a museum gift shop. Dinosaur models and rubber dinosaur children's toys sat atop the filing cabinets. Above us, a few raptors hung from the ceiling by fishing wire.

A thin man wearing lenses the size of playing cards plodded into the lobby from behind a door. His head bent so far forward that his chin dipped down to his chest. He stood almost over us, the room was so small. And he peered up from behind his glasses without lifting his chin. He was an Asian fellow, with a bush of black hair above either ear. Other than that, his head was shiny and barren. His eyes wandered over us as though he were looking over limp lettuce at a casino salad bar. A cascade of bags hung below his eyes, each successively bigger and darker as they got closer to his lips. A lit cigarette dangled from his lips and he gnawed at the filter.

"Buy or sell?"

"You do trades?"

He nodded. "I do everything. What you trade?"

"Honda Element."

"Where?"

We took him around to the back and showed him the Honda.

"What will you trade for this?"

"This piece of shit?"

"It's a good car."

"How many mile?"

"Like 350."

"350,000 mile? Piece of shit."

I nodded. "Hey, can you not cuss in front of the girl?"

He rolled his eyes and the bags below them jiggled. "What happen here?" He pointed to the front.

"Somebody backed into it."

He chewed his cigarette. "You got papers?"

"I got the papers."

He scratched the side of his face with one hand. "Let me look." He took a look inside the car and walked around it.

"Piece of shit start?"

"It's a Honda," I said.

"I give you two grand."

"Just two grand?"

"Come on," he said, looking over us. "Someone back into it?"

"Like I said, we need a trade."

He rubbed the side of his face some more and gnawed on his cigarette. "I only got one car."

"We don't want a car," Melanie said. "We need something - "

"Big?"

Melanie nodded.

"Something can sleep in?"

"Yes."

"I see now," he said. He flicked his cigarette. "Come on, I show you perfect thing."

The perfect thing turned out to be 1986 Volkswagen Westfalia. You know, the boxy '80s version of a VW bus. It was grey or blue, I couldn't tell. It looked like a sixteen year old had tried to touch up the paint using house paint rather than auto paint in a half-baked plan to cover the rust around the wheel wells, doors and bumper. The front hub caps were missing and so too was the gas cap cover. But curtains hung inside and they could be pulled around the windows for privacy and sleep.

"This thing start?" I asked.

"Does for you," he said. "I put in new starter yesterday."

"If it runs, you got yourself a trade," I said.

We went back into the office.

"Mister," Aubrey said.

"What you want, little girl?" the man asked.

"Mister, something is wrong with your dinosaurs."

"You like dinosaur?" He leaned forward, his eyes combing over Aubrey.

"I do."

"What wrong with my dinosaur?"

"They're missing their feathers."

"Feathers?" he leaned back, looking at Melanie and I. "This your daughter?"

"Dinosaurs had feathers."

"Dinosaur no feathers, little girl." The man shook his head. "You say Mr. Liu not know about dinosaurs? You come to office to tell Mr. Liu this?"

"She's sorry," I said. I put my hand on Aubrey's shoulders and gave a little squeeze. "Aren't you, Aubrey?"

"They did, they had feathers." Aubrey looked up at me. "It was recently discovered."

"Little girl think she so smart and me just stupid foreigner," Mr. Liu said.

"She's very imaginative," Melanie said. "Please, we are so sorry."

"This is joke?"

"Not funny," I said.

"Very unfunny," Melanie echoed.

The man looked at us, then down at Aubrey. He scratched the side of his head. "Feathers and dinosaurs," he laughed. "This stupidest idea I ever hear. White girls always too confident. No one tell them truth."

"It's not stupid," I said. Melanie jabbed an elbow into me.

The man looked at me. "What you say?"

"I mean, she's just a kid."

"So, the trade," Melanie interrupted. "We're kind of in a rush."

"I like this lady. She only focus on the money." Mr. Liu smiled. "Okay, we do trade."

We did the paperwork for the trade in the man's office. After, Aubrey and I waited in the lobby while Melanie used the bathroom.

"They have feathers," Aubrey whispered to me.

"I believe you," I whispered back.

"I saw a Montana license plate once," Aubrey said.

"Yeah?" I said.

"The state flag is blue."

I nodded. "I didn't know that."

"Yep. I've never been there."

"Me neither," I said.

"Blue is the most popular state flag color," Aubrey said. "I think. Or maybe it's white."

"What are you guys talking about?" Melanie asked, grabbing a seat beside Aubrey.

"Montana."

"Why?"

I shrugged.

"Because that's where you said that man went, Mr. Clark."

Melanie laughed. "Yeah, yeah. That's right."

"It's quiet there," I said.

Aubrey scrunched her eyebrows. "You said you've never been there."

"I haven't," I said.

"Then how do you know?"

"Oh, it's just a song."

Melanie turned to me. "What song?"

"Another Hero for a Day song. It's a lyric."

"Which song?"

"'Don't Forget Me, Molly'," I said.

Melanie stood. "How does it go?"

I hummed. "Fly to Montana or something. It's quiet out there or something."

"Yeah, yeah. We listened to that one, right?"

"Great song. Why?"

"That's from the same album, *Through Being Quiet*, right?"

"Emory's favorite album."

I popped my eyebrows up in frustration. "We established that. Where is this going?"

"It's quiet out there," she said.

"Yeah, that's not the lyric. But, it's something like that."

"Let's get our stuff and move it into the Volkswagen."

"Can we name our new car?" Aubrey asked.

"Sure," I smiled.

"Cool," she said. "Let's call it Westy."

"Like short for Westfalia?"

Aubrey nodded. "That sounds bor-ing."

"Westy it is," I said, patting Aubrey's head.

Melanie grabbed Aubrey's hand. "I want to see those clues again."

"Why, what's up?" I asked, standing.

"Because," Melanie popped her eyebrows. "Get some help."

The three of us waved goodbye to the man and left the trailer.

"What about getting help?" I asked as we walked to Westy.

"Earlier you said, maybe it wasn't who to get help from, but where to get help."

"Okay."

"The song was kind of fast. But I think that's what the singer sang."

"Well what did he sing?"

"Come on, don't you know it?"

"I don't."

"I thought you loved that album," Melanie stopped. She looked at me from behind her glasses and I wasn't sure what she was seeing.

"Oh yeah," I said. "How stupid of me. I haven't been able to think straight after hitting my head. I told you I fell and hit my head running after Clark, right?"

Melanie pursed her lips. Her eyes narrowed. Then she asked me how I was feeling. I told her I was fine. I just had a bit of a headache. Melanie nodded, her mouth cocked to one side. "You know those lyrics through and through."

"Yeah, I do," I said. "He sings about going to Montana to get some help."

James Wallace Birch

JUST WATCH THE FIREWORKS

Chapter 31

I sat in a lazy chair, the chair reclined and my eyes closed in a small office in an old building with a droopy doorway. The building was huddled on University Avenue at the edge of bar row. The windows wore that historic wrinkly glass that you can't see through. Before the Civil War, the building served as a hotel but it became a makeshift hospital after one of the nearby battles. As the story goes, the place is haunted with dead soldiers.

I was here because my department chair told me to come after I didn't show up to teach for two full weeks after my wife died.

"Look, I'm going to be honest with you," she said. "You look terrible. You smell like a bar. You need some help."

"Help?"

"Grief counseling."

"That's not for me."

"Well, make it for you if you want to keep your job," she said as she stood from her desk. I got up from my seat across from her. "I feel for you, James. I really do. But I've got a department to run. Enrollment is down and budget cuts are coming. I'm going to have to let three adjuncts go next semester."

"Layoffs?"

She nodded. "Look, the students like you. So don't make the decision for me."

Two days later I was sitting in an easy chair. A low voice was talking on a tape with butterfly music in the background. Then, it ended.

"Was that calming?"

"I guess so," I replied.

I heard a pencil scratching on paper. The counselor instructed, "Why don't you describe how you feel." She was a short black woman with a very pink nose and she wore a white lab coat as though this were a psych ward in *One Flew Over the Cuckoo's Nest*.

"I guess I feel abandoned and alone."

"What do you mean, you guess?"

"I feel abandoned and alone."

"Your wife's sickness was not your fault, James."

"I know."

"She didn't abandon you. She passed away."

"She did. She told me she never wanted to see me again. She made me move out two weeks before she went to the hospital at the end there."

The counselor nodded. "And why is that?"

"I don't know."

"Well, what was the main source of tension in your marriage?"

"Time, I guess."

"Time?"

"The more that passed, the less we understood each other."

The counselor nodded.

"Did she say anything to you that might help unpack her feelings?"

"No." I opened my eyes. "Well, there was one thing when she found out she was sick. A few weeks after that she started telling me to develop a mind that clings to nothing."

"Nothing?"

"Nothing."

"Why do you think she said this?"

"I don't know. You're the counselor."

"James."

"I guess she was saying nothing mattered between us anymore. Like, give up. There's nothing worth living for."

"There's always something worth living for." I sat in silence a bit and the counselor did too.

"I…um..."

"Yes?" the counselor asked.

"I um, I drove - um - I drove through a stop light today. On purpose."

The counselor nodded. She waited a while for me to talk but I didn't. "And?" she asked.

"The intersection wasn't em-" I trailed off.

"The intersection wasn't what, James?"

"Oh, nothing," I said. "Never mind."

We sat, separated by silence. The counselor didn't push or pull. She just looked at me, her hands crossed, a practiced smile on her face. Finally she said, "So tell me about your late wife, James."

"She was so pretty and smart and funny. It's like, what happened? Time. That's the only thing I can think of that keeps me from going crazy. Otherwise, you know, it's like I can't figure it out."

"There was nothing else? Think for a minute."

"Well, she was tired of me always talking about Emory Walden and giving these talks about his book."

"And who is this?"

"Oh, he was this friend of mine. I published his book. Long story. But she said I was obsessed and couldn't go live my life. Like I was stuck in the past."

"I see. I see this a lot, where one partner is looking one direction in time and other is looking the opposite direction in time. Some disagreements are normal in a marriage."

"It didn't feel normal."

"No, I'm sure it didn't. Any other issues?

"We tried to have a baby. But it didn't work."

"Did that breed resentment?"

I nodded.

"On your side or hers?"

"Both, I think. But, even before that. If I'm remembering correctly - I can't seem to remember anything right these days -, we just seemed to be growing apart. Well, not apart. It was like we were two boats broken from our anchors drifting in the sea. We just drifted away from one another. It wasn't growth. It was just waves." I wiped my eyes. The counselor handed me a box of tissues.

"So, yeah, she wrote this letter to me. Her brother gave it to me at the funeral."

"What did it say?"

"I haven't read it."

She nodded. "Grief takes time, James."

"Tell that to my dead wife."

"What do you mean?"

"Oh, nothing. She was always discounting my feelings."

"And how did that make you feel?"

"Far away."

"I see. So tell me about the letter."

"Sure. Yeah, well, I can't stop thinking about it. But I can't read it. I haven't opened it. I just hold the envelope and stare at it and wonder what the letter says. I stare at it for hours. All night sometimes. I sit on my kitchen counter and drink and stare at it and try to build the courage to open it. But I always put it in the drawer before I get the courage."

"Why don't you read it?"

"Because once I know what's in it, well, I'm afraid."

"Afraid of?"

"Everything."

"Maybe it will offer some answers, James."

"That's part of what I'm afraid of. And then, I'm also afraid that it won't, and then where will I be?"

"It is okay to live with uncertainty."

"You don't understand. I'm paralyzed. I can't do anything but look at that letter and wonder. It's a miracle I'm even here, that I even left my apartment today."

"So if you weren't here?"

"I'd be sitting on my kitchen counter starting at that envelope."

"And how does it feel to be here?"

"It feels good. It's like being unstuck, if only for a short while."

She nodded

"But I'm afraid."

"Afraid?"

"That when I go home I'll get stuck again."

"It's healthy to do things to take your mind off of everything."

"Yeah," I nodded.

"Well, I think we have a possible way of coping then. At least until you start to feel better."

"We do?"

"Yes. Simply find something to do. Keep your mind occupied."

"How?"

"It doesn't matter, James. The point is, do something. Go the movies."

"But, a movie only takes a few hours. Then what?"

"Well, then exercise, or go for a run. Grade papers. Show up to work. Stay busy and you'll keep your mind occupied."

"But when it ends."

"What?"

"The work day. The run. When it ends?"

"Get creative, James. You're a capable adult. I'm sure you will be able to think of something."

Chapter 32

In some ways, Westy was an upgrade. The Volkswagen had more room for the three of us and I could see that we would actually get some sleep living in it. In other ways, it was a downgrade. It smelled faintly of cat food and moths and it didn't have a CD player. When I pointed this out to the man who sold us the car, he threw in a tape with a wire sticking out of it. The wire, he said, could be put into the audio jack of a portable CD player. Then, all we had to do was put the tape in the tape player and it would play the audio coming out of the CD player. Problem was, we had no portable CD player. So we went looking for a pawn shop.

We found a one near the mercado that we had slept behind our first night back in Progressville. It was a musty place, and dimly lit, but we found a CD player and a cigarette power adapter for it. In the van, we plugged the CD player in just like we were supposed to and lo and behold it worked.

"Okay, let's hear the Hero for a Day song," Melanie said, rubbing her hands together. I put on the song 'Don't Forget Me, Molly'. Melanie pulled up the lyrics on her phone and she read out loud as the song played.

Somewhere by the East River,
Maybe you'll find me cold.

On the rocks or by the boat,
Is where I always go.
Where you never go looking and never wonder if it's
found.
Some three days ago, I lost it,
And I heard that it has drowned.

And my teacher, she said to me:
The trains and the skyscrapers
And everything downtown.
The planes and empty papers
And everything around.

Boy, get some help.
Boy, get some help.

Go out to Montana.
Go out where it's quiet.
Go out where names mean nothing.
Out where everything's alright.

So you never know that it's lost,
Until it ends up in a box.
And the teacher's got it,
And she says it's growing moss.

It doesn't really matter, when you're banging on a
door.
And you're begging to her father, or screaming on the
floor.

So leave these lights behind.
And never let her know.
That you gave it so carelessly.
And it sank down below.

Boy, go get some help.

"Okay, play it again."

I reached for the CD player. "Wait," she said. "Let me get the clues." She reached into her shoulder bag, fumbled around a bit, and took them out. "Okay. Press play."

The song ended.

"That's it," Melanie said, waving the clue cards. She turned and looked at Aubrey in the back. "You want to go to Montana?"

Aubrey screeched. "Do I? Of course I do!" She bounced to her feet and hopped up and down in the van. "We're going to Montana, we're going to Montana," she chanted.

"Wait a second," I said. "Montana? Montana is far. Very far."

"You said you wanted to know what happened to Emory," Melanie said.

"I can't tell you how badly."

"Well, he went to Montana."

"To cross into Canada," I said.

Melanie reached across the aisle and grabbed my wrist. "Exactly. Idaho was a diversion. But going to Canada wasn't."

"And how do you know that?"

"Look," Melanie said handing me her phone. I read through the song lyrics. "See." She pointed to the screen. "'Get some help' and 'three days ago' are both parts of lyrics in this song."

"Lyrics in a song where Montana is mentioned," I replied. "That's all you're going on?"

"The guy literally sings that he should go to Montana to get some help."

"Well, the teacher says that," I corrected. "He doesn't say that."

"So what?"

"So what? And what does three days ago mean?"

"Maybe it means we are three days behind him."

"Or maybe it doesn't mean anything," I snapped.

"Maybe it is just meant to prove that the clue is a reference to this song."

"Maybe. Maybe not," I said. "What about the East River? He sings about that."

"No, not the East River. Montana. It's Montana."

"Why don't we go to New York to the East River? Or better yet, why don't we go to every place ever mentioned in every Hero for a Day song? Would you like that?"

"Because, the river represents where he usually goes to hide," Melanie said. "But that's not working. So he's got to go somewhere new."

"So this is it? You want to drive across the country to some place none of us have ever been to on the fact that Montana is mentioned in this song? This makes you think we should risk our lives in some mountainous wilderness with bears and wolves and all that?"

Melanie snatched the phone from my hand. "No," she said. "The other clue makes me think that. The NF-871."

I shook my head. "That's not a song lyric."

"I know. I searched Montana NF-871 on my phone and this is what I found." She pushed the phone into my hands. I looked down at the screen and saw the first search result. It read 'Montana Highway Map - Montana Natural Resource Information System'.

"Scroll down," she said. "Click the link that has 'Montana Reveries' in it."

I clicked the link. It was a blog post. I read down to where NF-871 was mentioned. NF-871 is described as a forest trail in the Federal Kaniksu National Forest. The author is almost poetic in describing how the road tracks right up to the Canadian border, "dislikes what it runs into" and turns south.

"Can we find this on Google Maps?" I asked.

Melanie searched and found the spot where the road seemed to bounce off the Canadian border as thought the border were a wall and the road were a rubber ball that America had thrown against it[7].

"It's literally on a mountain in the middle of nowhere. The closest thing to a town is called Yahk and all it looks like it has is a general store. It's the perfect place to cross undetected."

I took the phone from her and looked at the map. "I don't know if it's possible to even get to this place. He'd have to hike across a small forest, cross that barren spot on the mountain. And - "

"Yeah, and follow one of those forest roads down the mountainside to, what was that, Hawks road?"

I pinched and zoomed on the phone. "Hawkins Creek Road. That's a forest road - gravel. That whole time a ranger truck could come by and pick him up. He'd need five or six days of food and water at the least. Not to mention bears and whatever else is up there."

Melanie took the phone back. "You're right. But wouldn't you try if your life depended on it?"

"He was into backpacking. So yeah, if I were him." I turned and looked out the window at the buildings and the buses and the busyness all around. "What makes you think the money is going to be there?"

"Why else would he be leaving us these clues?" Melanie answered. "Either he's there, or the

---

[7] See the spot for yourself here: http://bit.ly/gmaps-nf871.

money's there, or something else - another clue maybe."

"Yeah," I said. "Maybe you're right. I just, I guess I'm afraid."

"You are?" Melanie's tone softened. "But, but you want to find him, right?"

"More than anything. All I've thought about for years is what happened to him?
But I'm too terrified to go looking for him. I think about stuff. What if I don't like what I find? What if his past caught up to him? What if, what if he's dead? What if - lots of stuff?"

Melanie slipped her fingers between mine. "It's okay." She leaned over.

"Are you going to kiss?" Aubrey called from the back.

"Yes," Melanie said, her eyes locked on me. The way she looked at me reminded me of the time when we first saw each other that August day nearly two years before. It was as though her eyes had never left me and here we were in some strange, distant world - a world I never thought I would share with her.

Chapter 33

"What do you think the last line of the poem means?" Melanie asked as we drove up I-270 towards Hagerstown Maryland.

"No clue," I replied from behind the steering wheel. "What does it say again?"

"Just up the lane, James lost his..."

"Another band name?"

"Can't think of any."

We merged onto I-70 and took that to I-68 West, where we headed into West Virginia. We were westbound to Montana. The air was warm coming through the cracked windows and the sun shone through the cabin of the Volkswagen like we were in an airplane coasting high above the clouds.

We turned north on I-79 at Morgantown and passed into Pennsylvania.

"Pennsylvania!" Aubrey chanted. "Another new state."

At Washington I turned onto the I-70 East.

"We're backtracking," Melanie said.

"Detour," I said.

"What? Why?"

"There's something - I just need to do something."

I turned off a winding road onto the cracked pavement of the cemetery and passed the statue of the Virgin Mary.

"Wait here," I said as I stopped the car. "It's somewhere around here."

I got out and wandered around a bit, tiptoeing between gravestones, my eyes searching.

Melanie got out of the van and walked softly over to me. "Can I help you look?"

I nodded.

Finally, I found it. My wife's grave.

"Can I sit?" I asked my wife.

I sat down.

Melanie stood off in the distance a moment before fading back to the van.

"I miss you," I said. "I feel like we never talk anymore."

A bird landed on a nearby gravestone and picked at the granite.

I lay down beside my wife and gazed at the sky.

"Do you remember our first Star Night? On the cliffs by the river?"

The bird flew off overhead.

"I think I ran away from you or maybe I pushed you away. Or both," I said. "I've been thinking a lot about how I remember things. I think I've been - I guess I was angry. Afraid. I think I've been seeing these last few years, our lives - I blamed you."

I listened as more birds flew by.

"What I mean is, maybe things were different. It's like I tell the story back in my mind and it's just the fights and the silence. And it whirls and whirls.

Fight. Silence. Louder, louder. But we were happy, right? There was so much fun, so much love. Why can't I remember it? Anyways, I know you wanted me to do something. But I don't know what. I haven't read your letter. I'm trying. I promise. I love you. Please. I want to remember."

The birds were gone, the sky empty. Tears filled my eyes. Everything above was blue and blurry.

We stopped at a rest area in Wisconsin or Minnesota to use the bathroom and as we were coming out Aubrey said, "Look, Emory."

Melanie and I turned our heads at the same time to find Aubrey pointing at a wall that was decorated in tiles. The wall was weather worn and the edges of its top were softened from years of visitors sitting on it. Tiles along the wall read "emory of ob Ne h rt". In several spots, tiles were missing.

"Not quite. But good eye." I leaned down and pointed to the places where the tiles were missing. "I think it is supposed to say, "In Memory of Bob something.""

"Maybe Newhart," Melanie chimed in.

"Good guess."

Aubrey sighed. "Darn. I thought we found a clue."

"I'm afraid not," Melanie said. "But you're doing a great job. Keep looking, okay?"

We walked on to Westy. "It's funny," Melanie said to me. "Emory is just memory without the M."

"Yeah," I nodded. "I never realized that."

Aubrey stopped. "That car was at the last two rest stops, too."

Melanie stopped beside her. "What car?"

"The black one." She pointed to a town car with dark windows several spots down.

Melanie squatted and put her hands on Aubrey's shoulders. "Do you mean a car that looked like that car?"

Aubrey shook her head. "The same car."

I squatted down too. "Are you sure?"

Aubrey nodded.

"It has the same Virginia license plate."

For the rest of the day we drove, our eyes locked on rearview mirrors and window mirrors. We got gas. We ate. And at night Melanie and I slept in shifts, the other sitting in the driver's seat keeping an eye out. But nothing happened. So the next day we drove some more.

That night we parked under a lamp in a grocery store parking lot in Rapid City and made camp. Melanie and I decided it was safest to hide in well-lit spots, avoiding rest stops and trucker parking lots off the highway. After dinner, we lay in the back of Westy as we suffered through the hours, the hum of the lamp outside and the start and stop of cars at a nearby traffic light keeping the seconds and minutes. Eventually Aubrey's breathing fell into a pattern and the comforting sound of her occasional snores helped to bring a sense of calm to the cabin.

"What are we going to do when we get there?" I whispered. "Those mountains are huge and we're not experienced backpackers. And Aubrey, what about her? What if we can't even get the van onto that road?"

"We'll figure it out," Melanie said, tracing her fingernails along the back of my neck. "I bet it's going to be breathtaking up there."

Two beams of light washed over Westy. They yawned across the length of the van from back to front before fixing their position on the driver's side window.

Melanie's fingers froze. "What was that?"

I crawled to my knees, peeled a curtain back, and snuck a glance. "The town car."

"Seriously?"

I nodded.

The car lights beamed at us. Its engine idled as though at any minute the driver might slam the pedal down and bulldoze into us. It was a naked feeling to be in that van with those lights watching over us.

Melanie pushed herself up on her elbows. "What do we do?"

"I don't know. Let's just wait them out."

We kept still as the cows in the fields we had passed on our journey west, me at the corner of a window squatting on my knees and Melanie propped on her elbows. But we were no cows and soon our bodies ached.

"It's been like an hour," Melanie said.

"I think it's been two."

"What time is it?"

"It's just after 3 am."

"I'm so tired," she said.

"Me too."

"Who is it?"

"I can't see."

"Do you think it's Penny?"

"Who else could it be?"

"That savage bitch," Melanie spat. "Where the hell did she get a car?"

"It's probably an Uber," I joked.

Melanie snort-giggled. She leaned over and opened the cabin door and began to crawl out.

"What are you doing?"

"That's enough of this girl's shit," she said.

"What's going on?" Aubrey called, rubbing her eyes and sitting up.

"Nothing to worry about," I said. "Go on back to sleep."

"Where's Melanie going?"

"Don't worry."

Melanie rounded the front of the van. She marched directly into the light. "Leave us alone," she yelled, crossing her arms above her head and waving them wildly. She yelled it over and over with each step towards the town car. The town car awoke. It shifted into gear. "Leave us alone," Melanie yelled. She spread her legs a few feet from the hood of the car. The car revved. It growled in the cool spring air of the high plains.

I threw open the door. "Melanie!"

She turned back towards me. The car jolted forward. I leapt from the van, my bare feet smacking the asphalt. The town car leapt. It skidded. It stopped an arm's length from Melanie's thighs. The gears shifted. The tires spun. The car zoomed backwards and let out a scream. It swung around and sped out of the parking lot, swerving into the street like a bowling ball that had jumped a lane before disappearing down the road. Traces of tail light trailed behind it before vanishing into the night sky like fireflies scattering. But of course, there are no fireflies in places like South Dakota.

The next morning we awoke to find a filling parking lot. We caught a few sideways glances as I cooked on the fold-out griddle while Aubrey and Melanie shoved pancakes in their mouths, their legs dangling from the floor of the open sliding door. We used the bathrooms in the grocery store, stocked up on essentials, and got ready for the trip into Wyoming and then our goal. Montana.

"Wanna drive a bit?" I asked Melanie.

"Sure."

She hopped in the driver's seat but the Volkswagen wouldn't turn over.

"Is it the battery?" I asked.

"I don't know. Sounded like the starter wasn't turning."

"I didn't know you knew cars," I complimented.

"My dad," Melanie replied.

"Let's try and jump it, just to check."

We found someone to give us a jump and the Volkswagen came to life. Soon we were on our way. We left South Dakota and entered Wyoming, the altitude creeping up. And soon we saw Montana.

"Wow," I gasped. "We're really gonna make it to Montana."

"Should we stop for a photo?"

"Photo, photo," Aubrey chanted from the back.

We pulled over on the highway, hopped out and took turns getting our photos taken. Aubrey and I got a great shot where I held her up on my shoulders as she pointed to the word Montana in a big white circle on the blue sign[8]. "See, it's blue," Aubrey squealed.

"What is?"

"Montana's flag is blue," Aubrey howled. "And so is its sign."

And she was right.

"Can I sit in front for a while?" she asked. So I hopped in the back and watched 'the big sky' state from the back seat for a while. Something about it

___

[8] You can see the sign where we took the photo on Google Maps here: http://bit.ly/gmaps-montanasign.

was beautiful in a way the East Coast could never understand. The soft blue sky lit every corner of the auburn prairies and jutting rocks. In Montana, it felt like you could see forever.

We whizzed past towns where nothing happened and everyone was left alone to just live. And soon the altitude began to climb again. Little mountains jutted out of the land here and there. We crossed through the Northern Cheyenne Indian Reservation and kept on towards Billings where we stopped for lunch. After Billings, the land turned greener. Great pastures of grass by the road gave way to jagged mountains in the distance.

"I can't believe we're doing this," I called, popping open the rear window to take in the Montana air. As it swirled through the cabin we opened our nostrils and sucked it in - it's clean, crisp taste awakening us to the moment.

"I love Montana," Aubrey sang from the front seat.

"Me too," I called back against the swirling wind. I laid back, shut my eyes, and let the air wash over me.

"I can't believe how beautiful it is," Melanie declared as she rolled down her window.

And so we drove further into the pure, welcoming beauty with no need to say anything more.

We wheeled into Missoula well after dark. We slept in shifts, fearing the town car might still be following us. The plan was to gear up in Missoula. Melanie and I had our hiking packs but we needed to buy one for Aubrey at a camping store. We also needed tents, rations, water, and the proper clothes. We needed hiking maps and forest access road maps of the Kootenai National Forest and the Northwest Peak Recreation Area, the parts of Northern Montana near NF-871. We needed a new car battery. But our savings were down under $100 dollars. So Melanie and I went looking for work.

Melanie found a job as a server in a diner and she talked the owner into giving me a job washing dishes. While we worked, Aubrey hung out in the diner and doodled with crayons on the back of paper placemats until she got bored on the third day. So I bought her an old Gameboy and a few games from a pawn shop for $20 and that kept her busy. When she got bored, I went back and bought more games. We managed to pass two weeks like this and, working every available hour and living off of the customer's uneaten food scraps, we managed to save just over $300. So we bought everything we could with the money, but it wasn't enough. We still needed a quality tent that could fit all three of us.

We were living in an RV Park outside of town. Safety in numbers seemed like as good a strategy as any. The campground was lined with pine trees and sat at the end of a dusty road a ways off the highway. It was my first RV Park and not at all what I expected. It was orderly and quiet. The people were joyful and friendly. The facilities were clean and well-lit. There were even water hookups and places to pump out human waste for the real RVs. Best of all, at night the adults would bring out fold up lawn chairs, grill, and strum guitars while the kids ran around and threw footballs or played tag. It made me feel like every night was the Fourth of July.

On the night we bought our gear, I put Aubrey to bed after the girls she was playing with were called home to their camper a few rows down. Melanie climbed into the van. "You okay?" I asked.

"I think living off of food waste is messing up my stomach. I just puked in the grass." She wiped her mouth with the back of her hand. "I don't know how Renton did it for so long."

"I have a plan," I said. There had been no sign of the town car the entire time we had been in Montana. Despite this, Melanie and I were still sleeping in shifts and before I went to bed for a few hours I wanted to pitch my plan to her. "I think we got to steal the tent," I said.

"Are you serious?" Melanie asked.

"We can't stay here much longer eating uneaten eggs and soggy bread, right? I think we steal it and get out of town."

"I kinda like it here," Melanie admitted. "Well, not the eating situation."

"Melanie."

"What? It's nice. It's pretty. It's relatively cheap. The people are friendly. It's got a lot going for it."

"I can't believe you. You're the one that pushed us. We've come so far. We're so close."

"Maybe this is enough," she said. "It feels right. I feel - I don't know - at peace here with you and Aubrey. God, she's so sweet. And, you're so good with her. And it just feels, it just feels right. Our own little family."

"I do too. I'm happy here," I admitted. "But we're so close to - "

"To what?"

I wanted to say, 'To possibly finding Emory, or at least seeing where he crossed into Canada. Won't that be incredible - just to see it, to have that feeling?' But instead I said, "To finding the money. You said that was our ticket to freedom."

"It's like you said," Melanie replied, settling down beside me. "It's a big risk to go out there in the woods, especially with Aubrey. What if something happens to her? To us?"

"Look," I said. "Just go with me on this. Will you do that?"

Melanie nodded. She slipped her hand in mine and we sat in the van cabin in that RV Park, our feet stretched out before us and aglow in the bars of moonlight that slipped under the curtains.

"I love Montana," Melanie whispered. "I love us. It's perfect."

Chapter 34

_Emory

Chapter 35

I didn't have a plan to steal the tent from the camping store. I just said I did. So I spent my shift staring through a crack in the curtains while I tried to come up with one. Then, Melanie woke and I slept. In the morning we drove to the camping store. I took the temporary license plate tags off of Westy in the parking lot and tossed them in the back.

"Stay in the passenger's seat and don't get out for any reason," I told Aubrey. "Okay?" She nodded, her hands fidgeting on her lap.

"We need to go buy one last thing and then we are going to drive a bit further for our big hiking adventure. Does that sound like fun?" Aubrey nodded again. "Okay, I'm going to leave Westy running. Melanie and I are going to go inside. I want you to keep your eyes on the front door. When we come out, I need you to open the passenger door and the driver door and then hop into the back and put your seatbelt on. Can you do that?" Aubrey nodded a third time. "I need you to say 'yes'," I said, putting my hands on Aubrey's shoulders. Aubrey said yes, her hands fidgeting, her eyes avoiding mine. "Okay, what are you going to do?"

"I'm gonna open the doors and get in my seat."

"Good. And what else?"

"Put my seatbelt on."

"Right," I said. "Good. We'll be right back."

Melanie and I hopped out of Westy and began crossing the parking lot on our way to the automatic doors at the front of the camping store. The sky felt extra big, even for a Montana sky, and the sun shot rays of light down between the clouds. One ray seemed to target us and another hit bullseye on the door of the camping store. My heart raced. Sweat seeped through my pores. It ran down my wrists. My armpits felt hot. My feet felt cold.

I stopped about halfway to the door. "I need you to know something," I said.

"There's something I want to tell you too," Melanie replied.

"What is it?"

"You go first."

"Okay," I said. "There's a gun. I've got a gun."

Melanie grabbed me, tugging me back. "What? Are you suicidal? A gun? Where'd you get that?"

"A while ago. Before all of this," I said, pulling away. "It's in my sweatshirt pocket, just in case."

"So armed robbery, that's the plan?"

"No. I'm not going to use it. But, you know, just in case."

Melanie patted my sweatshirt pocket, her hand pressing against the unforgiving edges of the pistol.

"Promise me you won't use it."

"I won't." I put my hand on her wrist and pulled it gently away from my pocket.

"Okay, your turn."

"What? Oh, never mind," she said. "I'll tell you later." She reached out and grabbed my hand. "Better than an amusement park, right?"

"We'll make our own magic," I said, squeezing her hand. "We can do this together."

I don't think we breathed the rest of the walk across the parking lot. We walked side-by-side into the store. I bent over to catch my breath. "Okay," I said. "Stations."

I scooted to the tent aisle while Melanie perched near the doorway where she could see me, the cashiers, and the whereabouts of floor staff. The plan was no plan, really. She was just supposed to stand there and make a judgment call on when she thought I had the best chance of slipping out of the front door with the tent.

Meanwhile, I slid two rubber bands from my pocket. I weaved them around the plastic security device that was designed to set off an alarm when someone walked out the front door with stolen merchandise. It was the same kind of device that clothing stores put on clothes with a pin that went through the fabric with two plastic clasps on either end. I eyed the features on the tent bag as I wove the rubber bands tighter and tighter. Soon, the pressure began to work the clasp on the security device off the pin until it dropped harmlessly to the floor. I pulled the pin through on the other end and placed it on the shelf. The old trick Emory and I used to steal clothes from the mall back in high school still worked.

I rested the tent bag onto the shelf. I explored a few other tents while I darted my eyes at Melanie every few seconds. Finally, she gave me the signal which was an overarm stretch and a fake yawn. I clutched the tent and headed for the exit when I noticed something odd, something that seemed a touch different than the flow of people, the noises of cashiers, and the aisles and aisles of stuff. A big man held post across the way in the kayak section. He stared at me. I froze. Then, a panic hit me. So I started walking again, pacing down the aisle as I eyed the man. Who was he? He was familiar but out of place. He was someone I knew and didn't know. From what crack or crevice of my life had he crawled out of?

I flung my gaze towards Melanie and gave a tilt of the head in hope she would get my signal. She didn't. So I jabbed my head to the side a bit. She turned her head in the direction of the man. She turned to me, her palms up.

I kept walking towards the door. I could see sunlight. I stared into it. I stared out through the sliding glass doors and into the parking lot. Each step drew me closer. Each step my heart thudded against the cage of my ribs. Each step the sweat of my hands drenched the tent bag. Look casual, I told myself. I told myself a lot of things like act normal. Act like you are supposed to be walking out of this door with this tent in your hand and no one will notice.

And it was true. No one noticed. I was an unseeable thirty-something. I stepped through the door threshold and out into the Montana sun. I had done it. I didn't look back. With each step towards the van I wanted to take off running. But I didn't. I stepped deliberately. Three, four, five, six, seven steps in the parking lot. Then, I heard a voice. The voice was in my head - it must have been - but I heard it through my ears. It said, "It's the linebacker."

"Yes," I replied. "You're right." I turned around to see Melanie easing her way out of the store. I turned to Westy. I turned back again to Melanie. "It's the linebacker," I yelled. She kept on walking. "The guy in the store," I called. She walked towards me. She passed me. As she passed facing straight ahead, she scolded under a sharp-tongued whisper, "We don't know each other, remember?" I reached out to grab her arm. She leaned away. "Pick me up at the pickup," she called back.

She took a turn and darted around to the side of a donut shop on the far side of the parking lot. I paced towards Westy. When I got to the van I hopped in and announced to Aubrey, "Okay. All our shopping's done."

She didn't reply.

I punched the car towards rear of the donut shop. "You okay back there?"

Nothing.

I turned around. That's when I knew. It was the linebacker. Aubrey was gone.

In a panic, my foot kicked the gas pedal. The van accelerated. Melanie was standing where she said she would be. I skidded to a stop. "She's gone," I hollered.

Melanie jumped into the van. "What? Where?"

"The linebacker!" I slammed my elbow against the car window.

"What linebacker? What are you talking about?"

"From the fancy hotel."

"What hotel?" Melanie stopped. "You mean? No!" Melanie smashed her fists on the car dash. She swung her head forward and back. "How could you let this happen to her? How could you do this?"

"I didn't do anything," I shot back. "They took her while we were in the store."

"God. What do we do?"

"I don't know."

"Are you sure it was him?"

"It was him," I spat.

Chapter 36

"I like your sweatshirt."

I stood in the checkout line at a big box hardware store in a town near the university. They sell candy bars at jacked up prices in the checkout line, and I was staring at them.

"I like your sweatshirt."

"What?" I asked. "You don't sell Charleston Chew, do you?"

"Your sweatshirt. Great band," the teller said, pointing at my chest.

"Oh, thanks."

"That's like a throwback, my man."

"Is it?"

"Late 90s, early 2000s, right?"

I nodded. "That's when I peaked."

He laughed. "Long time ago."

I nodded. "Too bad, right?"

"Most of these college kids around here don't know good music."

"Yeah," I said. "You're right."

The clerk looked to be a few years older than me. He had tattoos down his arms and gauge earrings. Had his hair not been salty and his face punched a bit by time, I would have thought he was much younger.

"So this it, brother man?" he asked.

"Yep."

"Okay. One can of spray paint. That will be $4.43 with tax."

I pulled out my wallet and threw down a five dollar bill.

"It still snowing out there?" the teller asked as he handled my change.

"Just a little," I replied.

"Snow in April." He shook his head. "Unbelievable." He tossed the spray can in a bag and handed it to me. "Hey," he said as I turned to leave. "Don't go vandalize anything, my brother."

"Huh?"

"Just playing with ya," he said. "Someone comes in here buying spray paint at 9 p.m. on a Saturday night and pays cash. Well, you know, usually they're teenagers doing their thing."

"Oh," I said. "Yeah. Well you don't have to worry about that. Just a project in my garage."

The teller laughed. "Well, have fun." He leaned in. "Sure as shit would be more fun though to be sixteen again."

I nodded. "Beats house work."

He winked. And as I walked out of the automatic doors he called, "Have fun, brother man." I jogged across the wet parking lot as a few flakes of snow fell on my cheeks and nose and hopped in my car. I started it, turned up the volume on the CD player, and began the one and a half hour drive to Washington DC.

SHOULDER TO THE WHEEL

Chapter 37

"We got to find her, we got to look for her. Oh, God, our little Aubrey. What are you doing? Drive! Drive! What are you doing? Drive the freaking car, James. Jesus! Drive the car! We go to find her!" Melanie seethed, spit flying from her mouth as she raged. Her head and shoulders pointed like a dagger towards me.

"Where should I go?"

"The linebacker. Where is he?"

"I don't know. He was in the store."

"Did he come out?"

"Listen. I. Do. Not. Know."

"We gotta go back in and look."

"We can't go back in the store, Melanie. We just stole a tent."

"God." Melanie grew quiet. Suddenly, she jumped out of the car. She ran out in the open in the middle of the parking lot. I flung Westy around and went after her. She spun in circles. Then she stopped. She pogoed and pointed. She turned back towards me and waved, then turned and pointed. I glanced in the direction she was pointing. A black town car vaulted out of the parking lot and onto the street. I swung the van alongside her. She hopped in. "Follow that car," she hollered, clawing for her seatbelt.

I kicked the pedal. We swerved through the parking lot. The van shot out onto the street just in front of a green pickup truck. The truck slammed its brakes and honked. A glance in the rearview mirror gave me a glimpse of a middle finger shoved out of the truck's driver side window. We barreled forward.

The town car held a defendable lead on us - maybe five or six cars. I wove between cars when openings presented themselves as we jostled through downtown Missoula. We streaked past the comfortably spaced buildings and the manicured pines that stood between them.

"He's turning," Melanie pointed.

"Good eye." I took the turn.

"Where'd he go?"

"I don't know." We spun our heads in every way possible. But we didn't see him.

"Gone just like that, really?"

I followed the road. The car was nowhere in sight. Soon, the buildings receded behind us. The pine trees grew more plenty.

We felt a thud. Our heads lashed forward as Westy jolted. My head smacked the steering wheel. I looked at Melanie. She rubbed her forehead. "What was that?" she asked.

"We got company." I pointed in the rearview. The black town car lurked behind us. It flashed its lights.

"I think he wants us to pull over."

"No way."

"He's got Aubrey, James. Pull over."

I began easing Westy to the median when the town car flashed its lights again.

"What's that?"

"I think he's trying to tell us something. Keep driving."

"Something is vibrating," I said. "What is it?"

Melanie looked at her phone. "Not mine. Must be yours."

"No one ever -"

"It has to be. Find it."

"I'm driving."

"Where is it?"

"I don't know. Sounds like it's back there."

Melanie climbed out of her seat and into the back. She rummaged around a bit as I lumbered down the road, the town car coasting behind us. "Here it is," she finally said. "What do I do?"

"Answer it."

"You answer it." She shoved the phone at me. I grabbed it and said hello. A faraway-sounding voice instructed me to drive a few more miles and then turn right up a mountain road.

"Why," I asked. "Who is this?"

"I've got a message for you."

"What did you do with her? Is she okay?"

The phone was quiet. "Hello, asshole? I want to know that she's okay."

The voice replied, "Just do what you're told." Then the line went out.

I turned to Melanie. "He said to drive two miles and go up this mountain road we're going to see."

"Was it the linebacker?"

"No clue."

"Was it the car behind us?"

"I guess."

"What should we do?"

"I don't know. He just said he had a message for us."

"About?"

"Didn't say."

"And Aubrey?"

"Didn't acknowledge her name."

Trying to buy time, we cruised along for the next few miles at maybe twenty five miles per hour, a good twenty miles per hour under the speed limit. We debated what to do. We listened to our hearts pounding. We wondered what would happen. But we didn't do anything other than let time and Westy take us to the mountain road. I let the momentum take the turn for us, leaning on the wheel just enough to turn it.

We climbed the road with the town car close behind. Soon, the mountain grew steep and Westy coughed and chugged along as she dropped gears and whined.

We climbed higher and higher. Westy grew tired and complained more now. "He isn't calling. How much further do you think?"

"Let me see your phone," Melanie said. I handed it to her. "No service," she said.

"Shit."

We ascended the mountain. Eventually the town car flashed us and flicked its blinker on. I pulled

Westy over at a bend. I'm sure she was happy for the break.

"Take the gun," I exhorted Melanie, shoving the pistol in her lap. "Stay in the car no matter what happens. I'll get out and if something happens to me, I want you to either drive the car out of here or run. Run towards the trees. Hide in the brush. Wait till dark and work your way down the mountain. Avoid the road. Find someone to get you to the police."

I turned before she could reply. I stumbled reluctantly from the van out and onto a patch of wildflowers alongside the dirt road.

"Wait," she called as I flung the door closed. She leaned across from her seat and pushed my door open. "I have to tell you something."

"Now?"

"I'm pregnant."

"You're what?"

"I'm pregnant."

I leapt into the van and crashed into her. I grabbed Melanie around the waist and pulled her tight. We kissed hard and fierce. She pulled back to catch her breath. "I had to tell you," she panted. "Are you happy?"

"Of course," I gasped.

"I think - I think I'm falling in love with you," she said.

"You are?"

"Yes. Yes I think I am." She clenched her mouth and her lips closed completely for the first time. "Do you think?"

"Yes, yes I do."

"Say it."

"I am falling in love with you."

The horn on the town car burst through the van. "What do I do?" I asked.

"I don't know."

"Wait here," I said. "I'll be right back."

"Promise?"

I nodded, hopping from the van. "I'll just get the message and we'll go." I could feel her eyes on my back. I could feel that they had not left me for some time.

I turned towards the town car. What was about to happen? I hid my trembling hands in my sweatshirt pocket. I stepped out away from Westy and walked into the dirt mountain road. I stepped closer to the town car. Each step made a little more buffer between me and Melanie.

The door opened. A foot crashed onto the dirt.

"What's the message?" I called.

"Turn around," the voice demanded. "And sit down on the road with your hands in the air."

"No way," I called back. "Show your face."

"Do it," the voice boomed. "Or else."

I turned around and sat down.

"Arms to the sky," the voice called from behind me. I put my arms up.

Steps grew close.

Melanie, run, I thought. But I couldn't yell. My throat was locked by fear. Just then I heard a banging. I looked up.

"Quick, quick." Melanie banged on the back window of Westy. I caught her eye. "Quick," she pointed behind me. I swung my head around.

It was Nick. It was "Nick" she was saying. He stood right behind me. His arms cocked back, a bar of some sort high above his head. He swung. I ducked. The bar swished through my hair just missing my skull. His body swung around with the momentum. I popped my head up. I dove at him, my shoulder ramming into his stomach. He stuttered back and fell. I plummeted forward and we crashed with an 'uff' to the ground. I lunged for his arm. The bar was gone. I glanced up. It had rolled off somewhere. But I couldn't see it.

The thud of a fist struck my right cheek. My body toppled over, my shoulder landing on his face. He bit me through my shirt. He sunk his craggy teeth into the meat at the base of my neck, twisted his mouth, and yanked savagely. I howled. The flesh ripped away. I dug my teeth into his neck. I bit. I sunk my teeth in as far as I could thrust my jaw and clenched down with every bit of primal rage and yanked and whirled my head side to side like a predator giving a death shake to a bird. He squealed in pain.

We toppled over a few times in the dirt and dust. For a moment I was on top. I turned to the back window of Westy and screamed for Melanie to run. I couldn't see her in the window. I punched him several times. His head did not give way to my fists. His eyes grew wide. The color of his eyes were flooded out by the blackness of his pupils. His thick neck throbbed. He lifted his head. He jabbed it towards me, trying to use his strong forehead as though it were a frying pan. I leaned back. I made a fist, placed my hand upon it, and struck him across the face with my elbow the way I had struck Clark on that forest floor in Virginia weeks before. Again, his head did not give way. His eyes widened further.

"I found you," he spat, blood shooting from his mouth like buckshot. It splattered my face and chest. He grinned. Blood seeped through the gullies between his teeth. It coalesced on his lips where it ran like a river down his chin. "I found you!"

He struck me. We rolled over. Nick got on top. His hands closed in on my neck. I wiggled and withered. I tried to break free. But his hands closed in. Then they were around my neck. "That goddamn book."

He squeezed. Everything narrowed. My breathing felt like it was through a straw. My vision darkened at the edges like I was looking through a straw. At the end of that straw tunnel was Nick's face, his jaw open, his wretched teeth flared out, blood washing down his neck and soaking into his shirt. I tried to speak. All that came out was a cough. The tunnel narrowed. All I could see was Nick's open jaw, teeth flaring. Then I couldn't see anything.

So this was it.

It was over.

Time to die.

As I told you early on, none of this would have happened if Nick had just shoved me harder way back in my crummy apartment with the sticky linoleum floor the night Melanie first brought me the book. I could have hit my head real good that night and that would have been it; the end of the story. That's all I wanted then: For someone to help me do what I was too afraid to do myself. I could have waved a nice thank you to Nick as I drifted off, a contorted smile across my face, blood seeping out of my ears.

I imagine he would have looked down, confused by my smile. And in the rush of his anger, or perhaps the sobering fear that would have washed over him, he would have missed my thanks. Maybe the police would have been called and he would have been arrested for my death. Had I my say in it all, of course, I wouldn't have pressed charges. But sometime later when he had time to stop and take it in, perhaps from the cold of a prison cell, the clarity would wash over him and he would realize that he was set up. But that linoleum floor was far away now and that night so long ago. And now, dying like this? Well, I didn't welcome it.

Chapter 38

The snow fluttered against the windshield, whooshing about and swirling by as I sped down the highway. The headlights on the Honda lit each flake up as it swirled around before being smacked and broken into droplets of water by the car's grill. The music muted the traffic racing alongside me down Route 66 East. Then, the last song on the CD finished and the music stopped. It was 9:57 p.m. I eyed the backpack in the passenger seat beside me. On top of it lay a new can of spray paint that I bought an hour earlier at the hardware store.

I flipped on the radio and flicked through the stations. But there wasn't any good music, just a carousel of new stuff. The new music was so frenetic it must have been thrown together by artists in between panic attacks. It was nothing more than corn syrup sounds for teenagers to chug down with their energy drinks, proof that we don't listen to music anymore, we consume it.

Soon, I landed on a news station. The broadcaster said, "Today, Saturday, April 14, the animus between the Trump White House and Former FBI Director James Comey continues to grow in a very public manner. Comey's new book, *A Higher Loyalty*, accuses the president of building a White House that is a 'cocoon of alternative reality'." I knew what the date was. But it still shook me to hear it spoken aloud.

I kept on driving. I spilled into the maze of streets and intersections and was flushed out into the city. I navigated the car through the sloshy streets of Washington DC. I passed a cemetery and turned onto 2nd Street Northeast. At the tail end of that, I followed the road as it bowed and fused with MacDougal Street. And there it was before me: The gas station that I had found on Google Maps the night before. The gas station where I was sure that Emory Walden had once hid in those days before he fled, never to be seen again.

I pulled over in front of a row of houses. I opened the backpack and got out an envelope. It was the envelope which held inside it the secret of my wife's last words to me, the words she wrote and gave to her brother to give to me after she died. I had tried to open it a hundred times in the nearly four months since my wife passed away. I would slip my pointer finger under the edge of the envelope and ease the glue apart just enough to hear it start to tear. Then I would stop.

I held the envelope in both hands. I smelled it. It smelled only of paper, though I closed my eyes and tried to imagine that it smelled like my wife. But how did my wife smell? I put my finger in the worn edge of the envelope and felt for the spot where the edge was torn. I ran my finger back and forth over the seal where my wife had once licked. "I've got to open you," I said. "I've got to do it tonight. Before I…" I stopped.

"It's me, your husband," I sniffled. "I wonder if you miss me. It's been a year since our last Star Night." I drew in air, wiped my nose and let go a deep sigh. "If I had known that it would be our last one together, I would have - well, I would - I don't know what I would have done. I guess I just regret that our last Star Night happened like it did."

The snow fell. It collected on the hood of the car. "I wonder if you feel the same way. I guess I'll never know. Anyways, I um - I don't know why I'm saying this. It feels skitzoid to talk to no one, except the snow I guess, and this envelope. It's weird. I know you're gone. I know that. But if I don't read this letter then maybe, maybe you're not dead. Does that make sense?"

The snow piled on the windshield. A white film was forming like a frozen wall. I looked at the other windows. The white wall was forming on them too. The world outside faded away. "So, I guess. So anyways. I guess what I'm trying to say is goodbye." I turned the envelope over in my hands and looked at the front. "Jamey" was written in my wife's handwriting. I ran my finger over it, tracing the letters. She had such perfect cursive. I knew it so well. I turned the envelope back over and poked my finger into the edge of the envelope where it was slightly torn. I gave it a tug. The edge of the envelope tore an inch. The sound of the tear filled the cabin. I looked down at the peeled back corner of the envelope. Then I opened my backpack and tossed it inside.

Chapter 39

Then it hit me. Here I am. Still alive. And it seems that I should continue to live. After all, there is someone who needs me.

I coughed and wretched for air. The lights came on. The tunnel widened. The Montana sky, big and blue as ever, gazed down on me. I rolled over and vomited. Nick's body lay a few feet away motionless. I rolled back onto my back. I pulled my head up. Melanie stood with her hands covering her eyes. Suddenly, I heard her wails.

She leaned down and grabbed my shoulder. "Wake up, babe, wake up."

"I'm okay," I called, but nothing came out. She shook me. She stood. She reached into her bag and brandished her phone. She held it over her head and waved it.

I stretched for her leg. I couldn't reach it. She turned towards the van. I rolled towards Nick.

He was gone.

I rolled back towards Melanie. She stood waving her phone in the air. Nick shuffled into my field of vision, his leg dragging behind him. He lunged at Melanie from behind and tackled her to the floor. She kicked frantically. She yanked away from him. She crawled away and stumbled to her feet. Nick lunged and screamed in pain. "Darling, you hit me. Why? Goddamn that hurts!"

Melanie glanced back, her face blank. I lifted my hand in a wave. We caught eyes, her eyes widening like a flash, her mouth tightening into a circle. She looped around Nick and knelt beside me. "James?"

"Get out of here," I pleaded.

"Why?" Nick yelled. "Why?

"Wait here," Melanie told me. She shot up and darted towards the Volkswagen. Then she stopped. She turned, ran back, and slid me the metal bar. She jumped up and raced back towards the Volkswagen. She climbed into the van and hopped out. The gun fell out into the wildflowers. Melanie dropped to her knees. She patted around for the gun. Nick pushed himself up. He struggled to plant a shaky knee under him. The knee gave way and he fell on his face. He started again. He shook his head and, grunting and clawing, got his knee under him. Then he pulled the other knee and straightened his back.

I pushed myself up with the same struggle as Nick. My legs were fine, but my head throbbed. I stumbled about as though the ground shifted beneath me. Nick was on his feet. He slid like a zombie across the dirt road towards Melanie. She was crouched and pawing under the van.

I staggered after Nick. He clawed at his chest, ripping his jacket open. He yanked something out. It was a revolver. One of those snub nose jobs.

"Darling! I just want to be with you," Nick clamored. "And you hit me. Why?" He pointed the revolver at Melanie. "I fucking love you, darling. We can get on the Peanut. We can leave. We can sail away. We can go searching for whatever stupid thing - not stupid, not stupid. We can - I'm enough. You know that. You fucking know that!"

Melanie raked at the wildflowers. Her eyes were locked on the barrel of the snub nose pointed at her and the man standing behind it.

"Tell me you love me," Nick demanded. "Tell me you love me. It's just us now. Come home."

"Hey," I called.

He spun towards me, his face stretched in surprise. "Aren't you dead already?" he snarled.

"Not yet," I called.

He raised the gun and pointed it at me. "Not a problem we can't solve," he laughed.

I threw my hands in the air. "Don't shoot," I said.

"No time to negotiate, poser," he replied. He called back to Melanie, "You gotta see this, darling. I'm saving you."

"Please," I begged.

He thumbed back the hammer. His voice sank so that only I could hear it. "She still talking about those stupid Mexican kids?"

I nodded.

He laughed a bloody laugh. "Guess they were worth dying over."

"Look," I shouted, pointing in the distance. He turned around. But there was nothing. I threw the metal bar at him. I looked over at Melanie. She was scraping at the ground under the van. "Run," I yelled.

She flashed a glance at me and then at Nick. Nick faced the trees, his gun pointed out in front of him. Melanie scrambled to her feet. Nick swung around towards her. He fired the gun. It kicked back. The bullet clanged off the hood of the van. He fired again. The bullet pierced Westy. Melanie tumbled to the far side of the van. She skittered towards the trees.

Nick swung back towards me. "She's always running off somewhere, isn't she?" he laughed, staggering. "I'll find her." He yelled towards the woods, "I'll find you, darling!"

I darted towards the far side of the van for cover but stumbled and fell. I rolled over. I looked up. Nick stood a few feet away. He laughed as he staggered towards me. "You ruined my life," he said.

"I didn't do anything to you," I pleaded. "You're the drug addict. You did this to yourself."

"Nah," he said, rubbing his chin with the gun barrel. "You did this. You sent me this laced shit. You got me hooked." He lifted the gun, pointed it towards me, his hand wobbling. "You're the reason darling left." He crouched down. He placed his hands on his knees as though he were winded. The gun rested on his bad knee. "I love her," he said. "Why? Why won't she help?"

I crawled like a crab, my chest up, my hands and knees beneath me. Nick righted himself as best he could, his body sagging forward. He lifted the gun and pointed it at me. "This ends here, poser," he said.

Bang.

I opened my eyes. Nick stood erect, his eyes white. He pawed at his stomach. The gun fell from his hand the way a child might drop a toy when he's about to cry. He staggered forward. He seemed to linger a moment. Then he crashed to his knees. Like a statue being yanked down by a rope, he toppled face forward. His arms were not out to catch him.

I seesawed to my feet. "Melanie?" I called, spinning around. But Melanie wasn't there. "Melanie, he's down," I yelled. I looked down at Nick. A pool of blood seeped out from under him, spreading in every direction from the center where the hole ripped through his back. "It's okay to come out." Still nothing. I waited in silence. I yelled again. "He's dead." Still no sign of Melanie.

I heard an engine from below. A car poked its way around the bend. It stopped a few dozen yards away. It was a black Cadillac SUV.

"Where's the girl?" I heard a voice say. I turned around. A man walked out from the brush on the other side of the road, the side opposite of where we had parked and where Melanie had fled into the woods.

"What?" I asked.

He holstered a gun. It was the linebacker. "The child. Where is she?"

"You tell me," I gasped. "Wait, what the hell just happened?"

"I shot him," he said as though he were telling me his name. "Was it not obvious?"

"Oh, it was pretty obvious," I shivered, pointing at Nick. "I think it was the puddle of blood that gave it away."

"Now tell me where the child is."

"I thought you had her."

He shook his head.

"What?"

He shook his head again.

"At the store. I saw you."

"That's correct."

"Is she with Melanie?" The linebacker started in the direction of the trees where Melanie had fled.

"No," I said. "I'm confused."

He stopped, turned around, and jogged back to me. "Have a seat," he said. He walked to the van and opened the sliding door. He helped me to sit. "You got some water?" he asked.

"Yeah. In the front." He fetched me the water. I gulped down half the bottle and caught my breath.

"My employer needs me to find her."

"Look, I came out of the camping store and she was gone," I said. I could not stop shivering.

"I know that."

"What do we do about him?" I asked, pointing at Nick's body. "What do we do about his car?"

"Don't worry about that," he said. "Let's just focus on finding little Aubrey." He turned towards the Cadillac and waved it up. The SUV eased up the dirt road, its shiny black detailing dusted by the

Montana soil. The Cadillac stopped in the middle of the road. A man in a black suit jumped out, walked around to the back passenger side, and opened the door. A leg popped out. Then another. Two heels stabbed the dusty road. The man in the suit held Ella Alice's hand as she emerged from the backseat, dark sunglasses wrapped around her face. She walked towards me, her ass swaying the way only Ella Alice's ass did, with the man in the suit holding her hand on the uneven road. Her blonde hair was pulled back in lines as straight as darts and it hung down behind her head in a ponytail. She wore tight black pants that cut above her ankles, the white gold of her skin smooth across the bone. Her top hung loose in layers. And platinum dangled like ornaments from her wrists, neck, and ears.

"Hello, James," she said, gazing down at me as I sat on the floor of the van.

"Ella fucking Alice," I replied. "So you're here for the money, eh?"

"What kind of a woman do you think I am?"

I shook my head. "Oh, I've read all about you, remember?"

"James, you impish, myopic fool." She laughed. "That pittance? No. No, I wanted it back then when I could have made something of it. And I could have built something and put my name on it. But I'm married to Geoff now. He's got all the money I'll ever need. And power. Yeah, that's right. Power. And what good's power unless you use it, right hunny?"

I wiped blood from my neck with a towel I the linebacker had handed me.

"Congratulations. Can someone take a look at my neck?"

The linebacker leaned in and surveyed the gash. "You'll live."

Ella looked over at Nick's broken body and the pond of blood he seemed to be floating in. "What I want is my little girl back."

"What? Why?" I spat. "You don't even care about her."

"How dare you," Ella snapped, stabbing a heel into the dirt. "You know nothing about love. You know nothing about loss. You're just like Emory. You just take and take."

I waved her off. "It's true. That's the kind of person you are. You just want Aubrey because Aubrey doesn't want you."

She spun towards me. "And you're a kidnapper," she scolded, jabbing a finger in my direction. "That's the kind of person you are."

"I'm no kidnapper, lady. I was saving Aubrey from you."

"You're not capable of saving anyone," Ella roared.

"You know some child trafficker tried to take her right on your front porch? What kind of negligent parent let's that happen? Or did you not know that?"

"And I would have done to them what I did to Nick and what I will do to you and that nobody pencil of a girlfriend of yours if I don't get my daughter back."

"Oh, piss off," I sang.

"Emory stole my life from me," Ella charged towards me. The linebacker grabbed her by the elbow. "You think I'm gonna leave my child with anyone associated with him and that, that book?"

"So that's what this is? Just some way to get back at Emory, huh?" I stood. "Look, I don't know where Aubrey is. And even if I did, the only person I'd give her up to is her dad."

Ella stepped back. The linebacker tried to calm her. "Her dad is dead, you fuck." The words flared from her mouth.

"He died? He was with you that night at the hotel."

"No, you idiot. Geoff isn't her dad. Well, legally, yes. But not paternally."

"Then who? Brock?" I hopped to my feet.

Ella reached out and slapped me. "I could only wish." The linebacker yanked her back.

"Emory? No way."

"That's right," Ella seethed, shedding the linebacker with a shake of her shoulders. "We were together. A couple times. He didn't write that in his little book, did he? Hmm," she exaggerated a shrug, her palms upward. "I wonder why."

I plopped down on the floor of the van where the sliding door was open. "No way," I muttered. Really? Emory, a dad? "Did he know?"

"Of course not," Ella said. "Would it have mattered?"

I wasn't sure if it was a question or a statement. I wasn't sure if Ella wondered if things would have been different had Emory known.

Ella turned to walk away and then turned back to me. "Midnight. I want my little girl back. Get her to me by then, or you and the pencil girl are dead." The driver reached into his suit jacket and brandished a flip phone which he tossed at me.

I rolled it around in my hand. "What's this?"

The driver didn't respond.

I turned to Ella. "What's this phone for?"

"A burner," Ella said. "What does it look like? You'll get a text with the address." She shook her head. "Fucking amateur." She turned and extended her elbow out. "Mike, go find that Melanie skank. And have this mess cleaned up." The linebacker nodded and trotted off in the direction of the trees into which Melanie had fled. The driver locked his arm in Ella's and escorted her to the Cadillac.

I sat there in shock with my blood-stained hand pressed against my neck as Ella climbed into the Cadillac. My neck stung. My face throbbed. My body was numb. Soon, the Cadillac started with a hum, turned around to face down the mountain road and backed up alongside where I sat with my legs hanging out the van. The back tinted window rolled down. Ella, smoking a cigarette, leaned out. "Hunny, here's free advice. You might want to get out of here," she said, pointing the cigarette in the direction of Nick's body and his car which sat idling with the driver's door open. She closed the window and then opened it just slightly so that I couldn't see her. "Oh, and one more thing," she said, her voice quivering now. "If you find Emory Walden, tell him about the wake he cast." She closed the window and the SUV sped down the mountain and out of sight.

I hopped into the driver's seat, started Westy, turned onto the mountain road, and kicked the gears into neutral. Westy rolled down the bumpy road with the sense of defeat and confusion that I felt. Where was I going to find Aubrey? What happened to her? As I neared the bottom of the mountain road I heard a buzzing. I stopped and found my phone. But there were no missed calls, no texts. The buzzing started again. I searched through the seat cushions and cup holders and finally found Melanie's phone under the passenger seat. There were two text messages. Both from Penny.

The first read: "I found somebody who is looking for you."

The second read: "Meet us at the bake shop of West Broadway in town."

I headed down the road towards Missoula. A thought struck me between the eyes. Before leaving, I didn't stop and look for the gun that Melanie couldn't reach under the parked van. I pulled over and weighed whether or not to go back for a while. Every thought was heavy, every decision a labyrinth. The light in my head flickered. I forgot why I was sitting on the side of the road. I had this feeling that I had been dropped into a moment by a helicopter, like a troop thrown onto a battlefield in a fight that had been waging for some time but that the soldier was suddenly in the middle of, disoriented and blown over. It was like waking up into a fist fight. And then I remembered why I was sitting on the side of the road, swollen, bloodied, bones sagging underneath tattered seams. The gun. It was back on that mountain. What should I do? Going back was a bad idea. What if someone had gone up the road and found Nick's body, his car, and my gun and then I came cruising up there? What if the police had been called? On the other hand, what if no had gone up there yet and I could still recover the gun before it was found and ultimately traced to me? They could do that with guns, couldn't they? Trace them? So I turned around and drove back to the mountain road and turned up it. I coaxed Westy into chugging her way back up to that terrible place.

As I rounded the last switchback before arriving, an odd sight was laid out before me. This was the place where I had parked, where Nick had died, where his car had been left with the door open and the engine running, wasn't it? Because it was all gone. Nick. The car. The only thing left was the last trickling of a river of water that washed over the place where a pond of Nick's blood had pooled. I ran to the place where Westy had been parked, the tire tracks a clear giveaway. I threw myself to the ground and raked through the wildflowers. But I did not find the gun. I hopped up and kicked at the ground between the tall grass and flowers. But the only thing I struck was a rock. I bolted to Westy, jumped in and got out of there.

Chapter 40

I grabbed the bag and jumped out of the Honda, the wall of snow on the window falling to the ground as I closed the door behind me. I crossed the road and turned left on Michigan Avenue and walked the sidewalk alongside the gas station building. At the far right there was a roof access ladder. It was dark. The snow fell gently on my shoulders. It melted harmlessly. The roads were sloshy and the avenue was empty. Even the gas station pumps sat vacant.

I scurried up the access ladder and plopped over the top and onto the rooftop. My heart ticked like a bomb. I was really here. After all this time. I climbed on hands and knees over the roof hoping to find some evidence of Emory, some connection across time.

In the far corner stood an electric box. I crept over to it and looked around. But there wasn't much to see. At the edge of the roof a pile of refuse slouched onto a few cinder blocks which were plopped on top of a small, snow-covered mound.

I eased my back up against the electric box and watched the snow convalesce on the cinder blocks and a smile snuck up on me. Emory hid on this roof, perhaps in this very spot. This was the closest I had been to him in years. How strange it is to be somewhere with someone when all that's keeping you apart is time. How slim the distance between the past and the present becomes.

"Hey Em," I said, looking over as if he might be there shivering beside me, a can of cheap beer in his hand. I heard him say back, "Heya, Jammy James. Long time, huh?" I reached out for the can of beer. "Can I get a swig?" I closed my eyes and suddenly we were not on a gas station roof, but on the roof of his parents' house all those years ago in high school. He took a gulp and handed me the beer. "Damn, we had it good," he said. "If only -"

I opened my eyes and tears flooded out. I reached into the backpack and extracted the spray paint can and the pistol I bought the day of my wife's funeral. I stood and gazed out over the street below, the orange light from the streetlights illuminating the large, wet snowflakes as they glided lazily to the ground. The canopy of clouds above was bottom-lit from the orange streetlights and light reflected back down over the city like an artificial moon. Buildings jutted into the skyline like broken puzzle pieces. But the streets were empty and all I could hear was the distant whirr of crosswalk signals beckoning for an audience that wasn't there. For a second I felt like Emory must have felt to be above it all, to break apart from the world.

I looked down at the gun. Then, I lifted it and tasted the metal of the barrel. I ran my tongue over the metal and poked it into the little hole at the end. Something about it tasted familiar and then I laughed at the realization that blood and gun barrels both taste of metal. I pulled the gun from my mouth, shook the can of spray paint and bent over and started spraying my goodbye message when something caught the corner of my eye. Something was on the electric box. I stepped over and could just make it out in the orange glow. Something was spray painted.

I put the gun down and wiped my hand over the white film of snow on the electric box. It was a crude graffiti cartoon, no taller than my forearm.

A message from Emory?

That's what I thought at first. But, I knew Emory's work in and out. I was there when he started painting and helped him pull off many of his early stunts. And I quickly saw that this tag was not done by him. That I was sure of. Still, there was something familiar about the way it was drawn, as though I knew the artist well.

The tag looked something like half of a female figure, the left side missing on the upper half as though it were unfinished. It had one eye and it seemed to be looking at me as if it had something to say.

"What do you want from me?" I asked the troll with one arm painted across the electric box. But she just stared back. I looked down at the gun as it rested peacefully in the snow. I looked up at the painting. And still it stared. "What is it?"

I followed its eye. It wasn't looking at me. It was looking towards the trash pile. I crouched and crawled towards the pile. What was it? I lifted a few of the cinder blocks, pulled away a piece of aluminum siding, and brushed away some snow. Beneath the pile was a smooshed black trash bag. Wait, I thought.

Didn't Emory write something about hiding his stuff in a black trash bag? I crawled back to my backpack and felt around. But I had forgotten to bring my copy of *Discontents: The Disappearance of a Young Radical*. I crawled back to the pile and ripped the bag open. A second trash bag was below. I ripped through that. Inside, was a zipped up duffle bag. Was it? Could it really be? This has to be it, I thought. Emory's belongings. Maybe some money, but who cared? Maybe there were answers. Maybe there was a note.

Chapter 41

One of those bells that hang on a restaurant door chimed as I entered the bakery shop on West Broadway in Missoula. I had my hood up to hide the holes in my neck and my sunglasses on to hide the swelling on my face. It reminded me of a line in Emory's memoir, when he was dressed like this and Ella Alice jokingly told him he looked like the Unabomber.

Penny sat in a booth by a window that overlooked the wide road and an empty lot next to a rent-a-car shop. Across from her sat Aubrey, eating a donut and sipping a soda. I walked in, wiped as much dust off of me as I could, and sat down next to Aubrey.

"Are you okay?" I gasped as I threw my arm around her and squeezed her close to me, the scent of her hair rising into my nostrils.

"She's fine," Penny said. "Why're you so salty?"

"What happened?"

"Something was bad," Aubrey said. "I was waiting, like you said to. There was a car. Someone was going to try to steal me again. So I ran and hid."

"Did you try to kidnap her?" I whispered sharply to Penny.

"No. It didn't go down like that," she said, leaning back. "I scooped her at a gas station down the road."

"How'd you know who she was?" I asked, incredulously.

"She asked me to buy her some grub. I asked her if she was okay. She said she was lost. I asked her who she was looking for. And she said James and Melanie."

"Bullshit."

"You cuss like that in front of the kid?"

"I'm sorry, Aubrey," I said. "Is it true?"

Aubrey nodded. "Miss Penny said she would help me find you."

"I keep it 100, don't I kid?" Penny winked at Aubrey. Aubrey smiled and gave her a thumbs up. "You give this kid a shower lately?"

"That's none of your business," I said. "What are you doing all the way out here?"

"Seriously?" Penny said. "Are you low key trying to do this in front of the kid?"

"I'm not letting her out of my sight," I snorted.

"Your call." Penny sipped her coffee. "First, I want the money. Second, I want the truth about Clark."

"I don't know a thing about either," I said.

"Oh, that's too bad," Penny said scooting out of the booth. "You really want me to do this?"

"Do what?"

"I'm turning you in for child kidnapping." She stood. "And maybe they'll find something else to pin on you. And what'll happen to Aubrey? State's ward, I bet. End up in an orphanage, maybe bounce around a couple of foster homes getting fondled by sweaty fifty year olds with sex dungeons."

"What are sex dungeons?" Aubrey asked.

I turned to Aubrey. "Nothing. Pretend you didn't hear that please." I turned to Penny. "You shouldn't say stuff like that in front of a little girl. You'll give her nightmares."

"Right now it's just a nightmare. But with a phone call, that's her future. So you decide, are you going to give me the money?"

"Money?" Aubrey asked.

"Aubrey, please. We're just making adult talk."

"Is Melanie a grown-up? Are you a grown-up?"

"Sorry, um. That's not what I meant."

Penny turned to leave.

"Okay, sit down," I begged Penny in a whisper. Penny sat and folded her hands in front of her. She cocked her head to one side as if to say, "I'm listening." I turned to Aubrey and gave her a big hug, then placed my hands over her ears. "I don't have the money. But I know where it is. It's a few days hike up near the Northwest Peak. About an eight hour drive. You come with me, we find the money, and you can have it as long as I never see or hear from you again and you promise to forget about Clark."

"Forget Clark? You just want me to forget him? He's gone, he's really gone?" Penny was shaking. I stabbed my head in the direction of Aubrey. Penny got up and ran off. I leapt up after her. But she disappeared into the women's bathroom.

"Is she sick?" Aubrey asked.

"Maybe," I said, sitting back down. I sat with Aubrey and watched the women's bathroom for some time. Finally, Penny emerged. She labored over to our booth and flopped into the seat.

"Are you sick?" Aubrey asked. Penny didn't respond.

I covered Aubrey's ears. "Penny, I'm sorry. I don't know. Yeah. I mean, don't forget him, forget him. Just. You know what I mean."

After a long pause, she said, "Clark was my BAE. My partner. And you just want me to pretend?"

"Don't talk so loud," I shushed, nodding towards Aubrey.

"He's gone. He's really gone." Penny put her elbows on the table and pressed her hands against her temples. She looked like a tarot card reader processing the cards before her. "Why is this happening?"

"He attacked me." I leaned in and whispered, "It was me or him."

"That's your excuse?"

I put my hand to my mouth. The sight of Clark's bloodied face as I pulled his mask off came into focus. I shook my head and it blurred from view.

"I loved him," Penny said. "He loved me."

"Some kind of love," I said.

"Wow," Penny said, peeling her elbows from the table. Her suddenly erect body told me she was glaring at me, though her eyes were obscured by her bangs as always. "Wow. I see. I see how you see me now. You think I'm this, this, this cunt. Let me guess, Melanie put that idea in your mind?"

I shook my head. "I don't care why you're doing what you're doing. I know you have reasons."

Penny's body loosened. "Is Melanie still in the shade about my mom?"

"Yes," I said. "I never said anything."

"Why?"

"I don't know," I said. I looked around the placid donut shop. "Melanie doesn't know about Clark."

Penny nodded. "Okay," she said. "I see. Okay."

"Look, it's not worth anything, but I'm - I didn't mean to." I turned and looked out the window and watched a logging truck pass down the road. "I. I'm sorry."

Penny rubbed the palm of her hand up her nose. "Something's gotta come from this," she said.

I pulled my hands from Aubrey's ears. "Aubrey, can you wait here a second?"

"Don't leave me," she protested, tears welling in her eyes.

"I'm not going anywhere. Penny and I are going to go get something to eat. Want another donut?"

Aubrey nodded.

"What kind?"

"Pink frosted."

"Good choice. You can see us the whole time and we'll be able to see you."

I got up and Penny followed my lead. We walked to the ordering line. "Jesus on a bike, what happened to your neck?" Penny whispered. "Didn't wanna scare the kid, but did you get attacked by a wolf or something?"

"Something like a wolf," I whispered back. "I got a big problem. Aubrey's psycho mother tracked me down. Said she's gonna kill me and kill Melanie if I don't return Aubrey to her."

Penny nodded.

"So I need to take Aubrey back to her by midnight." I grabbed Penny by the elbows. "I think they got Melanie."

"Bullshit," she said, pushing my hands away. "You're just feening to get out of here."

"No bullshit," I said. "Look, don't believe me? Come with me tonight. But you gotta give me Aubrey back or there won't be any money."

"You'll probably do me like you did -"

"Do you know what it's like to carry that around? Look, we need each other right now," I said. "Okay?"

"So this is business?"

I nodded. "It's just business."

"It's nothing personal?"

I nodded.

Penny nodded. "Okay," she said. She nodded again, as if nodding at her nod. She reached her hand out and we shook. "Hundo P," she said, "Business. Just business"

"So you'll come? Is that what Hundo P means?"

"Something good's gotta come from this," Penny said. "Yes. Yes, you owe me that money. There's still time. There's still time."

I looked over my shoulder at Aubrey.

"The kid's bananas. That's tragic you gotta return her," Penny smiled. "Listen, you're not a bad person. I know that. I'm not either."

I looked over Penny's mop of hair and searched through the layers for her eyes. As if noticing what I was doing, she combed her hand through her bangs and I saw her soft, pale irises and the purple-black bags below them.

Then we bought some donuts and ate with Aubrey as she licked the icing off her pink frosted donut.

At 9 p.m. the text came with a link to GPS coordinates.

"What's up with your van?" Penny asked, eyeing the busted rear bumper and the dent in the back hatch as we finally left the bakery. The bakery had been empty of other customers for some time but the sweet old lady in cowboy boots who ran the place was too nice to ask us to leave and we had nowhere to go.

I excused Penny's question with, "Fender bender."

"Fender bender?" Penny asked, pointing to the bullet hole.

"Fender bender," I said.

The three of us climbed into Westy and headed to the location. Google Maps took us out of town and off into the dark Montana countryside. We drove for half an hour, winding about as we watched scant lights in the distance grow closer then fade off behind us. The air was cool, the sky crisp and moonless. The stars were so plenty and bright that the canopy above looked like the sprawling cities of distant solar systems all connected through the dotted highways built by some greater intelligence. It was such a lonely sight when cast against the dark road that rolled out before us.

"Can you pull over?" Penny asked. "I gotta make buzz before we lose reception."

"No way," I said. "I don't want you telling anyone where we are."

"No one knows I'm here."

"Come on," I said.

"Please," she said. "Just do me this kindness."

"Kindness?"

"Clark's gone. You know that. Please."

I pulled Westy onto the dirt median.

"BRB." Penny hopped out.

"How do you know I won't just leave you here?" I asked, as she stood on the dirt in the open door.

"Because," she said. She shut the door and disappeared into the Montana night. A few minutes later, the door opened and Penny climbed in.

"Ready?" I asked.

She nodded, her head facing the black landscape.

"I know it doesn't –" I started the engine. "I lost my mom when I was seventeen," I said. "I know it doesn't help."

"She's still alive," Penny said. "There's still time." She pushed her palm up her nose and took a deep breath. "It's just a God-fumble. All of it."

"I know," I said.

"You do your whole life for someone else. And then," Penny said. "I'm all she can rely on. My dad said he'd... Jesus on a bike, why I ever believed anything he said. And William, he's - well he's. It's just a God-fumble. All of it."

Soon we arrived. We drove up an unpaved road, crossed a gentle creek, and climbed a hillside. The road was then swallowed by giant conifers on either side as we entered a tunnel of trees. The road, wide as before, ran like a gravel valley through the tree trunks which loomed on either side. As our headlights hit them, these tall, ghostly statues cast eerie shadows on the forest floor.

Then the rain came in over the mountains. It had not rained the entire time we had been in Montana. And I had forgotten about rain in a sense, as though it were something that only happened back east. But here it was, familiar again. I rolled down the window and took in its scent. Westy began to cough and groan and threatened to quit. "Just a little further," I coaxed. "Keep going."

Up ahead, lights flickered through the passing trees. I turned Westy around at the bottom of a narrow dirt driveway that looked to be the address. She was pointing down the hill, her idling engine seeming to struggle to catch its breath.

"Okay. Wait here," I told Penny.

"No chance, I'm coming with."

"Look you got our car. I'll leave the keys. Where we gonna go? If I show up with some stranger," I paused, "that you-know-who doesn't know, she'll probably -" I looked over my shoulder at Aubrey and then back at Penny. "Look, I already had my chance to get rid of you, remember?"

Penny looked up the driveway at the cabin above and the light glowing through the big windows. "How much you think this Airbnb costs to rent?"

I climbed into the back of the van and sat down next to Aubrey. I told her I was sorry, but that I had to return her to her mother. She screamed and cried and pounded my chest. I told her it was the law and that she needed to be in school and that it was the right thing for her. She said she didn't care. She said she didn't want to leave me. I said I didn't want to leave her.

"Will you come visit?" she asked, her screams gone now and in their place a chorus of tired sobs. I lied and told her I would. It was the worst lie I ever told.

I opened the sliding side door and stepped out. "Let's go. Your mom's waiting."

Aubrey oozed out. "Give me a big hug," I said. I picked her up and she squeezed me tight, resting her chin on my shoulder and pressing her knotted blond hair against my ear. How safe it felt to hold her. "You're a good dad," she whispered. I squeezed back and closed my eyes and told myself to never let go. But I knew I had to do it to save Melanie and the baby that bloomed inside of her.

"You're a good kid," I replied. "Never let anyone tell you different. Never, ever."

"I won't."

"Be brave."

"I will," Aubrey whispered, "just like you." I put her down and took her hand and together we clambered up the driveway. Aubrey softly sang, "Happy faces, happy places, I can see happy faces."

"It's going to be okay," I assured her. "Your Mom missed you." We climbed some steps onto a porch. With hesitation, I knocked on the sliding glass door and pulled it open.

Inside, Ella Alice sat on a cream leather sofa by a fireplace, her dark sunglasses wrapped around her face, the light of the roaring fire dancing on the lenses. She sipped a glass of white wine from her good hand, her paperweight hand resting on her lap, and said, "My little Aubrey."

Her driver stood in the open kitchen uncorking a bottle of wine. The ceiling was high and slated in stained wood. The walls were stained wood, too. The place was decorated like a luxury cabin stereotype with animal busts, a chandelier above made of antlers, and high-end country-style furniture. A brown fur carpet was pinned under the heels of Ella's silver pumps. A gray wood farm-table with two long, wood benches idled in the kitchen.

Scotty sat facing the fire in a rocking chair. The chair creaked on the hardwood floors as Scotty rocked slowly, his feet pointed inward. His back was to us and his round shoulders bobbed in that familiar and soothing rhythm that kept time in the far off world that Scotty occupied. It looked like the same rickety chair from back east.

"Here's your flip phone," I said.

Ella didn't respond.

"Okay, I guess I'll - I'll leave it here." I set the phone down on a gray wood table by the sliding door.

Ella sipped her wine.

"So, what now?"

"Aubrey, I missed you," Ella said.

Aubrey looked down. "Hi Scotty," she mumbled.

"Aubrey, come sit by your mother."

Aubrey squeezed my hand. "Do I have to?"

Ella gasped. "Aubrey, how could you say that? You unappreciative little brat. Do you know what I've done for you? Do you know the sacrifices I've made?"

"I'm sorry, mother. I didn't mean it."

"Didn't you miss me?" Ella peered over her wine glass. Her face drooped. "I'm sorry," she said. "I missed my little girl."

Aubrey nodded. "Can I go see Scotty?"

Ella's face stiffened. "I just saved you from this, this rube and a life of poverty and sorrow and destitution. Where is your sense of gratitude?"

Aubrey let go of my hand and stepped forward. "Oh, you look disgusting," Ella sighed. "Stand there." She turned to her driver. "Richard, go run a bath for Aubrey. She certainly needs it." The driver gave a "yes ma'am" and disappeared down the hall. "I see your injuries are settling in," Ella sneered, waving her paperweight hand in my direction. I touched the knob below my cheek and the other perched on my upper lip.

"Where's Melanie?" I demanded. "I'm not leaving here without her."

"Come again? Your words are a bit, well cloudy. Must be the swelling," she chuckled.

"Melanie. Where is she?"

"Oh," Ella brought the wine glass to her lips. "Yes, her. I'm sorry, she's so, so forgettable that it slipped my mind." She sipped her wine. "Melanie is outside in the woods with Mike."

"Why?"

"In case you try to pull something."

"Pull something?"

"Aubrey, how did you let this troglodyte kidnap you?"

"He didn't kidnap me, Mother."

Ella laughed. "You gullible little fool."

"He loves me. He took care of me," Aubrey cried.

"He loves you? He loves you? What about me? What about what I've done for you?" Ella howled. "I am your mother. This man doesn't love you. He's using you. He's using you to feel good about his sad little life."

"He loves me," Aubrey sobbed.

"I love you," Ella stammered. The veins on her temples flared. "That's who loves you."

"I want to be loved," Aubrey sniffled.

"Love isn't about cuddling and toys and smiles and fun," Ella yelled. "It's about opportunities. It's about protection. It's about doing what you have to do. Any other kind of love dies quick and hard. You'll see that someday." Sweat broke through the canvas of makeup on Ella's face. Little beads collected on her nose, forehead and cheeks. Her face betrayed her, tinged in crimson. She dabbed at it discreetly as if tending to spilled wine at a cocktail party. "I love you. That's who loves you."

I reached out and grabbed Aubrey's hand. "Give me Melanie back."

Ella guffawed. "Or what?"

"Or I take Aubrey and leave."

"Aubrey, go to the bathroom and close the door," Ella pointed. "I have to explain something that your boorish companion here is not getting."

"No," Aubrey protested, stomping her feet.

"Children," Ella sighed, putting her wine glass down on an end table. "People always act like they're so magical, don't they James? But the truth is, they're just little shits like you and me who are given too much wiggle room. We love them an ounce more than we want to strangle them." She stood, looming over the room, and in a devastating tone said to Aubrey, "If you don't love me by doing as I say then so help me God I will lock you in a closet and you will live on celery and toilet water for a month. And when you come out, if you do come out that is, you will be begging me to forgive you for what a petulant little disease you are as you crawl pathetically across the floor."

"Scotty?" Aubrey called. "Please help."

"You are insane," I chided. "How could you talk to her like that?"

"Do you have children, James? I thought we've been over this. You do not have children. So shut the fuck up and come back to me when you've got an ounce of experience."

I turned to Aubrey and squatted. "Do you know who your dad is?"

"She knows Geoff," Ella interjected.

"No, you're real dad. Do you know who he is?"

Aubrey shook her head.

I stood. "She doesn't know?"

"It's not her business," Ella said. She stepped towards us, her heels clicking. "Now let go of my child's hand and turn around and leave. And when you leave, I will signal Mike to let Melanie go."

"No," I said, stepping back. "I want to see Melanie first."

Ella took another step forward. "Not going to happen."

I straightened up. "Make it happen."

Ella rubbed her eyes with her thumb and pointer finger. "You're not understanding, James." She stepped forward. I pulled Aubrey towards me.

"No," I objected. "You're not understanding. Give me Melanie or I take Aubrey."

Ella stopped and snickered. "Just where are you going to go, hunny? You go out that door with Aubrey and it's over for you and that pencil girlfriend of yours."

"Mother! Why are you saying that?"

"It's unfortunate you're hearing this," Ella said to Aubrey, "but I told you to go into the bathroom and close the door."

Ella lunged forward and grabbed Aubrey by the arm. I tugged. Ella tugged back. I grabbed Aubrey by two hands and tugged. Ella reached to grab Aubrey with her other hand, and quickly realized that she couldn't. Her fake hand just clawed at Aubrey. But it could not squeeze. I yanked. Aubrey and I fell back onto the wood floor. I glanced up to see Ella menacing over us, the scar across her face flickering in the light from the fireplace. Her sunglasses had fallen off in the tousle. Her empty eye glared through me. She reached to her side, swiping for a purse that wasn't there. She spun and looked towards the couch. By then I was on my feet. I saw her phone on the armrest of the cream couch. "Richard," she screamed. "Call Mike."

"Scotty!" Aubrey screamed.

Scotty stood shakily. He glanced around the room, his arms crossed, his toes pointed at one another. He lumbered towards us.

"Scotty! Help!" Aubrey screamed. Scotty looked through crossed eyes at Ella. She looked at him. Her jaw loose. Her face sagging. Her body damp and heavy. Scotty cupped his hands over his ears and swayed, his head sinking forward.

A shot rang out somewhere outside. The sound of its bang ricocheted off the high wood ceilings and panel wood walls. The sound froze us all a moment. I rushed to the door, threw it open, and burst onto the deck, the rain crashing all around me. In an instant I was soaked through.

"Melanie!"

I ran down the steps. I glared into the direction of the shot. All I could see was darkness and the ghostly trunks of a few nearby conifers.

"Melanie!"

The rain poured down.

A shadow emerged from between the trees like a convict emerging from a tunnel. It was Melanie. She sprinted towards me. Her arms flailed above her. "James!"

"Melanie!"

"Run!" She grabbed my arm as she flew by. I turned to follow.

"Down the driveway," I steered her. She stumbled as she turned. But she caught her balance and I ran after her down the hill. I stopped, turned back and gazed at the cabin above. Rain pelted the sliding glass door. It cascaded down the door in oozing waves leaving behind a blurry outline of Ella Alice as she stood looking out, the chandelier light cast over her. Then, a silhouette slid up beside her about waist high. A nose pressed against the glass. A hand waved. I waved back from the darkness of the driveway. The rainwater carved tiny canyons down the hill between my feet. I waved, sad and certain that Aubrey could not see me.

"Let's go!" Melanie yelled.

I spun around and chased Melanie down the hill. We careened into the side of Westy. Melanie hurled open the passenger door. She dove in. "What the hell is she doing here?" she screamed. Penny sat in the driver's seat.

I jerked the sliding van door open and jumped in. "I'll explain later," I hollered. "Penny, start the car, start the car, let's go!"

Penny froze. "I can't."

"You better or we're all dead!"

"I can't. I can't drive."

I screamed for her to get in the back. She climbed over the seat. I climbed up front. "Where the hell are the keys?" Penny dug around in her pocket. She shoved the keys into my hand.

I turned the key. Nothing.

I turned it again. Westy gurgled.

"What, what is it?" Melanie called from the back.

"The battery?"

"No, no, no. Try it again."

"I already tried. Twice."

"Why the fuck didn't we get a new battery?"

"Shitty, shit." I banged the steering wheel.

"They're shooting at us?" Penny screamed. "I heard a gun."

"Shut up, Penny," Melanie scolded.

"I heard a gun," Penny wailed.

"Do something, James."

"Let me try again."

I put my left foot on the brake and hovered my right foot over the gas pedal. I turned the key and pumped the pedal.

Westy gurgled and coughed. Then, she awoke. I flicked on the headlights, and barreled down the gravel road.

"Tell me what she's doing here," Melanie demanded as we crossed the creek. We swayed out onto the main highway.

"She followed us." I said.

"Obviously. Why's she here?"

"I can answer that," Penny said.

"Don't," Melanie interrupted.

"Why do you think she's here?" I asked.

"You bitch," Melanie barked at Penny.

"That your best insult?" Penny shot back. "You know I just like seeing you shook."

"So how'd you follow us?"

"Not until I get the money."

Melanie seethed. "It was the computer, wasn't it?"

"What computer?" I asked.

"That computer she gave us."

"I don't remember any computer."

"Because we never used it."

"Shitty-shit," I said. "I do remember it. It's somewhere back there."

"James, pull over and toss her out and toss the fucking computer."

"Kindness, James," Penny said.

"Alright. Shut up, the both of you," I shouted. "We're not gonna toss Penny out. And that's that."

"That's our money," Melanie said.

"You said you didn't even want it anymore," I said.

"Well I don't want her to have it," Melanie countered.

"Enough!" I banged the steering wheel. "We need to figure out where we're going now. How do we make sure Mike's not following us? How are we going to get rid of this car?"

"They're not following us." Melanie slouched in her seat. The blood sank from her face and pooled into her trembling hands.

I turned to her. "How do you know?"

She reached into her jacket pocket. She presented the gun. My gun.

"Oh," I sighed. It was a flat, airless sigh; I felt the oxygen get sucked out of my chest as though my lungs were being shrink wrapped. The three of us drove along the dark Montana roads for some time, our lungs empty. The rain pummeled the roof. The rat-tat-tat of the raindrops hammered around inside our heads.

James Wallace Birch

335

CLARITY

Chapter 42

The snow continued to fall. I stared at the black duffle bag inside two trash bag layers. I tried to pull it out. But the hole in the bags weren't big enough. So I tore the trash bags away and tugged at the duffle bag. It was heavy. The straps strained as I tugged at it. But I got it out of the trash bags and dragged it over by a roof HVAC and, panting, unzipped it. Inside I found a folded note sitting as if on a throne atop stacks of white envelopes. I picked it up but saw that it was taped to one of the envelopes.

So I picked up the envelope. And as I ripped the note off of it, a bounded wad of cash fell out onto the wet rooftop. I shoved the damp cash in the bag and glanced around as if someone might be watching me. I pulled the cash out again and flipped through it. I didn't trust what I was seeing so I tossed it back in the bag and pulled it out a third time. It was as it was before, a wad of cash the size of which I had never before held. I stuffed it back in the bag and unfolded the letter. Snowflakes collected on the paper as I read:

> *James,*
> *If you're reading this, if you came all this way, then I know you care enough to help me. Please publish my book. Inside you will find the money Fletcher Spivey gave me. It's dirty to me and I don't want it. But it may be of some use to you. Then again, maybe not. So burn it if you like. Just don't let it fall into the hands*

of Ella or Brock or anyone else - there's nothing worse than money in ignoble hands. Whatever you do, move this money before you publish the book or someone's going to come find it.

The letter continued. But I looked up from the letter as tears poured out. My vision was blurry. It was too dark to read all that well anyways. So I slipped the letter in my pocket. I checked my phone. It was fifteen minutes past midnight.

I laid down on the rooftop and watched the white flakes fall from the gray-melon clouds above. "Wow," I sniffled. "I'm still alive." I fumbled around and grabbed my backpack. I pulled the spray can out. Above and a little back from where my head lay was a lip that jutted out from the HVAC. I shook the can, sat up, and sprayed the date on the bottom side of the lip: 4/15/18.

Star Night had come and gone and I was still alive.

I grabbed the black duffle bag, hauled it across the rooftop, and waited for the traffic to die down. I threw the bag down into the dumpster behind the gas station. I parried down the ladder on the Michigan Avenue side. I slipped behind the building and around to the dumpster where I hid with the duffle bag filled of money for some time. Finally, the road was completely clear. I grabbed the bag, its weight dragging me down, and scrambled across the road to MacDougal Street. Grunting, I hurled the bag into the back of my Honda Element.

Chapter 43

In the depths of that black night, as Penny slept on the floor of the van, I shook Melanie awake and motioned her to follow me outside. The rain stopped. But the ground was wet and we sloshed along barefoot out of earshot of Westy.

"You okay?" I asked, wrapping my arm around Melanie's waist.

"Yeah, I'm fine. They just threatened me a bit."

"Is the baby okay?"

"The baby's the size of a seed. She's fine."

"I was afraid that -"

"Why is she here?" Melanie asked in a low, caustic tone.

"Look, I um –"

"I don't want to hear a lie," Melanie pulled away.

"She's, um, she had Aubrey. She found Aubrey. And I made her a deal. I had to give Aubrey back to get you back from Ella. Ella, well, the Mike guy. See, Ella told me if I didn't get Aubrey back she'd have Mike kill us both."

"God."

"Yeah."

"That breaks my heart about our little Aubrey."

"I abandoned her. I threw her away." I shook my head. "What is wrong with me?"

"You didn't abandon her. You cared for her."

"It's devastating. You wouldn't believe how Ella treats her own kid." I paused. "Maybe I should go back for her."

"James, you didn't abandon Aubrey. You helped her. You helped her more than you know."

"What are you talking about?"

"Maybe she was just supposed to be a part of your life for that short period. Did you think of that? And maybe that was the role you played in each other's lives and you're both better for it. Maybe she wasn't yours to save. And that's okay."

"Maybe," I shrugged.

Melanie looked off towards the van. "Let's get rid of Penny. I'm back now."

"I can't," I said. "I just can't."

"James. What's going on?"

"There's something you should know."

"What happened? What happened to Nick?"

"Oh, um, jeez." I stopped and tried to build the courage. Finally, I got it out, "Nick. Mike shot him. He's dead."

"He's dead?" Melanie turned around and stepped away. "This is your fault."

"What is?"

She turned back towards me. Her face looked different. "How did you know where Ella Alice was?"

"What are you talking about?"

"Don't lie to me. You knew where she lived that whole time and you didn't tell me."

"Me? I never said I knew where she lived. What about you? How did you know where she was?"

"You knew," she said. "You knew that street too well. Don't try to turn this on me. I asked you a question."

"I, um," I looked away and rubbed my swollen jaw. I had this feeling like I was being bulldozed over. It was time to be honest. "I had already found her some time before, before you showed up at my door. I wanted to, um, confront her. Ask her some questions. I thought it might help me, you know."

"No, I don't. Tell me, James. Help you what?"

"Help me put all of this Emory stuff behind me. Move on."

Melanie stood and swallowed this down. I watched her cradle it in her stomach for a while. "You sent the book to my house," she spat. "It was you. You wrote the poem. You set all of this up. It was you. You lying, psychotic - oh and I let myself think that I was falling in love with you - what is wrong with me?"

"What? You've got to be kidding me. I didn't write that poem. I didn't set this up. Come on, please. Don't say that."

"You got Nick high. On what, what was it? Meth? PCP? You knew he'd come looking for me and that he would lose it if he saw me with you."

"Hey, I didn't put any pipe to his lips. The guy had a drug problem. And a serious inability to control his rage, mind you. What's that got to do with me?"

"Yeah, yeah, both of which you exploited."

"I didn't do that. I've never even talked to the guy I don't think. I didn't exploit anything."

"Well you got him the drugs. You got him hooked. I'm not sure how, but I know you did it."

"You're talking crazy," I pleaded. "You're in shock from everything."

"Don't you dare call me crazy. And I am in shock! I'm in shock of how blind I've been of you. I'm in shock of what a psycho you are. Yeah, I'm in shock. I am in shock of how your actions killed my boyfriend and nearly got me killed."

"I didn't do it," I pleaded.

"You're the crazy one."

"What the hell? You're blaming all of this on me? You came to me, remember? You begged me to take you away. You're the one who said you wanted to go find somewhere where you can know what most people will never know. Or, whatever the hell it was."

"Yeah, I was naive; naive to believe in anything. But this is the world we're in and that's all there is. No fumes, just the world. Nick was right. And I was naive. He only ever got a little violent when he was blasted, but never like that. That wasn't coke. That was something else. He had his flaws, but he didn't deserve - and now he's dead. He's dead James. And it's your fault. You drugged him. You convinced me to leave him there behind that building. You put the ideas in my mind. And look what else - look what else you made me do. There are dead people, James. And it's your fault."

I grabbed Melanie at either elbow. "Get a hold of yourself. This is ridiculous. I feel terrible about what happened - utterly destroyed. But it's not your fault, it's not my fault. It's just - it's unanticipated stuff that happened. I didn't write that poem, I didn't plant those clues. We gotta stick together. We have a pregnancy to think about."

"Yeah? Well, how do you explain this note from Emory?" Melanie reached into her pajama pants pocket and brandished a folded piece of paper. "I found it in your bag."

Chapter 44

And still the snow fell. I sat in my car on MacDougal Street across from the gas station for a long time staring at the note Emory had left me in the duffle bag.

Whatever you do, move this money before you publish the book or someone's going to come find it.

But Emory was wrong. No one had come to find the money in the many years since I had published his book. The note continued:

Goodbye James. Thank you. You'll never see me again. I'm off to West Virginia and then Montana. I plan to -

But the letter was torn off below that line. Where was he off to? Where did he go? Why did he tear it off? I sat and tossed the question around and finally the answer came to back me. He wrote down where he was going and then changed his mind and tore it away so that no one could ever find him. That had to be it.

I dug into my backpack and pulled out the envelope my wife's brother gave me after she died. Open it, I thought. Just open it. But, still I couldn't. Then I glanced in the rearview mirror and saw the duffle bag sitting in the back.

Chapter 45

We arrived in the afternoon of the next day at the Kootenai National Forest in northern Montana. It was the most beautiful place I have ever seen. The landscape was unencumbered by the decay that follows humans everywhere they go. Birds with wingspans as long as a person is tall soared above. The jagged edges of mountains were smoothed into waves of green conifers, as though a giant hand had sandpapered them with moss. And then there were mountains that didn't have more than five trees on them, their crags and blemishes boldly exposed in nude confidence.

Elk sauntered unafraid across the road. The path, South Fork Road, weaved up, down and through a tapestry of flowers, plants, trees, and boulders. There were giant trees with trunks as wide as Westy. You could come around a bend and a field would open up that was the length of two trains. Off in the distance a mountain would remind you that around the next bend there was another wonder to discover[9].

Westy was miserable. She moaned with every hill we climbed and sighed in relief with every hill we

---

[9] For an example of what I'm talking about, look at this street view of the South Fork Road on Google Maps: http://bit.ly/gmaps-southfork1. Then, move forward a little bit (northbound) and behold the field to your left (or, you can just click on this map to see it): http://bit.ly/gmaps-southfork2.

descended. Finally, we made it to Yaak, an outpost at an intersection with a few red-roofed buildings. We stopped at one and got some food, then traveled down a dirt road a ways and made camp.

"I'm not sure how we're supposed to do this," Melanie complained over a can of beans that she cooked on the stove we had hooked up to the griddle. "Penny doesn't have any hiking gear."

"I'm a go. Hundo P. I'll be totally fine," Penny said, defensively. "I've got my sneakers. And if you let me borrow a clean shirt, then I'm good."

"My clothes are too tight for you."

"Are not."

"Are too."

"Girls," I interjected. "Enough." I shook my head. "Melanie, let her borrow some of your clothes."

Melanie climbed into the van, grabbed a red sweatshirt, and tossed it at Penny.

"Thanks," Penny muttered.

"It's not just the clothes," Melanie said. "We only have two adult hiking packs. We only have enough food for two people. We only have enough space to carry water for two people. It's not possible to pull this off. It's suicide if something happens out there."

Penny squeezed the sweatshirt over her head. "You're just trying to get rid of me."

"Yeah, why are you here?"

"We all know why she's here," I said. "Let's just figure this out."

"Can't we just buy a new pack?"

"Do you see a store?" Melanie chided. "This isn't a city. We're in the middle of nowhere. They don't have one-day Amazon Prime delivery out here, you city-idiot. You 'citiot'." Melanie turned to me. "She doesn't even have a head lamp for when it's dark."

"We can share," I said.

"Exactly," Penny echoed. "We can share."

"Do you even know where we're going?"

Penny took a bite of her beans. Her face wrinkled and she swallowed hard. She nodded. "We're rolling up to get the money."

"We're hiking there. We're not *rolling up* like it's a Starbucks drive thru. We're driving to the road and if we can't make it up the road with this old piece of shit van —"

"Hey," I cut her off. "She's got a name. It's Westy. And she's a good van. Aubrey named her."

"Sure, whatever, Westy." Melanie tossed her empty can of beans down. "If Westy can't go any further because it's too steep, or its muddy, or the road's closed off, or, or, or, the road's too narrow, or it's not even freaking there - I mean, after all, we've never freaking been there before and all we got are some paper maps of forest roads to go on - then we're gonna be hoofing it. In fact," she huffed, "and maybe I'm the only one who thinks this, but we probably shouldn't be leaving our van on a road where we might get stopped by some park ranger who's going to be asking us what the hell we're doing there looking all under-prepared. And he'll probably radio us back to the ranger station just because the place is so freaking remote that they keep tabs on this kind of stuff for emergency purposes."

"Alright," I said. "I hear you. We hear you. What do you suggest?"

"I suggest that Penny stays with the car and you and I hike out and get the money and come back."

"No chance," Penny said. "You're shook if you think I'm letting either of you out of my sight."

"Why do you talk like that?" Melanie groaned. "You're twenty four years old."

"Talk like what?"

"Shook? Hundo P?"

Penny rolled her eyes.

"Shit," Melanie said. "I'm starting to sound like Old Man Birch."

"Well, wait a second," I said. "Why not?"

"Why not what?" Penny asked.

"You'll be with the van. Where are we going to go?"

"No chance," Penny said. "You said this road we're going to hike along goes right up to Canada, right?"

I nodded. "So?"

"Well, maybe you'll cross into Canada. Just like you said Emory did."

"So what do you suggest we do, Penny? I'm not going out there tomorrow under-supplied," Melanie said. "And my advice to the two of you is to do the same."

"What was that?" Penny asked.

"What?"

Penny shushed us.

We stood and listened. It was the quietest quiet I ever heard, although I didn't hear it the way I normally have heard things when I thought everything was quiet. Even in the stillest moments, isn't there always a heater running, a light buzzing, a computer fan whirling, a car chugging off in the distance? Yet here, we found soundlessness. There were maybe fifteen people within fifty miles of us and the big Montana sky swallowed what little sound they might have made. I felt so tiny and yet oddly a part of this verdant landscape that spread for hundreds of miles, leaving me with this calm sense that I were a terrestrial giant. Then, somewhere in the valley below we heard the howling of a band of wolves.

###

"For real, you're going to stay here?" Penny asked Melanie as she hoisted the hiking pack over her shoulders.

Melanie nodded, "I'll stay with the van. You two go ahead and I'll wait here."

"And if a park ranger comes?" I asked.

"We haven't seen anyone this whole time," Melanie said, climbing into the back of Westy. "But if someone comes, I'll do what you told me to do back at that gas station in DC. Flirt."

We were west of the Northwest Peak Scenic Area in northern Montana. We made it to NF-871 through a circuitous series of forest and secondary state roads. It was several hours of bumpy, white knuckle driving through the most beautiful, unadulterated landscape you can imagine. We drove through valleys that carved through towering mountains and over little bridges that straddled small creeks. We saw the snow runoff collect into the creeks and slide effortlessly down the mountainside. We passed Rock Candy Mountain, its broad bare chest flexed like a rocky citadel high above us. Then we climbed up the valley, slithering up switchbacks with painful slowness as Westy rebelled with every turn of her wheels.

We crossed the Pacific Northwest Trail. But we didn't see any hikers. We didn't see anyone the entire drive. I had imagined we would see some loner in his pickup truck all decked out with a camping rig in the back. He would wave us over, say hi, and want us to meet his dog. But that didn't happen. Instead, we were company to trees; endless forests where conifers stretched out their branches for hundreds of miles. The only waving we saw occurred when a breeze passed through the conifers and their needle branches bent in unison, as if the trees were drunkards propping one another up on a long walk home. Then there was the dust of the dirt road and the rocks that kicked up under our wheels and pummeled Westy's underbelly with rattling dings.

We passed for a bit into Idaho, though boundaries didn't seem to matter out here. How arbitrary. How manmade. The wilderness cared little for them. As I drove, Melanie meticulously tracked our whereabouts. We had the GPS of her phone, which worked only once for five minutes. But back in Missoula we had also paid a parcel store to print forest road maps and dozens of pages of the Google Map satellite view of the entire route from Yaak. Melanie organized them with little color tabs. Still, a few times the road would branch, and because they were often not marked, we would take a spout on faith and once we drove for almost an hour before panicking and turning around. It was impossible not to get lost. Impossible not to feel that one would die in a maze of green drunkards and dirt roads, all of which looked the same. We drove along a ridge for what seemed like two hours.

And then, in time, we crossed unceremoniously back into Montana. We weren't even sure we were in Montana until we passed what might have been a turn off for an overgrown road that seemed to fall down off the cliff's edge. We spied that same turnoff on our map.

We stopped and ate. I wanted someone else to take over driving for a while. But I was also afraid to not be behind the wheel. So I drove again when we started back up. The road straightened a bit and we rumbled ahead.

We failed to mark the time when we entered the forest roads. It might have been four hours ago, it might have been six. But we were making progress, if ever so laboriously. And then it happened. We saw it in the distance, but we probably didn't recognize it until it was maybe twenty feet ahead of us. A tree trunk lay dead across the road. It was maybe three feet thick. There was no moving it and no getting around it.

We puttered to a stop and debated what to do as the dust settled in our wake.

"How far do you think we are from the border?" I asked.

Melanie looked over the printouts. "It's hard to say."

"Don't they have like a thing in the corner that offers some kind of scale, like every inch is two hundred feet or something?" Penny asked from the back of the van.

"No. These don't have a distance on them. I can read, you know."

"If you had to guess," I asked, "how far do you think?"

"I said I don't know."

"Well, guess. Ten miles? Twenty miles?"

"Could be five miles. Could be fifteen miles."

"I think this begs a bigger question," Penny said. "Where exactly is the money? For real? Where exactly? Listen, we've been driving for hours and we're in the middle of the middle that's inside the middle of nowhere. I didn't even know there was such a nowhere as this nowhere."

"Yeah, yeah. We're with you, Penny," Melanie sarcastically called, swatting the air with the sleeve of printouts in her hand. "We know that this is bumfuck nowhere. Can you shut up so we can think?"

"The money," I announced, "Is going to be where the road meets the Canadian border." Then I added, "Hidden, of course."

Melanie looked at me from the far edge of her vision and her near eyebrow twitched slightly. This was the first I ever said about any precise location of the money. This was also the first I had said with any certainty that there was money. And I think that Melanie was trying to hide her reaction from Penny while also trying to read my face for what I might know. "The money," Melanie finally said. "At the border." She nodded as if taking this news in and said, "It'll be at the border."

"So we actually got to hike?" Penny asked.

"Looks like it," Melanie mocked.

It was just after one p.m. We debated whether or not we should head out or wait until early the next morning. But we were all too anxious to wait any longer.

"There's not enough gear," I said, "in case something happens. It's going to get pretty cold at night way up here. We're short a bag."

"I can carry water in my arms," Penny offered.

"For how long?"

"You guys go ahead," Melanie suggested.

I turned to her. "What?"

"I'll wait here. You go ahead. The two of you." Melanie flicked her tongue across her teeth. This was the first that I ever saw her do this. So I had no reference for interpreting it.

"Wait here? Are you sure?"

"You're going to bounce," Penny said. "You're going to drive off you sly cunt."

Melanie spun around. "No. I'm not going to *bounce*. God, you're fucked in the head."

"You will. You've wanted to drop me this whole time."

"Well, you stalked us across the country. You're trying to extort money from us. Forgive me for not wanting to give you a big hug and a pat on the back."

"I'm trying to save Politifuel. It's nothing personal. I'm not doing this to you. I'm just doing it because it needs doing." Penny stomped her foot. "You don't know anything about business, you shit bag. It's eat what you kill."

"Eat what you kill?" Melanie groaned. "What are you, Steve Jobs?"

"Maybe. Maybe I could be. Like I said, none of this is personal."

"That true? Finally something exciting is happening in my life and you can't be okay with that? You've got to shove your face in it. You've got to steal it from me."

"You're such a cunt. Not everything's about you."

"About me?" Melanie gasped. "About me? Are you going to put this in your stupid fucking memoir, you self-aggrandizing little -"

"Little what? Little what? At least I've got the balls to -"

"You're a woman, why do you need balls? Why are you trying so hard to be a man?"

"I'm not trying to be a man. I'm trying to be better than men."

"But you're the one that is all about Tinder," Melanie groaned.

"Well, a girl like you needs Tinder. But I don't. Look at these winners you've been with. Nick? What a joke. You let men hold you down."

"Wait a second," I interrupted. "I'm a man and I'm not holding her down."

"Of course you are," Penny said. "With your promises of money and whatever else you promised her."

"I haven't promised her anything." I turned to Melanie. "Have I?"

Melanie shook her head. "No. I... I don't know." she paused. "No, I don't think so. Maybe. Does it matter?"

"It matters to me," I replied. "You're the one who showed up on my doorstep with the book, the one who egged me along, remember? The one whose boyfriend attacked me?"

"I remember," Melanie said sharply. "But why was the book addressed to me? -" her voice trailed off.

"What? I thought you said it was my mail."

"It had your name on it, but my address."

"You never said that."

"You snatched the envelope before I could."

I thought back. Yes, she was right. Had I not bothered to look at the address on the envelope?

We sat in the van, victims of a silence that washed in with a breeze that came down the mountainside to our right. The conifers swayed drunkenly. But the dead tree trunk remained splayed across the road, unmoved by our spat.

Finally, Melanie spoke up. "Look, you guys take the keys with you. If that makes Penny feel better, then that's cool with me. I just want to get this over with so I never have to see this backstabbing bitch again."

"Okay," I said. I pulled the keys from the ignition, put them in my pocket, and zipped it up. "Let's gear up." So Penny took Melanie's backpack and wore Melanie's hiking clothes. And her and I climbed over the tree trunk and began our dusty voyage together.

We hiked in silence along NF-871. Westy and the tree trunk faded into the distance behind us and we turned just the slightest bit with the road a little to the left, a little to the right. In time we looked back and Westy was gone and so too was Melanie.

"Any word about your mom?" I asked.

Penny rubbed her palm up her nose and shook her head.

"My mom was a teacher," I said. "She was shot by one of her students. It was just after Columbine."

"I'm sorry," Penny said.

"I had to complete my senior year at home. I just, I don't know, I couldn't bring myself back into the school."

"God-fumbles." Penny adjusted her bag, pulling the straps off her shoulders momentarily to wipe away sweat.

"I was getting in a lot of trouble with Emory before she died. Partying. She thought I was going to fail out. When she died, I was determined to graduate. I just wish she could've seen. You know? I just wish I could've made her proud."

"God-fumbles," Penny muttered. She walked on ahead.

My mind wandered with each step. I thought of Aubrey. I thought of pancakes. I thought of her running down the aisle in the grocery store clutching a syrup bottle. I thought of her kicking me in protest when all she wanted was to play. I thought of reading eBooks to her at night and running my hand through her hair until she fell asleep in the back of the Honda. I thought of feathered dinosaurs. I thought of Missoula and how she ate food scraps, how she spent hours alone playing Gameboy, how she danced and played in the evenings with her friends at the RV Park, and how much she just wanted to be loved. I thought of the last time I saw her, her eyes searching for me through the rain as she pressed her nose against the sliding glass door of that cabin on the mountainside, her mom looming above her. I thought of the song she sang, "Happy faces, happy places, I can see happy faces." I thought of how I abandoned her.

No. No, that wasn't right. Melanie was right. I helped her. I helped Aubrey. And she helped me. She needed to be loved. And so did I. That was our purpose together. It was over. And that was okay. It was okay for things to be over.

My mind leapt back in time to the kitchen in my old apartment, the one with the sticky linoleum floor. I saw the kitchen counter that I sat on every night as I drank my life away. My mind wandered back to that junk drawer with my wife's letter inside and the gun that sat atop it. It wandered back to Melanie knocking on my door and how she said that fate drew us together and brought us here, to a desolate forest road and to this moment hiking alongside someone I did not know. Someone who held something over me.

Then my mind hopped to something Melanie said earlier that day when we were sitting in Westy at the fallen tree. The package with the copy of *Discontents* bearing the riddle which had spurred this whole journey had my name on it, but was addressed to Melanie.

My mind wandered back to my wife. What did she look like? I couldn't remember. How strange the way our mind has the urge to protect us, the way we want to protect a child like Aubrey.

No. See her. Stop thinking and see her, I told myself. Stop thinking of the past. Stop trying to tell yourself the story of the past. Let the past be the past.

I saw my wife. Her pigtails dangled behind her. I saw the red in her dimpled cheeks and the brown in her eyes. I saw that little scar on her chin. I saw her long neck, crisp collar bones, smooth skin down her chest to the V in her T-shirt. I looked down. Her small hands wrapped into mine, her nails pinching the back of my hand. I looked up. Her mouth agape, she laughed. "Of course, Jamey," she giggled. "Yes, yes, yes I want a family. You know that."

"I thought you didn't really want kids," I said.

"Are you skitzoid?"

"Don't you remember that night, that Star Night and we fought? And I asked you if you really wanted kids and you just shrugged?"

"We never fought on any Star Night, Jamey." My wife tugged me close. "Besides, I'm the one that asked you to have kids."

"Wait, what? You never asked me."

My wife laughed. "Yes, of course I did. We always made love on Star Night. But, I think it was our fourth. And the condom broke. And I told you I didn't care. And we stayed up all night talking about having a family."

"No, no. That's not what happened. There was the red light on the fire alarm in our bedroom. It was blinking, and blinking."

"You mean the green light? The fire alarm light was green. I was staring at it that night while we talked. I'll never forget." My wife shook her head, her pigtails billowing behind her as if weightless. "What are you talking about?"

"I. I'm not sure," I said.

"Jamey, I want to show you something," my wife said. I could feel her presence - as though it was not Penny hiking beside me, but my wife. Was it, really? Was my wife guiding me here? It was as though one of the many pebbles that I stepped over as we hiked was hit by the back of my heel and went tumbling off the forest road and on down the mountain, gaining momentum as it tumbled, and that little pebble carved a wide path down to the valley floor. It was as if I was looking down the valley and I could see back to the beginning and I could sense my wife was standing there at the beginning, just as I could sense that she was here with me now on this ridge, so far along on this journey - so much farther than I would ever dare to go alone.

What had my wife asked me in that coffee shop the day she told me she was dying of cancer? Not to help her, not for sympathy, not for solutions. She just wanted to know the name of the young woman with "the cute haircut".

We hiked on. What was the last riddle? I searched my mind and finally I saw the poem typed on the opening pages of *Discontents*. It read: "Just up the lane, James lost his...." What did it mean? Here we were, wandering up a lane of sorts. A forest road to be exact. What should I be preparing for?

"Let's hydrate," Penny said, shaking me from my thoughts.

I nodded. "Good plan." My mouth was dry, my throat coated in dust. The sky was ever-blue, the air cold and crisp, but the sun burned as strong as ever. It is funny how the sun gives us all our energy and takes it away with the very same light.

"How long has it been?" I asked.

"About two hours," Penny replied.

We stopped and drank and then started back up. Soon we saw something in the middle of the road up ahead. "What's that?" Penny pointed. It was red. Blood red. We approached. Giant antlers reached for the sky in a call to the heavens. It was a caribou carcass laying as if exhausted on its side, its ribs exposed, its body mostly gnawed and torn away except for the neck and head. A splattering of blood reddened the dirt in front of its mouth as if its last breaths were coughs of blood. I leaned down and looked into its onyx eyes and saw my reflection in the marble coating.

My thoughts jumped to Clark. I shoved him from my mind. And right behind him on the next mental slide was Nick. I saw Nick charge me in my kitchen. I saw him grab me in the dark as he lay propped against the dumpster behind the abandoned building where Melanie and I tried to discard him. I saw him stagger, his pupils bleached, before his knees gave out and they slammed to the ground on that mountain road. I saw him topple forward. I saw the pond of blood. He lay face down, floating in it.

What was Nick in all of this? Collateral damage, that was all. Surely, that was all, wasn't it? He had been set up. I had been set up. Melanie. Melanie had been set up. This had all been set up. No, Nick wasn't collateral damage. But his death surely was.

It was all becoming clear to me as though the pebbles and dirt of this forest road were the pages of an unfolding book. It was a hike of Clarity. *Clarity*, I thought. What a great album by Jimmy Eat World. My wife loved that album. I smiled at the thought. I smiled at my wife.

Then I thought again of Clark and this time I could not push him away. Surely, he was collateral damage. My wife had never heard of Clark or Penny. I guess that made Penny a loose end.

"What happened to it?" Penny asked, covering her mouth as she turned away.

I shrugged. "Wolves, if I had to guess."

"Wolves?"

"Yes, wolves are real Penny. And we are in the wilderness, did you notice?"

Penny pulled her hand from her mouth and tried to loosen her shoulders. "Don't try to scare me."

"I don't need to," I said. "The wolves can do that themselves."

We hiked a bit further, descending slowly with the mountain. An hour or so passed. Then suddenly we found ourselves at a right bend in the road. A small clearing sat at the bend. A white marker stood in the far right edge of the opening. I reached into my pocket and pulled out a stack of folded papers. I unfolded them and shuffled through them until I found the printout of the Canadian border[10].

This was it. We stood near the border. I could see in the back of the clearing a line cut away in the trees similar to the way the power company cuts a line through the trees and the power lines follow the cutaway through a forest. On the near side of the cutaway was the United States. On the far side of the cutaway was Canada. The cutaway was the border. All Emory had to do was walk to the cutaway, turn right, walk a few hundred yards and he would be in a vast opening where once there was a forest fire; a place where tree stumps and a few new trees scattered the mountainside. Then he would connect up with a dirt road, follow it down to Yahk Meadow Road, and walk to freedom.

I stopped and stared. It was silent except a shushing sound that rolled as a breeze through the trees. Penny stopped too.

For some reason it hadn't occurred to me, but this whole time we walked the same wild road that Emory walked to his escape. I looked down as if his footprints might still be cast in the dust below me. I looked back behind us and saw the endless forest of

---

[10] It looked approximately like this. We hiked from NF-871 coming from the right side. The line through the trees is the Canadian border. Above that is the United States, below that is Canada (This map is upside down such that the top of the map is south): http://bit.ly/gmaps-canadianborder.

green standing alongside either edge of the road. Had Emory looked back before kissing America goodbye?

I envisioned Emory, his hands waving triumphantly in the air as he stepped off of NF-871 and into the clearing. Here we stood. Together. Reunited at the same clearing. I made it to the journey's end. I walked into the clearing to the Canadian border and stopped. I looked right and watched as Emory walked through the cutaway down the mountainside. He faded from view. But before he did, he turned and waved, a cockeyed smile painted across his face. I lifted my hand and waved back. And I knew with certainty, for the first time since he had sent me a letter asking me to publish his memoir all those years ago, that Emory Walden made it to Canada, survived, and was still alive somewhere.

"Why are your eyes welling up?" Penny asked. Just like that, I was shaken from peace and forced to remember that the journey was in fact not yet over. "And where's the money?"

"I'm thinking," I said. "Can't I have a moment?"

"James, it's going to get dark soon. Where's the money?"

I looked over to the sign that marked the border. "It's over there."

"Where?"

"The sign. It's just behind the sign in the woods."

"Well go get it."

Something shifted in me just an inch. "Fuck you, Penny. I'm not your errand boy."

"No," Penny rebuked. "Fuck you, James. Listen, I come out on top on this one. Men like you always think you can tell a woman what to do."

"It has nothing to do with me being a man and you being a woman, Penny. I'm telling you because we're in the middle of nowhere and I'm getting tired of hearing your shit. Whether you were a man, a woman, or a caribou, I'd say the same damn thing to you."

"That a threat?"

"It's whatever the hell you want it to be," I jabbed. "You go get the money. You want it, then march over there and grab it."

"Well, what's it look like?"

"Money, Penny. It looks like money."

"Funny. What is it, in a bag?"

"I got to think that it's in a bag."

"Well, how we gonna carry it back?"

"I don't know. You should have thought of that before you came all the way up here."

"Well, how am I gonna know what it looks like?"

"It's going to be the only thing out here that isn't a tree or a rock. When we find that, we'll know we found the money."

"Alright." She stomped her feet. "I'll go find it."

"You give me a yell when you find it," I said. "It's supposed to be just behind the trees there."

Penny marched towards the sign. When she got to it, she turned around and called, "This sign?"

"Yep. That's the one."

She turned to the trees and stepped into the woods. I crept up behind her. She was bent over scouring around, lifting sticks and poking around tree trunks. I let my bag fall off one shoulder, reached in, and felt around for my gun. But it wasn't where I packed it the night before. It fell to the bottom of my bag, I thought. I eased my bag down and placed it at my feet. I glanced up to see Penny still scouring for evidence of the money. Quietly, I reached down to the bottom of the bag. I felt through a densely packed maze of tent gear, clothes, and food. No gun.

"What're you looking for?"

I looked up. Penny stood at the edge of the woods no more than ten feet from me. She held a hunting knife out in front of her. The knife was pointed at me. "I said, what're you looking for?"

I straightened up. "Nothing. A map."

"Enough!" Penny stepped towards me. "Toss the bag over there." She pointed. I tossed the bag where she told me to. "Show me where the money's at. I'm over you dragging your damn feet. I've won. Accept it. Now get in there and get the damn money and help me carry it outta here before it gets dark."

"Okay, okay. Please put the knife away."

"Not a chance," she said. "You've been suspect this whole time. What the hell's the money doing way up here, anyways?"

"This is where Emory crossed into Canada."

"So? Why'd he stash money here? Wouldn't he just mule it with him?"

"Good point," I said. "We're not here for the money."

"We're not?"

"No," I smiled. "We're just here because I needed to see it."

"Because you needed to see it? Why?" Penny waved the knife at me.

"To stop clinging."

"To what?"

"Don't worry, I'm just realizing all of this myself. I knew we had to come here but I didn't know why. But now, now that we're here, I understand."

"I don't care," Penny screamed. "Stop! Stop! Stop!" She stomped her feet the way Aubrey would when she was upset. "Where's the flipping money, James? Show me the flipping money or I'll cut you and the damn wolves can finish you off."

"There is no money here," I said.

"No money?"

"No money."

"What do you mean there is no money here?"

"You said it, why would Emory have left money here in the middle of nowhere?"

"Because he was an idealistic loser. That's why."

"Think about it, Penny. How would Emory have dragged all that money up here while carrying everything he needed to hike for days and days?"

"I don't know. Stop trying to game me."

"I'm not trying to anything. Look around. Do you see any money?"

Penny peered around at her feet as if expecting to find something. "No." She seemed to shrink when she said this. Her spine melted and she slid to the ground, her knees collapsing against each other. "Jesus on a bike, you dragged me way the crap out here so you could look at a bend in the road?"

"You didn't need to come," I said, stepping forward.

"There's no money," she sobbed. "Politifuel is dead. I'm a failure." The sobs chugged like Westy's tired engine. "Oh momma," she bellowed.

I took another step towards her. "Get away from me!" she barked. She swung the knife like a drunk swatting gnats. I jumped back.

"It's okay," I said. "It's just a company."

"Shut up! What've you ever created? Nothing! You're not capable of understanding what it takes to make something. You subsist off Emory's deeds, you ratchety-ass leach. Without him, you'd shrivel up."

Penny gazed up at me, tears in her eyes. Her hand that held the knife quivered and fell to her side. "I've got nothing left to live for."

I looked over the melted woman before me, the hiking pack on her back the only thing propping her up.

"It ends here," she insisted.

"It'll be dark soon." I stepped forward. "Give me the knife. You can go home and be with your mom."

"I can't," Penny said. She lifted the knife and slashed at the air. "This is your fault." She climbed to her feet. "This is your fault. You killed Politifuel."

"I killed Politifuel?"

"You said there was money and there wasn't." She slashed the knife through the air. I stumbled back. "At the whiskey bar. You said you were gonna get the money."

"So what?"

"I blew valuable time following you." Penny lunged at me. I lurched back. "I'm not dying here alone."

I threw my hands in the air. "Penny, stop."

She lunged again.

I turned and ran.

I ran and ran. I ran past the caribou carcass. I ran past where we ate lunch. I ran until my lungs were on fire and my legs throbbed. I ran until I grew too tired to run. I turned. Penny lingered not far behind. She was bent over catching her breath. She must have tossed her bag because I didn't see it. But the knife, clutched in her hand as it hung by her knee, glistened in the Montana sun. I gasped for air. I walked on glancing over my shoulder every few steps. She stalked me, the knife waving by her side. Finally, I saw the tree trunk spread across the road. Westy rested on the far side of it. I turned around. Penny was gone.

I jogged towards the van, climbed over the tree, opened the van door and climbed inside. "Melanie, let's go," I yelled. I looked around the van but Melanie was gone. I jumped out of the van and ran around back. "Melanie!"

"What?" Melanie was climbing down a hill out of the woods. "What is it?"

"We gotta go, Penny's got a knife."

"What? Why?"

"What the hell were you doing in the woods?"

"A girl's gotta go sometimes," she shrugged.

"We gotta go. That's who's gotta go. Come on," I begged.

"What are you talking about?"

"We gotta go," I said, "quickly."

"What's going on?"

"Can we talk about this later? Let's go."

Melanie and I came around the back of the van. Penny stood by the driver's side door. "Give me the keys," she said. "Toss the keys on the ground by my feet and walk over there."

"No," I said. "Let's all just calm down and we can all leave here together."

"I'm rolling out of here. You losers are staying here to try your luck with the wolves."

"I thought you couldn't drive," I said.

"I'm a survivor. I'll do what I have to do."

"Wolves?" Melanie asked. "What wolves?"

"I'll get that money. Some way or another," Penny said. "There's still time. There's still time."

"There are wolves," I said. "There's a bloody caribou carcass up a ways."

"You'll meet them soon," Penny barked, her nostrils flaring. "There's no money here."

Melanie turned to me. "There's no money?" She pulled my gun from behind her where it had been tucked into her rear waistband.

"She's right," I said.

She looked at Penny. "None?"

Penny waved the tip of the knife up and down as if using it to nod a yes.

Melanie stepped towards Penny. "Seriously?" She stepped closer. "He drove us all the way out here and there's no money?"

Penny nodded.

"He drove us all the out here in the middle of the middle of fucking nowhere in some endless fucking forest infested with wolves and there's no money?"

Penny nodded again. She and Melanie stood just a few feet from each other. They faced me. "This idiot," Melanie lifted the gun and waved it towards me, pointing with the muzzle, "tricked us into driving all the way out here? What for?"

"It'd be news to me," Penny said.

Melanie snort-giggled. "You don't know? Why don't we ask him?"

"Let's ask him," Penny agreed, snickering.

"James," Melanie said, the gun pointed at me. "Why are we here if there's no money?"

I stammered. "I, um, I. I just. I just followed the clues. I don't know."

"Oh yeah," Melanie said. "The clues. And where did those clues come from, James?"

"I don't know. Where do you think?"

"Well, this whole time I thought they came from Emory. But now I'm not so sure."

"Yeah," I agreed. "Now I'm not so sure either."

"Oh," Melanie snorted. "That's funny."

"Melanie," I pleaded. "Think of the baby."

"I can understand why my friend Penny here is upset," Melanie professed, ignoring me. She turned to Penny. "You came here looking for money, didn't you Penny?"

"I am here on business." Penny nodded. "Wait, what baby?"

"But there's no money," Melanie declared.

"No," Penny said. "Just wolves."

"Just wolves. Isn't that too bad?" Melanie laughed. "Just wolves." She let the gun fall to her side.

"Melanie," I said. "Come on. Think of the baby."

She looked at me. "There's no money, James."

"What baby?" Penny asked.

"Better than an amusement park, remember? Please!"

"There was never any money, was there James?"

"He's a ratchety-ass liar!" Penny accused.

"We'll get there, I promise," I said.

"How can we go, if there's no money?" Melanie asked.

"We've got a van. We just drive."

"Drive?"

"We were so close, remember? Back in Missoula."

"Missoula," Melanie said, the word dancing on her lips like a song lyric.

"Yes, Missoula."

"Missoula? That shithole?" Penny asked.

"Shut up, Penny," I said.

"Why are we here, James?" Melanie asked.

"We're, we're, we're searching. We're learning. We're on our way to knowing, knowing what Emory knows that most people don't know. You've got to believe that. Maybe finding where Emory crossed is part of the process. It's got to be."

"I'm not sure anymore," Melanie said. "Maybe this is all there is."

"It's not. This trip, not just seeing where Emory crossed, but all of it, it has changed everything for me. It has to be the same for you. Isn't it? Don't you see we needed each other? We needed each other to leave. We were stuck back there. And now we're free. We can be free together and we can find that place, that somewhere where we can stop searching. We're almost there."

"Knowing? Searching? What the crap stupid talk is that?" Penny asked. "Are you buying this man's bullshit?"

"Penny," Melanie said, her head swiveling back and forth so that she had both Penny and I under her watch. "Did I ever tell you about the kids in Mexico City breathing all those fumes? The ones that stand in the busy street selling mango juice? All day they stand there."

"Mango juice?" Penny wailed, her shoulders bent forward, her butt sticking out in her feet stomping stance. But instead of stomping, she swung her little clubbed hands forward and back and pounded at the air in a tantrum. "Jesus on a bike, the two of you make no sense!"

"It's true. We make our own magic, together," Melanie said. She flicked her tongue across her teeth. "You tried to take advantage of us. You only care about yourself." She lifted the gun slightly.

"What are you doing?" I asked.

"Are you crazy?" Penny cried.

"I'm not crazy," Melanie said. "Don't call me that."

"Then, shoot him!"

"Melanie!"

Melanie pulled the trigger. An explosion. The boom rushed down the mountainside. It echoed through the valley below and clattered back up the ridge.

My eyes bulged. I stuttered forward, my hand closed over my mouth.

Penny wailed, grisly, tortured, and deafening. She thrashed in agony and fell over. Blood painted the ground where her foot had been planted. She grabbed her ankle and screamed. "You shot me! You shot me! You cunt!"

"Nothing personal," Melanie said. She smiled. "But I got a feeling you'll do just fine out here in the wilderness. Just another wolf, right? You know, eat what you kill and all that."

Chapter 46

The snow stopped. I put Emory's letter down and climbed into the back of the Honda. I opened the duffle bag and picked up the envelopes, weighing and shaking them in my hand. They were real. Emory left me this money. And it was much more than the few thousand dollars I imagined he would have left me as an incentive to publish his memoir.

As I dug around in the bag, my hand hit something that felt out of place; something that wasn't an envelope. It was a cardboard box. I pulled it out of the bag, grabbed my phone, and flipped on the flashlight app.

I turned the box over in my hand, hearing its contents slide. A piece of paper was taped across the box seam. I focused my light on it. I pulled the box close to my face so I could read what was on it. The words were typed, like they came from an old typewriter.

"Do not open," it began. I continued reading:

Take this to the post office. Have them open it and mail what's inside. Do not look when they open it. Pay and leave.

"What the hell," I gasped. Was it Emory? Was this how I would get in contact with him, or let him know I got the money? I kept reading:

Jamey, It's going to be painful, and it might not work out, but this is the only way I can think to help you. It's the only way I know how to save you from yourself. It's the only way I know how to help you stop clinging to the past. So just mail what's inside. I know it might be impossible for you to understand now. But I'm working on explaining it in a letter I'm writing you. It's just so hard to write. I promise I'll finish it soon. I'm going to have my brother give it you after I pass.

I fell back onto the floor of the Honda Element. How had my wife? When had she? How did she know I would ever finally come find the rooftop?

"Develop a mind that clings to nothing," she had said.

I hadn't come here on this April night wanting to find the money. I came here to find Emory and some debris from our past before saying goodbye.

As I stared at that note from my wife and that bag of money in the back of car, the snow a blanket of white cast over the windows, I accepted that I didn't have the strength to say goodbye on my own no matter how badly I wanted to. I was alive. I had the proof that I was clinging to in front of me: A bag of money in all its weight. What had Emory written about the money? "*It's dirty to me and I don't want it.*"

Emory wrote that he didn't want anyone else to have the money. So I drove it to West Virginia but I couldn't find anywhere to hide it. So I drove on to

Montana. I imagined Emory might get a kick out of that, wherever he was, if he was even still alive. Montana. He had the audacity to go to Montana, to fade into the wilderness and make his way across the border all alone. But I wasn't like Emory. I knew I would never go to Montana alone, no matter how hard I wanted to find out what became of him.

But Montana Avenue? That I could do. It wasn't far; just a short drive from where I sat in my car into Northeast DC. So I hopped in the driver's seat and drove. I took North Capitol down and made my way to West Virginia Avenue NE. I crossed to Montana Avenue Northeast. Just off Montana Avenue Northeast, I found a field, its trees in bloom. Across the way, there was a building housing a liquor store and a day care. And somewhere nearby there was a lot where broken things were cast aside and a few buildings with rusty roofs leaned against one another.

When I got done hiding the bag of money, I drove to a post office.

"Can you open this box and mail whatever's inside?" I asked, handing the postal worker the cardboard box my wife had buried in the bottom of the duffle bag.

The postal worker stopped. She peered at me over her glasses. "You don't wanna see what you about to mail?"

"No," I said. "I don't."

"You alright, hunny?"

"Hunny," I said. "That's ironic."

"Now why you say that?"

"Oh, it's nothing. There was this woman, Ella. She was in this book I read. She was always saying hunny," I said. "Never mind."

The postal worker cut the tape on the box. "So you saying you don't wanna see what you about to mail or who gonna get it?"

"No," I said. "I'm not supposed to. Just let me know what it costs."

"Okay, so we got two packages. That'll be $9.57."

"Two packages?"

"You wanna know or what? Now you got me confused."

"No, I'm sorry."

"You sure you alright, hunny?"

I shrugged. "I don't know yet."

I left and climbed back into my Honda Element. Then something hit me. I reached into my pocket and unfolded the note Emory had left in the duffle bag. I read the last line of the note again:

Goodbye James. Thank you. You'll never see me again. I'm off to West Virginia and then Montana. I plan to -

I ran my finger along the paper to the where the words ended abruptly. I felt the torn edge.

Chapter 47

Westy churned down the mountain, bouncing along the forest road as if happy to finally be heading down hill.

"Jessie," I said. "At the hospital. It must have really been her after all."

"Who?" Melanie asked.

"Forget it," I said. "It's in the past." That was where my wife got the drugs that Nick got hooked on, right? That was the last piece. I could see it all now. It was time to put the puzzle down.

"We didn't find him. We didn't find any clues. We didn't find anything," Melanie said, her shoulders sagging, her face heavy.

"We did," I said. "We found Emory."

"We did?"

"Yeah. He was there at the border," I said. "I waved goodbye to him."

"Are we done searching, then?"

"Yeah," I replied.

Melanie mouthed the words, "done searching".

We rumbled along through the endless forested mountains.

"Oh shit," I said, looking back over my shoulder and out of the rear window. All I could see was the dust Westy kicked up in our wake.

Melanie was driving. "What is it?"

"The letter. My wife's letter. It was in my hiking bag. I tossed my bag at the border when Penny pulled the knife on me."

"What letter?"

"A letter my wife wrote me before she died."

"What did it say?"

"I don't know," I said. "I never opened it."

"Never opened it?" Melanie asked. "Why not?"

"I was afraid."

"Afraid?"

"To let her go."

We passed into Idaho.

"Actually, I think I do," I said.

"Think you do what?"

I nodded. "Yeah, I know what the letter said."

"What did it say?"

"'I love you.' It said, 'I love you'."

Melanie looked at me and smiled.

We passed back into Montana.

"James?"

"Yeah?"

"The letter from Emory, the one I found in your bag - I thought it said? Oh, I see. The hot girl theory, all that was wrong — someone had already found the money?"

I gazed out the window at the passing conifers. A valley opened up before us and I could see the sun yielding to the big Montana sky as if being extinguished by a blanket of endless and deep blue. "Montana sure is beautiful," I said.

We drove on. It was just me, Melanie, and the baby inside of her.

About James Wallace Birch

<u>James Wallace Birch</u> is an author and freelancer from Northern Virginia, just outside the U.S. capital. His writing has been described as smart, elegant, insightful and poetically bittersweet.

If You Find Emory Walden, is the long-anticipated follow up to his publication of Emory Walden's story, *Discontents: The Disappearance of a Young Radical.*

Discontents: The Disappearance of a Young Radical is about the disappearance of James's old high school friend, Emory Walden, a political agitator and notorious graffiti artist who became a counter-culture icon and was hunted by the U.S. Government. In the summer of 2011, James received a letter from Emory asking him to publish Emory's account of what happened. The rest is history.

James enjoys coffee and tacos, though not together. His mind moves to late 90s and early 2000s ska, emo and punk. He's an over-analyzer, occasional social commentator, a 90s-obsessed millennial, and a twentieth century fiction junkie. His favorite novel is *Coming Up For Air* by George Orwell.

Stay in touch with James:

Instagram —
https://Instagram.com/JamesWallaceBirch
Goodreads -
https://www.goodreads.com/author/show/5068602.
James_Wallace_Birch
Web - https://jameswallacebirch.wordpress.com/

Share the love by posting photos of your copy of *If You Find Emory Walden* or *Discontents: The Disappearance of a Young Radical* on social media with #WheresEmoryWalden.

About Emory Walden

Once a well-known activist and graffiti artist, Emory Walden mysteriously disappeared circa New Year's Day 2011. In *Discontents: The Disappearance of a Young Radical*, Walden claims to have played a little-known but instrumental behind-the-scenes role in sparking the political unrest in the United States that began in the early 2010s and which has defined much of that decade. His claims remain unconfirmed to this day. For reasons unknown, little can be found today of his existence.

www.ingramcontent.com/pod-product-compliance
Lightning Source LLC
Chambersburg PA
CBHW062021190726
48284CB00014B/1549